Praise for the Novels of Red Garnier

"I knew it would be blistering hot and very erotic. What I didn't expect was the fact that I would have no choice but to think about *The Satin Sash* for days after I finished reading it. . . . [With] expertly written love scenes so blazing hot I blushed, *The Satin Sash* is at the top of my list of books that I will read over and over again. FIVE RIBBONS."

—Romance Junkies

"Red Garnier is the truth, the real deal, and everything great when it comes to hot-and-heavy romance."

—Joyfully Reviewed

"Reviewer's Choice Award. An explosive ménage story that gets off to a fast start and never loses its erotic pacing . . . if you love a wild ride, a fast-paced story, and brilliant characterization, you owe it to yourself to make *The Satin Sash* your next erotic read."

—TwoLips Reviews

"Oh my goodness! Red Garnier has just earned herself a slot on my 'Willing to spend my rent money on' list of authors."

—Fallen Angel Reviews

"Red Garnier is a breath of fresh air, bold and daring in her creations of enlivening characters that blaze along the paths of captivating story lines."

—Night Owl Romance

The LAST KISS

RED GARNIER

HEAT

HEAT

Published by New American Library,
a division of Penguin Group (USA) Inc.,
375 Hudson Street, New York, New York 10014, USA
Penguin Group (Canada), 90 Eglinton Avenue East, Suite 700, Toronto,
Ontario M4P 2Y3, Canada (a division of Pearson Penguin Canada Inc.)
Penguin Books Ltd., 80 Strand, London WC2R 0RL, England
Penguin Ireland, 25 St. Stephen's Green, Dublin 2,
Ireland (a division of Penguin Books Ltd.)
Penguin Group (Australia), 250 Camberwell Road, Camberwell,
Victoria 3124, Australia (a division of Pearson Australia Group Pty. Ltd.)
Penguin Books India Pvt. Ltd., 11 Community Centre,
Panchsheel Park, New Delhi - 110 017, India
Penguin Group (NZ), 67 Apollo Drive, Rosedale, North Shore 0632,
New Zealand (a division of Pearson New Zealand Ltd.)
Penguin Books (South Africa) (Pty.) Ltd., 24 Sturdee Avenue,
Rosebank, Johannesburg 2196, South Africa

Penguin Books Ltd., Registered Offices:
80 Strand, London WC2R 0RL, England

First published by Heat, an imprint of New American Library,
a division of Penguin Group (USA) Inc.

First Printing, May 2011
1 3 5 7 9 10 8 6 4 2

HEAT is a trademark of Penguin Group (USA) Inc.

LIBRARY OF CONGRESS CATALOGING-IN-PUBLICATION DATA:

Garnier, Red.
The last kiss / Red Garnier.
p. cm.
ISBN 978-0-451-23313-4
I. Title.
PS3607.A7655L38 2011
813'.6—dc22   2011004454

Printed in the United States of America

As always, to Mr. Red.
Because you are, and always will be, the "One" for me.

ACKNOWLEDGMENTS

The release of a new book is always so exciting that I always feel indebted to the people who make it happen. A thousand thanks to Tracy Bernstein, Roberta Brown, Talia Platz, and the superamazing team at NAL Penguin, who always do a great job in putting my books together. I'm truly, truly blessed to have found such a wonderful team who believes in me and my stories.

And a big heartfelt thank-you to all of you wonderful readers who've taken the time from your busy schedules and have decided to spend it with one of my books. Enjoy *The Last Kiss*.

The LAST KISS

Prologue

A trail of blood, visible in the bright glare of a dangling headlight, blazed a red path to his sprawled body.

One hand lay open on the grass, while the other was curled into a fist, and it held something. Something important. He couldn't remember what it was; he knew only that it had been in his pocket. It was for *her*.

"Stay with me, a'right?" the truck driver said as he paced at the edge of the road. He peered into the distance before he spun around and shot him an apprehensive glance. "Just . . . don't do somethin' you'll be regrettin', now, a'right?"

It took an excruciating effort for Benjamin Newcastle to make sense of his words. With his body propped awkwardly against his wrecked car, the burning gash at his throat continued to drip blood across his chest, his hips, his thighs, oozing over the soil like the earth itself was stealing his life essence. Stealing his soul.

The old man's face looked ghostly pale in the darkness

as he kept an eye out for help. The collision had sent both vehicles careening down a slope at the side of the road. Now one man was standing; the other was on the ground. Struggling. Struggling to breathe, to remain conscious.

Above Ben's pounding head, the moon shone through the fog. The silence of the night felt endless as they waited to hear sirens, crickets—hell, anything.

"Promised . . . be back," Ben rasped, exhaling with difficulty. His breath misted the air. The need to be with her was something deep-rooted in him, and he felt the anxiety of being late, of making her wait, or worry.

The other man offered him a weak smile, taking care not to look beneath Ben's chin, to where his body was battered. Even if Ben had attempted to glance downward, he wouldn't have made out much through the cake of blood. But he felt it. Felt cold, felt numb parts, pained parts, and something he'd spent years trying to cure in others: his heart faltering.

"Help's comin'. The ambulance should be here soon," the man said, tapping trembling fingers impatiently on his cell phone.

"Her . . . birthday."

"Ahh . . ."

Ben squeezed his eyes shut, trying to summon an image of her face. A perky nose, small but plump lips. Smooth, rounded cheekbones. All set in a face that was calm and as warm as sunshine. But now . . . now he couldn't remember the exact shade of her eyes. "She . . . waiting. For . . ."

"She's waitin' for ya. I get that. But no more wastin' your breath, man. Help's comin'."

His head fell back when his neck couldn't support him, and it bumped against his BMW.

The other man flipped his cell phone open, his movements rushed and awkward sounding. Ben ached everywhere—he ached just to go home. All day, through patients, through surgeries, he'd ached to go home.

"Yeah . . . been in an accident . . . No, damn, I'm not gonna run—there's a dying man here. . . ."

A wry smile appeared on Ben's lips, then vanished when he couldn't dredge enough energy to keep it. He cracked open one eye. "Not gonna die . . . Relaaaaax."

The man slapped the phone shut, agitated as he glanced at his turned-over carrier truck. "Yeah, buddy, I know. Just hang on till someone gets here. So, what's that you're holding?"

The breeze felt hot against his chilled skin. He glanced down at his fisted hand, the metal warm inside his grip. "Can't remember," he murmured.

The man dropped to his knees. "Well, let's see, now. Want me to pry it off you? Ahh, a necklace," he said as he took it into his hand.

"Locket," Ben corrected.

"This for her?"

His teeth began to chatter. "F-for Emma."

"Your girlfriend?"

"My . . . *mine.*"

"Then you're gonna want to personally give this to her, right? What's your name? Whoa, there, stay with me. What's your name, buddy?"

Ben's throat felt drier than asphalt—it closed when he

attempted to answer. Couldn't say *Benjamin Newcastle*. Couldn't say *Ben*.

He knew the signs of cardiac arrest. Ironic that with such an extensive knowledge of the subject, he was as helpless as a newborn now. Even if he'd had an aspirin on hand as prevention, it would have only thinned his blood and ensured that he bled to death.

Assailed with unexpected rage, he stiffened his muscles and tried to buck upward, talk, do *something*. Would've been good if he were holding his wounds. Trying to stop the bleeding. Calm down, calm down; take action. Yet he couldn't command his hands. No longer felt his legs. His jaw felt stiff and cramped. *Emma!*

The squeal of an ambulance echoed in the distance, barely filtering past his thoughts of a warm bath, warm soup, and *her*. God, *her*. "C-c-call . . . !" he strained out through his teeth. "C-c-c-call!"

The old man cursed out loud, mumbled to himself, "This son of a bitch is dead," and then Ben felt the cold metal locket being pressed back into his palm, heard the man's footsteps racing across the grass into the tangle of trees on the deserted hillside.

"C-c-c-c-c-all Em-m-*mmm*-ma. . . ."

His breath became a wheeze. The chatter of his teeth hissed and clicked like a rattlesnake. And still the sirens approached. *Weeo, weeo, weeo.* He thought of . . .

Lips.

Pink.

Soft.

Sweet.

Lips.

And how they'd awakened him that morning. He'd seized those lips, had kissed them slowly, deeply. *Good morning*, those pink, soft, sweet lips had murmured against his, and they'd smiled, those lips, and nibbled, those lips, and kissed. *I have a mind to strap you to my bed and never let you leave me. . . .*

He listened to his pulse fade, heard his last struggling breaths spell out a mournful good-bye, and he wondered if she'd known. If *he'd* known. If they'd both sensed it. That this would happen.

That he might come to lie here on this ground and wonder whether he'd ever get to feel those lips again. That he might sit here and pray to see her big brown eyes again.

No. He couldn't have known. Because if he had, he would have made that kiss, their last kiss, last longer.

Chapter One

Texas
One year, eight months, and seven days later

Emma Wilkins stood at the entrance of the bar and tavern, clutching her small purse with one arm and barely clinging to her courage with the other. Her hair was combed. Her dress was buttoned. Her lips were glossed. But could she go through with this?

Oh, god, she had to.

Her breath rattled in her chest as she grabbed the doorknob and pushed into the Silver Fox. Music blared. People lounged by the bar, crammed the vinyl booths, hovered by the billiard tables. Boots thumped on the wood dance floor.

And slowly, one by one, just as Emma had dreaded, just as she had *feared*, the heads turned in her direction. Pairs and pairs of eyes began stacking, one atop another, until each new curious gaze felt like a sledgehammer on her breast.

Rooted to the spot, Emma swallowed the painful lump

that gathered in her throat. She didn't want their pity. Or their stares. Or their condolences.

She wanted . . . a man.

These people had been friends of hers, friends of *theirs*—hers and Ben's. But like everything else, everything that had been good and real in her life, it had all died with him that night.

That night almost two years ago.

Oh, Ben, why did this happen to us?

It felt impossible to go on after his death, but at the same time, if she didn't do something for herself—and soon—she would end up arranging her own.

She was tired of feeling gray. Of the wretched loneliness that had taken permanent residence in the home she and Ben had made together. She was tired of seeing him in places he wasn't, of *talking* to him as if he could still hear her, of dreaming of feeling his touch again, hearing his deep bass voice again. . . .

"Well, I'll be damned. Emma Wilkins!"

From behind the bar, Wooly grinned and waved her over, his silver tooth flashing in the lights.

Her stomach gripped in protest over the attention. Too soon. God, it was too soon for her to be here.

Wooly was not the owner of the joint, but he was the owner's cousin and he seemed to relish his post as bartender; he'd always had a hard-on for playing the psychiatrist and an even bigger one for gossip.

But Emma didn't feel like being diagnosed today. Just didn't feel like pouring her heart out to Wooly so all their friends could discover that her life was a mess, that she felt lost and lonely and frightened, and that she sometimes caught herself staring longingly at her medicine cabinet and wondering how many pills it would take to be carried back to Ben.

She didn't want Wooly to commiserate and pat her hand and say, "It's normal, a grief period. You'll get over it"—or anything else.

She was sure her grief would last forever and already envisioned herself an old, plump, lonely cat lady, telling whomever cared to ask about the love of her life, Ben, and how she'd lost him.

No. God, no.

Emma needed someone else tonight. Someone she could trust, someone who could *help* her. This man she needed, he'd be here today. But somehow he'd forgotten her. Why had he forgotten her?

"Well, don't just *stand* there! Come over, girl!"

Emma forced herself to smile at Wooly, but the smile felt alien on her lips. Sometimes it felt as if her mouth would never be able to curl anywhere but downward.

With effort, she convinced her legs to carry her to the bar, and her eyes scanned the crowd once more.

She spotted the tall, broad-backed man talking among a group by the jukebox, and she stopped in her tracks. Something warm and frightening went through her. *Carter.*

Her mind sparked up with a memory of slitted blue eyes, straight, sun-streaked, wind-swept hair, and a lone dimple on a bronzed face.

Emma remembered times when they'd laughed together, the three of them, when they'd been easy friends.

She remembered that when Ben died, when she'd been shocked and numb and spent days and days in complete denial, it had been Carter she'd cried with. What would she say to him now?

How could she find words to explain how badly it still hurt inside?

How could she begin to tell him how fiercely she needed him?

He turned, as though he'd sensed her scrutiny, and Emma held her breath when their stares clashed. She'd looked into that laser blue gaze far too many times. But today, across a sea of heads, his stare was a bit less friendly, more startling. Intense.

Her heart began to thump when that tall, familiar figure detached from the group and purposely began winding around the tables toward her. Anticipation flitted through her.

His eyebrows were drawn low over his eyes as though he couldn't quite believe he was seeing Emma at the bar, but the uncertainty ended there.

Carter moved with the sinewy confidence of one who owned not only this bar, but everyone in it. Today he wore boots, a black shirt, and faded jeans that hugged his narrow hips. That shirt showed off a lean, sculpted chest, which she knew firsthand was droolworthy and had caused many a traffic hazard when he washed his car shirtless in his driveway.

His smile had that same brand of charm that Ben's dazzling smile had had, except Ben had looked like a prince, and Carter looked like a pirate.

Those bad-boy, rugged looks and the permanent scruff

on his jaw fit Carter Bates like a black mask suited a high-wayman.

Emma felt her lips curl, strangely breathless when she basked in the sight of that sexy dimple, which made an appearance as he neared.

"Figured," he said then.

Like every word he spoke, the word was huskily sarcastic and coated with playfulness.

God, she'd missed him! "What figured?"

The dimple deepened as a row of white teeth flashed. "Even vampires come out to feed."

"I've been downgraded from princess to vampire now?"

"Zombie, then." He took her purse from her grasp and set it on the bar counter, and his eyes fell with tenderness on her face as he raised a large bronzed hand to briefly trace her jaw with his fingertip. "Welcome to the land of the livin', Em. Nice to have our princess back."

Looking comfortable in his own skin in a way Emma envied, he set his drink on the bar top with a *thunk* and rapped his knuckles on the wood.

"'Nother ice-cold beer, pal. And a Bloody Mary for the lady. Ain't that right, pumpkin?"

"Yes, that's right."

Falling silent, Emma watched Carter's profile as he spoke, nervously gathering her purse back to her chest for some reason.

She'd always kind of hated the way his straight, light brown hair fell into his eyes, like he'd just gotten out of bed and some woman had gotten her hands in there. She hated that her hands itched to do the same.

As he waited for their drinks and watched her with that unsettling smile of his, one that said he really *was* pleased to see her, Emma became aware of the attention they were garnering.

No matter how much this city had grown in the past few years, at times it still felt like a small town, population fifty.

She touched his forearm with the tip of one finger, quickly withdrawing her hand when his eyes fell there in puzzlement. "Bates, would you mind if we talked somewhere?"

His brows flew up in mock wonder, and a teasing glimmer appeared in his eyes. "So proper. I can hardly believe this is the wicked little nurse I know."

With a grin that made him look even more mischievous and pirate-y, he pushed open the door of the back office, holding it with the toe of his boot to allow her to pass, and extended his arm—mockingly, as usual. *"After you."*

He was Carter Bates, and now Emma realized he wasn't going to make asking for any kind of favor easy.

He flicked a switch as he followed her into his office, and all at once the room flooded with light. There was a large desk inside the room. A bookcase with everything but books. A set of electric guitars, a lot of clutter, and Carter.

He kicked the door shut behind him, a big slam, and Emma's tummy gripped. It had been ages since she'd talked to anyone—really talked.

Suddenly Carter felt too large, too knowing to trust. His size dwarfed her. His electric blue eyes quietly unnerved her as he leaned on the closed door, examining her, taking in every breath, every look, every move.

She racked her brain for a place to begin, and suddenly felt as though the friend she'd gotten to know during the past six years had died with Ben, and in his place stood a stranger. A stranger who'd totally forgotten her. Why had he forgotten her? Why had he been avoiding her?

"Well now," he said in that toe-curling drawl, his eyes sparkling with relish as he crossed his thick arms over his chest and widened his stance. "You've got all my attention—so speak."

The desperation in her eyes.

Carter waited for her to say something.

Expectation colored her face bright pink, and it nagged at his curiosity like a yarn ball nagged a cat. What could have possibly brought Emma to seek him out tonight?

Something.

Something powerful enough to make a woman like her, young and attractive, want to stop wasting away with her memories of Ben. Something that maybe, just maybe, involved Carter.

He'd known she'd entered the bar even before he saw her.

Decidedly impossible not to notice Emma had just come in—for some mind-boggling reason. Felt just like a hammer in the damned nuts. There had been an altering in his perception, a shot of alertness sliding into him and stiffening his back. Carter had turned to the entrance, and sure enough, she was in his bar.

He'd watched her, transfixed, as she entered uncertainly.

Other times he'd seen her, she'd looked worn out, like an old favorite sock without its mate, and not inclined to do anything to fix the problem. But this mighty fine evening there was something about the princess . . . something different. She looked . . . alive.

And the mere fact that she'd been standing there by the entrance, all lonely and sexy in his bar, got to his nerves.

Ben's death had left marks on her. Marks that made her body slimmer, her eyes bigger. Hell, even after a blow like the one life had dealt her, she managed to look prettier than anyone else in this bar.

She'd glanced around as she strode in, as if looking for someone—but her face jerked to Wooly when he called to her.

"Done mourning, is she?" someone had said, not without a hint of pity.

"'Bout time, too! How long has it been? A year?"

"Almost two," Carter mumbled. And Christ, this had been two very shitty years.

"Still good friends with her?" someone asked.

Carter shrugged and gazed into the empty depths of his iced beer glass. "I suppose."

But Emma had made all her friends go away, had banished everything from her life except what remained of Ben—his clothes, his pictures, his home. And Carter, who'd been there for her in the beginning, could hardly bear to look into her sweet oval face anymore.

"I swear my heart goes flat when I look at her," Heidi had said as Emma walked inside.

"We all miss Ben," another agreed. "Hell, I can't imagine what it's like for you and Emma, Bates."

Carter glowered at his boots. "Sucks the big one's all I plan to say."

They'd been too close, the three of them. Ever since she and Ben had moved to San Antone over six years ago. But tragedy had a way of pulling people apart.

Carter had tried to offer a shoulder. Be strong for her. Pretended it didn't knock him down like a bull when she cried, pretended it was all right that it was for Ben she cried. Until he just couldn't see her anymore. Every time he did he felt kicked in the ass like a rented mule, and he'd had enough.

He'd always known she wasn't meant for him. He'd had women, could have any woman he wanted. Except one. This one.

Off-limits. Because she was Ben's.

Sucked the big one, it did. To want the princess.

Now Carter was keeping a respectable distance between them. Three whole neighborhoods. But she was still close . . . still in his mind.

This minute she was *way* too close. Close enough to smell honeyed apples. His nostrils flared as he caught the scent, and he stayed put as he waited, his chest full of her. Damn she smelled right. *What's she doing here?*

Carter watched her with narrowed eyes, his body humming to the fact, the unmistaken sense, that Emma Wilkins wanted something from him.

A lady didn't put on a short brown dress with a line of

buttons down the front that tempted a man's fingers and a slightly flared skirt that ended in the middle of milky, slim thighs that screamed to be wrapped around your hips for nothing.

She wanted something—and she wanted it from Carter.

And yet Emma seemed to want to pretend otherwise, for she started shaking her head. "I don't know what I'm doing here."

But she did. Carter sensed, could almost see, something twirling in that sharp mind of hers. He knew for a fact Emma was little in stature but big on wacky ideas. Carter fucking loved wacky ideas.

The suspense was killing him, so he bit the bullet and asked. "You always talked to me before. Come on. Spit it out, Em."

She dragged in a breath, then went around his small office, absently stroking things as she went. "Why have you been avoiding me?"

A shot of raw, undiluted need swept through him when she stroked the leather handle of a flogger. He'd flogged a real plump girl on that desk over there—and he hadn't gotten nearly as hard as watching Emma stroke the damned flogger. His voice came out gruff. "Been things I've needed to take care of."

He watched as she struggled for more words, her finger trailing the leather tip, then tracing the length of a leather tassel. *Jesus.*

"I miss you," she said in a little voice, and her eyes searched his, and his traitorous cock pushed up against his zipper. "You're my friend—I feel like I've done something unforgivable."

"You haven't, I guarantee that."

His balls strained tight in his jeans and he'd bet his bar on the fact that they were turning blue. Now Emma was looking down at the flogger, lifting it absently, raking her fingers through those long lucky tassels. . . .

"It's been . . . three months. I even tried calling you here at your office," she confessed, her cheeks heating prettily.

Torture. "Like I said, been busy."

His mouth felt as stiff as his dick, and he found it difficult to speak while watching her teasing fingers plunge into those tassels in a way a man wanted to plunge into a woman. . . .

He almost groaned in self-pity. What would it feel like to spread Emma on his desk and work her up into a fever? To have those little fingers on his chest? To work those tassels fast and loving on her pert little ass?

He didn't consider himself a dom. Just a cowboy who liked to have some good ole adult fun. But this. Heck, this was the work of the devil. Sending Emma here just to tease him.

Damn, she was staring, waiting for an answer, waiting for him to stop thinking of her ass and her fingers on the tassel. His balls strained. His cock pulsed and thickened painfully. He gritted his teeth as he tried to get himself under control.

How could he explain his exasperating fantasies to her? Was he stupid enough to tell her that *she* was the star in every damned last one of them?

He didn't tell her he missed her, too, but he did. Damn, he missed Emma. And he missed the doc.

"Carter, I can't . . . I can't get over him." Her lips trembled, and the helpless torment in her eyes twisted a knife of fresh pain into him. *She needs Ben.*

She set down the flogger, her full attention on him now. Her chest shuddered as she exhaled. "It's like I'm waiting for him to come back so my life can begin again."

Conflicting emotions ran across her expressive face as she spoke. The sight made Carter's chest tighten. "Emma," he began. He didn't know how to put it, but then he just put it all out there, flat as it was. "Ben ran into a damned carrier truck. He's dead. Ain't no coming back from that."

A tomblike silence followed.

He sighed, rumpled his own hair. "Sorry if that was harsh, but it's been almost two years. He's not coming back, Em; why are you still clinging so hard?"

Her big eyes pulled at all his heartstrings, and his blood continued pooling, hot and wild, in his aching groin. "I don't know. It's like . . . it's the only thing I can feel. Wanting him back. I can't think of anything else. . . . I feel so empty. Carter, it's like my world stopped turning that night, and I don't know how to start it up again. I'm not sure I even want to, but I'm pretty sure I have to."

Her admission twisted him like the surest rodeo lasso yanked on the weakest rodeo calf. He felt it jerk, and tug, and pull, until he could hardly bear to stand there without doing anything to help her.

Emma was struggling, he knew. Struggling to continue with the life she'd made there. Struggling not to fall apart.

She was a nurse both by profession and by nature, and her compassion for her patients had always filled Carter with admiration. Emma was used to mending people, and now the poor little woman was struggling to mend herself.

But how in the devil could he help her? He was *not* Ben.

Carter had always thought she looked adorable after Ben kissed her, like a woman basking in a man's love. *Blissful.*

He'd even gone so far as to wonder if she'd look so rosy cheeked and warm after Carter kissed the heck out of her. Not that he'd ever really planned to find out, not now anyhow, with his friend gone and with no means of fighting fair and square for his woman. Just didn't seem honest.

Emma Wilkins was the kind of girl who'd grown up in a healthy atmosphere. Good parents, good friends, good schools. She'd had every reason to believe in happily ever afters, in miracles, and in soul mates.

Did she still believe that crap now?

If she did, then she had to know that she wouldn't be getting her happily ever after, that her soul mate had died, and that the time for a miracle had been almost two years ago.

Dammit. Now *he* felt depressed and empty.

And why the hell did she have to talk about this with *him*? Heidi would sure be happy to lend an opinion—she always had her mouth full of them. And Wooly, he'd have an orgasm just to have a go at Emma's little problem.

"Look, Emma, you got the wrong guy here. Not the brightest bulb in the box when it comes to examining feelings and shit. Maybe Wooly would . . ."

She shot him such a look of loathing he felt slapped. Then she grabbed her purse from where she'd laid it on his cluttered desk, affronted. "You're right. You're absolutely right. I think I'll have my drink outside and spill my guts to Wooly so the entire bar can know."

The door whacked shut behind her.

Back stiffening, Carter shook his head. He adjusted his pained shaft in his jeans, mumbled, "Very smooth, man," and determinedly chased after her.

In the noise-filled bar, he used the tip of his boot to yank out the stool next to hers and plopped down on the plush seat, folding his arms against the bar top. Her scent teased his nostrils. They flared as he sniffed her like a dog. His chest constricted. His nuts twisted, full of semen and crushed painfully under his jeans.

"What do you want from me, Emma?" His words fought to be heard through the loud rock music. "This ain't just a social call—you want something and I'd be appreciative if you spelled it out."

He waited expectantly, studying her profile. Even his nipples seemed to tingle against the cotton of his T-shirt.

"You want an apology? For back there?" he asked. Her mouth was about the sexiest thing he'd ever seen. His cock would barely make it inside. The fit would be snug. She'd probably give him teeth. Arousal coursed through his veins at the thought. If he shoved his hand into his jeans, he'd come with three strokes.

"I don't want an apology," Emma murmured, nursing her Bloody Mary between two small white hands.

Forcing his shoulders to relax, Carter shifted in his seat and angled his body in her direction. But still not close enough. He lowered his voice and bent his head to hers. "I'm glad you came, Emma," he admitted. He meant it so bad he might as well have just gone all the way and told her he loved her.

"Yeah, well." She shrugged. Was she blushing? The music came to an abrupt halt, and the band's lead announced a short break. Emma's eyes shifted to the back of the room, and Carter could see she was seeking topics of conversation. "I suppose the jukebox needs a little TLC," she said, with a half smile.

He glanced at the jukebox. Hadn't heard it play for a while. A year and eight months, in fact.

This used to be their favorite place. Hers and Ben's. Sometimes after the live band left, they would keep that jukebox playing all freaking night and when they were very drunk and got very amorous, they would play *their* song over and over. "Endless Love." Ben hated being ribbed about having a song, especially such a wimpy, maudlin song, but Emma had determined they must have one and had all but picked that one by herself. It had been funny before, for everyone except Emma. Now it was just sad.

"Does it still work?" she asked softly.

He shrugged. "You and Ben were the ones who loved poking it."

"Tequila! On the house." Wooly slapped two drinks on the counter and leaned over, eyeing Carter with juicy speculation. "You two need to catch up—I'll be sure to keep 'em coming."

"Here, princess—and in case you're thinking of thanking Wooly over there, *on the house* means *on me*."

Carter slid one shot glass over to her, and when she absently reached for it, their fingers brushed. It felt like being touched by a butterfly. Felt like having its soft wings flutter against your finger, and then going away—far away. Where you could never touch a butterfly again.

He curled his fingers into his palm and stared morosely into his tequila, then tossed back the shot in one gulp. Crap, the effect she had on him . . .

The bar had fallen unusually quiet. They were all whispering behind him, Carter supposed. They probably all knew he had a raging erection and a full blown X-rated film flicking through his mind. He glanced past his shoulders and yeah, they were all watching. He glared at them, all ten of their friends.

What the devil were they staring at? So what if a man wanted to make a woman feel better? So what if he had a thing for her smile? He had two balls big enough to admit now that he wanted to have something to offer her.

He fucking *loved* her. And why the hell couldn't he? She'd come to his rescue one day when he'd had a stupid accident with a Chardonnay bottle. Emma had given him a smile and three stitches on his wrist. One had gone to his mind. Another to his cock. And that last, heck, that last had gone straight for his heart.

He hadn't been surprised—to sit there, bleeding like an idiot, and watch her face as she worked, and think, *Damn, I really want to put my arm around this little woman.*

That realization of falling, falling, falling into someplace he'd never before been and would probably spend his life trying to get out of, had struck him when he'd first looked into her eyes, right inside this very bar, that first night she'd looked into his eyes and said, *Nice to meet you, Carter.* Holy hell, he'd badly wanted that sweet-smelling thing to say *Carter* again. But then he'd heard her say, *Ben's been talking about you,* and the admiration and love and respect she rendered to that word, to the word *Ben,* let's just say (and put it frankly) that Carter had never had any hopes of his feelings ever being reciprocated.

But now . . .

Now she'd said she *missed* him. Had come out of hiding just to come see *him.*

"Emma, what are you doing here? Tell me the truth," he urged softly. He was excruciatingly aware that their shoulders were almost touching. Hers, little and round. His, big and square.

"Carter . . ." She met his gaze, and her eyes were big and brown and as pretty as a deer's. The kind of eyes he'd remember tonight in bed. "I'd like for you to take me to the club you go to."

His breath stopped. The Club?

An emotion assailed him and squeezed his gut so tight it almost tore a groan out of him. *Emma strapped and helpless . . . being paddled . . . being pleasured by Carter.*

His dick pushed up against his fly. He could feel moisture threatening to dribble out the tip. He swallowed back a curse and reached out for her hand, intending to tell her she wasn't ready, it was too heavy for her. The Club was a place of fantasy and sex, of whips and bondage, of masters and slaves. Carter had never imagined Emma the sort of person who'd step through its doors. Though no one—let it be recorded, *no one*—would tan her hide as lovingly as Carter. No one would take care of her like he could. But his answer was still no. *Hell no.*

He hadn't yet grasped her hand to set her mind straight when he heard it.

The song, unmistakable.

He saw Emma tense, her eyes flare wide with shock as the haunting melody of "Endless Love" began playing.

He whipped around to the jukebox, but no one was there. No one was there! The words rang out loud and clear, troubling, gut-wrenching.

My love, there's only you in my life. . . .

And Emma, god, her eyes welled, and it was like watching a kitten being kicked to death. A sob caught unchecked in her throat and, stumbling to her feet, she grabbed her bag, ducked her head so no one could see her eyes streaming with tears, and stormed out of the bar.

Chapter Two

One year, eight months, and seven days ago

Ben Newcastle woke up in a strange room. The pain
was gone. No more blood on his chest or legs. Shit,
what time was it?

Bolting up on the table, he yanked the sheet off his body
and stared around the shadows. Where was he?

He had to go to Emma. Discovering that he was nicely
dressed, and in a monkey suit, too, he *knew* with unerring
certainty that there was no reason to stay there, so he yanked
the door open, walked out without any commotion, and
made his way home.

He was fine, felt wonderful. Light. But goddammit, he
was probably late. And so he ran.

The scene that met him at the house wasn't the domestic
one he had been expecting. A man stood in the middle of
the living room, a police officer, looming before Emma.

"Did I miss something?" Ben cocked a brow.

But Emma continued staring at the man before her with her face pale and her eyes rounded.

"There's some news about . . . Ben Newcastle," the man said.

"I promised I'd be home early for your birthday," Ben told her, sniffing through the kitchen, not hungry but feeling a craving for food. He could see she'd made their favorite risotto. "So here I am, I hope I'm not too late," he finished, almost drooling over the pot.

Emma spoke, her voice a teensy wisp—"What happened? Where . . . where is he?"

Ben glanced up and frowned. Concerned, he walked over to her, feeling things in an acute manner he'd never felt before. He felt her . . . fear. "I'm right here, Emma," he said softly.

"Ma'am, Mr. Newcastle is dead."

Ben almost fell over. He ran his hands over himself. His wounds—his wounds were gone. The pain—gone. But he was here. Here. How could he be here if he was—

"No," Emma said, a gasp as she gripped the chair behind her. "No no no no."

Ben was dead?

No way.

He was dead?

No! He couldn't be dead. He couldn't leave Emma, he couldn't. Holy fuck, he had *no heartbeat*!

"I'm sorry, ma'am."

"But he called me just before he left work; he said he was coming home!" Her voice broke, and the rest was cried out in a panic. "Sir, I don't think you understand. Ben never lies. *Never.* If he said he was coming home, then he's coming home!"

"I am!" Ben said. "I *am* home. I came here, for you. I came back for you!"

The officer grasped Emma's fragile shoulders and urged her into a chair. "I realize this is a shock, ma'am, so let's just calm down for a minute."

Dropping down like a deflated balloon, Emma let go a ragged breath—her big, soulful brown eyes unseeing, staring straight ahead, looking directly at Ben and past him and beyond him. Something about the lost expression on her face made Ben's mind scramble for ways to make her nymph-like smile return.

She buried her face between her hands, a sob catching in her throat. Her body shook violently. She said, "*Oh, god.*"

The feelings that arose in him as he watched her struggle not to cry defied description. Ben knelt at her feet and tried drawing her hand to his, but he couldn't grasp her. Damn, he couldn't *grasp* her.

"Miss Wilkins . . ." the officer began.

"I'm still here, Emma," Ben tried to soothe her. What else could he say? What else?

Emma. The first silly little fourteen-year-old who'd kissed him. He'd been sixteen. Neighbors their whole lives, and never apart. She'd just grabbed Ben's head that afternoon and kissed him, smack there, on his lips. *What the hell was that for?* a stunned Ben had said.

I just wanted to see if you knew how to do it, she'd chirped, looking smug because she'd caught him unawares.

I do, you little minx. Do you? he'd demanded, then he'd

pulled her right back to his mouth where she belonged and kissed the heck out of her.

She was not yet thirty now, but by the bent way she sat there, she could've been an old woman.

Ben couldn't take his eyes off the sad girl, the sad girl no one had ever been able to keep Ben away from. No one. He'd had simple goals because he was a simple man, and that goal had been to save lives and to be with Emma.

He'd waited until he got back from Harvard, and then he'd taken her, in all the ways a man can take a woman, he'd taken Emma, promising no one would ever keep them apart again. Even now, when nothing could possibly separate him more from her, he remained. Here. With *her*.

"Would you come with us to identify the body, miss?"

Head snapping back at the officer's voice, Emma seemed to struggle with the word *body* and caught her breath, her chest heaving.

"No, she will *not* be looking at bodies," Ben growled.

Fast as lightning, Emma's head whipped in his direction. "What?"

Ben felt something leap inside him as their gazes met. *Holy God, please tell me you see me.* "Can you see me? Baby, can you see me?"

Emma raised a trembling hand to his visage, watched, transfixed, as she placed her fingers at the same place where his lips hovered. She caught her breath, tears began rolling and rolling down her cheeks, and then she closed her eyes.

Ben knelt there, ragged emotion wrenching his gut as he waited for her to say something. Loss, anger, helplessness.

He thought of all the things they'd been through, and

after all the years, the misunderstandings, the quiet moments, the loud ones, and the ones you'd simply never forget, he knew they'd deserved a better end.

Ben had charged himself with the task of protecting her, had sworn to himself after her parents moved to France that he'd make Emma smile every day for the rest of her life. Now he was right here, mere inches from Emma, and for the first time ever he was unable to help her. He'd never felt so irked and frustrated. He'd never felt so bereft.

When she opened her eyes, Ben waited in suspense to see if she spotted him again.

She struggled to stand on her own two feet, ducking her head as though embarrassed. "I'm sorry, I'm fine, I'll . . ." Speaking seemed difficult, like she'd forgotten all the words inside her head. "I'll—I'll go with you."

Her eyes wildly scanned the living room, the kitchen, the foyer.

Was she looking for him?

Standing to her right with a protective arm around her waist, Ben murmured in her ear, "I'm right here, baby."

She didn't react—didn't see him.

They'd always shared an unearthly connection—always. *Look at me, Em!*

"I'll wait by the door," the stocky officer said with a curt nod.

Ben stood there, confused, watching Emma climb the stairs, one step at a time. A new feeling overtook him as she ascended. Abandonment. He felt like she'd broken up with him, or worse. Left him for dead.

She planned to go see his battered, beat-up body, and

for the rest of her life this was the way she'd remember him. Broken, battered. Dead.

He stood in his home. Dead.

Waiting for her to go see that he was . . . dead.

He kept expecting to wake up, for the ghost of Christmas Future to appear, laughing, and give him another chance. One he wouldn't waste.

Great lesson to teach that it was time to get married. Have a couple of kids. Great lesson to pay more attention to his family.

But it wasn't Christmas.

And it appeared that the ghost was he.

Present day

"Endless Love."

Everyone knew Ben had hated "his" song. He'd said it was sappy and depressing and that he'd never live it down.

" 'Endless Love'? Emma, for god's sake, *'Endless Love'*?"

He'd been outraged.

It figured, Emma mulled as she drove through the rain, that it would take a broken heart and many years to finally see the point Ben had stubbornly been trying to make. "Endless Love" *was* depressing.

And now Emma couldn't stop crying.

Had she thought that she could find a way to stop hurting? That Carter would produce a little box that enabled her to lock all her grief away?

Of course she had. She was a mess. Had been a mess for

over a year. Obviously she couldn't even think reasonably anymore.

Once, Emma had known a girl who'd loved a boy so bad she'd hitchhiked eleven hundred miles just to go see him. Once, she'd known a woman who'd packed her bags in two hours to follow her man and had secured a new home for them in the space of two more. And later, she'd known the woman who'd organized a funeral in a day, a woman who'd watched the rain hit the sleek wood of a shiny black coffin where the man she loved lay, and marveled how she didn't succumb to the urge to fling herself into that pit with the rain, with *him*, where no one would ever find her.

That girl. That woman. They'd left her, too.

Wiping her cheeks with one hand, she clenched the steering wheel as she pulled into the driveway of the home she'd lived in for the past eight years.

Behind the gray clouds above, the moon was the same. The sky was the same. The oaks lining her driveway, the same.

Maybe, just maybe, nothing had really changed.

Except missing from the garage was his black BMW. His keys weren't hidden in the flowerpot. And Emma knew that his long black coat wouldn't be on the coatrack.

Oh, god, Ben was gone.

She'd thought going out tonight would help her—but had it? When everything felt so wrong? When everything she did reminded her of him?

She'd tried to tackle her life—a life that had seemed fast and perfect with Ben, and now felt long and lonely and endless—she'd tried to tackle it the way Heidi, a sensible teacher, had told her to. With baby steps.

Baby step one: wake up; don't cry.

Baby step two: shower; don't cry.

Baby steps three and four and more: Dress; breakfast; visit her patients. Don't cry.

Baby steps had taken her through each and every day for the past year, but every second of each day, Emma Wilkins felt Ben like she felt a heartache.

She felt him whispering to her at night. She felt his eyes on her when she dressed. She felt him, felt him everywhere, and because of the wild expectation of one day seeing him pass through their front door, Emma was stuck in a hellhole of despair she was certain she'd never get out of if she didn't do something about the state of her life *soon*.

But Carter hadn't seemed too keen on her idea of the Club. He'd looked incredulous and then almost alarmed.

Why alarmed, dammit?

She was used to blocking pain: the wince of the patient when she tightened a stitch. Their sharp gasp at the prick of a syringe. If only she could block out her own.

Weighted down with frustration, she felt tiny soft raindrops slap her back as she walked up the gravel path and unlocked the front door.

She glanced bitterly around the cozy home they'd decorated with Native American pillows and rugs. She kept expecting him to appear.

But nothing materialized.

There was no sound except the creak of wood as she

closed the front door behind her and stepped into a home that had been bought for two—and was now only for Emma.

My love, there's only you in my life. . . .

Lifting the acrylic frame on the console table with cramped hands, Emma stared into Ben's strong, handsome face, the unique black eyes that seemed to stare all the way into you.

He used to say that they were special. That what they felt defied description and that they should never let anyone take that away from them.

Emma hadn't.

Emma *wouldn't*.

What she needed to do had nothing to do with the way she felt for Ben.

There was a knock. First one quick rap. Then silence. Emma set the picture frame back in place.

The knocks started more forcefully, like a bark for attention. Emma knew who it was, with every fiber in her body, she knew.

When she opened the door . . . he was there. A tall, handsome, wet Carter. Why did the sight of him make her want to topple?

"Hey," she said, her voice strange and craggy.

A gleam of concern flared in his eyes. He stuck a booted foot into the house with a big manly *thunk*. "You okay?"

The tenderness in his voice threatened to undo her. Carter didn't do tenderness. Not like this—like he meant it.

Lips thin and grim, he eyed her pale face and her damp hair and looked none too pleased. "Plan to leave me out here soaking or can I hop in? My word, I got no idea what happened back there at the Fox."

Emma ducked her head and stepped back so he could pass. Their elbows brushed and a sharp, warm shiver flitted through her. She frowned. "What are you doing here?" *Please let's just skip through this and take me to the stupid club.*

Carter's eyes met hers, and the acute awareness in his dark pupils reminded her of a caged tiger. He shut the door behind him. "Heidi call you, baby?"

Her heart leapt at the sexy way he drawled *baby*.

His hair was always rumpled, but now it was a little bit wet, and Emma felt a sudden need to reach out and straighten it for him. She curled her fingers into her palms. "No, she hasn't called."

The phone trilled in the living room, and he signaled. "Bet that's her."

Emma didn't move from her spot. Wasn't sure she wanted him here, with the way she felt.

"You might wanna answer unless you want her coming over, too. She was chewin' on her nails when you left."

Sighing, she went to pick up the phone and heard her friend's concerned voice. "Em, what happened?"

Carter let himself in, plopped down on her couch, and propped his feet up on the coffee table. His tumultuous-testosterone essence was suddenly all over the room.

Acutely aware of her male visitor, one who hadn't stopped by her house for three months, Emma gripped the receiver until her knuckles whitened. "Nothing—just—just wanted to come home."

"I'm so proud of you for taking this step, Em, so so proud!"

After short assurances, Emma told her they'd talk tomorrow, replaced the receiver in the cradle and turned, slightly annoyed, toward the man on the couch. Was he going to *baby* her, too?

He'd all but quit on her for three months and now he wanted to come here, pretty as you please, with that casual pose that fairly screamed take-my-boots-on-your-table-and-wipe-off-after-I-leave?

"Been thinking about it. And that does sound like a bit of a problem," Carter said. He rose to his full height with that deliberate laziness cowboys did so well.

"What is?"

He began coming forward, and Emma's heart began to thud. Instinctively, she backed away, breathless over the wolfish glimmer in his eyes.

She couldn't banish the thought, the sense, that something primal was pushing him on; something that seemed to have been nursed for a very long time. A pain, maybe not entirely unlike her own. "You came looking for me." The words rumbled up his hard chest. "Because you miss me. And what I see in your eyes right now, princess, ain't nothing."

"W-what do you mean?"

Her pulse skyrocketed to the roof. Oh, god, what was that crazy look in his eyes?

"I'll say you feel, Emma. I'll say you just feel *too damned much.*"

She hit a wall and had no other choice than to watch as one seriously alarming Carter took the last step toward her. A tremor went through her, a tremor of fear, of . . . awareness?

This had been a huge mistake. Epic. Sadly, she thought of Ben and how he wouldn't tease her if she had a problem like not feeling. If she cried, Ben would hold her. If she needed him, he'd know what she required without ever having to ask him for it. With Carter it was different. He pushed you to admit things . . . dared you to contradict him.

Now . . . oh, god. Now his body heat enveloped her. His proximity gave rise to all kinds of strange uncomfortable little flutters.

"Let's see now, princess." She felt the seductive brush of his hand ghosting across her quivering lips. His eyes took on a deep, thrilling quality as he caressed her with the pad of his thumb. "Do you feel that?"

"What are you doing?" she gasped. Her breasts beaded under her blouse. Her pussy clenched in shock. The look in his eyes was so primal, a flood of desire sluiced through her, watering her folds.

God, this was not the complication she needed. Not the kind of physical feeling she was looking for when she asked him to take her to that club. She didn't want to feel arousal—she wanted pain. Lots of pain.

"How about here?" His hand skidded up and down the tendons of her throat. The tantalizing caress of those long fingers made her thighs turn liquid.

She was startled by the sensation, pressed her legs tighter together as she fought to remain unmoved. Unstoppable, a rush of desire coursed through her veins. Her cunt started to burn. Squeeze reflexively. Longing for . . . penetration. Her nipples engorged and thrust up, sensitive.

"I . . . no." It was just a gasp. A choked gasp.

Something was happening to her. Something frightening.

Her nipples extended to a painful length. Her skin warmed to his presence and the little hairs on her arms stood at attention. Her insides rioted, coming to life in a way they hadn't in almost two years. She couldn't stop it. Couldn't control it, couldn't stop her pussy from feeling swollen and damp, couldn't keep it from blazing like a wet flame between her thighs.

"What about here, Emma?" He covered one breast and then the other, gently weighing the globes in his strong, calloused hands and fondling them as if they were fragile treasures. Her breath caught midway down her lungs. Her nipples screamed under the circling caresses of his thumb, pushing up, pushing for *more more more*. "Or here." His thumbs unerringly pinched the puckered buds. She bit back a strangled exclamation of pleasure.

Her every cell and fiber danced with female awareness, and unexpectedly, a wave of remorse surged within her.

Lust.

She didn't want to feel it.

Tears felt like they gathered inside her, all of them in a tight little ball contained in her throat. She couldn't bear to feel this again. Couldn't even bear to feel the touch of a man again, feel pleasure from it ever again.

"Aww, what is this? Tears?"

"No," she said, teeth clenched. "Stop this."

"You came all the way to my bar to cry on my shoulder, didn't you?" He groaned softly as his arms went around her, protectively drawing her against his rock-hard body as he nuzzled the top of her head. "You don't really want to go to the Club, you just want to be held."

Both nodding and shaking her head, Emma held on to him, burying her face in a neck that was thick and smelled of woods and raindrops. His big, strong hands massaged her back, gently, soothingly, as his husky whisper spilled into her ear. "You could've just said so, princess."

She fought not to cry, because she hated how her eyes swelled and she hated that she was a sniffler and that she'd cried oceans onto his shoulders already. "I don't want to cry ever again. I won't, ever," she said, a craggy breath against his collarbone as one large palm held the back of her head, while the arm encircling her waist kept her pinned to his body.

He ducked as he spoke. His lips grazed warmly against the shell of her ear, nipping softly as he said, "I've got one good ear—two in fact, and right now, they're all yours, Em. So tell me. What is it you need?"

Emma's focus sharpened on that low rasp. Her heart quickened. Carter sounded . . . No. He couldn't be aroused, he couldn't.

Concerned about the heat that swept through her like wildfire, she tried to quell it and buried deeper into his arms, seeking comfort. But a large bulge met her stomach. He was . . . hard. Oh, god, he was brutally hard. She should be doing something. . . .

Something other than slightly turning her head to his, bringing her mouth closer to his . . .

"Carter . . . ?"

"You feel this, don't you?"

He lowered his head and spoke in a murmur, a murmur against her lips. An electric bolt went through her as he planted a soft, close-lipped kiss against her mouth. A whimpering moan dredged up in her throat. He retreated and looked into her eyes with a heavy-lidded gaze. He bent his head again.

Her heart thundered in her ears. He brushed her lips, up and down, side to side. Slowly. Curiously. Her lungs strained for air, and he made a strange, deep sound, and parted his lips wider and began to tease her. Their breath mingled, hers fast and short, his deep and haggard. Emma didn't pull away as their air mixed, and neither did Carter. He angled his head and dipped closer.

"What are you doing?" she whispered, aware that her toes were curling, her nipples pricking so painfully she curled her hands over his shoulders to fight the urge to reach upward and massage some relief into them.

He looked tormented as he framed her cheeks between his large palms, his face taut and lust-filled as he slanted his head and slowly came down. "Something stupid . . ."

When his lips covered hers slowly, hesitantly, savoringly, a thousand thoughts exploded in her brain. *He's kissing me. He shouldn't be kissing me. . . .*

So hot. So very hot. She instinctively opened her mouth, dazzled by the mist of his breath, the silken graze of his lips moving coaxingly against hers. Arousal coursed through her blood in an avalanche.

Don't kiss him!

But his warm tongue stole into her parted lips, and her breasts swamped with heat, and for this very moment she forgot everything, even why she'd been on the verge of crying.

God.

God.

Her folds lubricated and her pussy swelled. Her hips rocked against his erection. His lips and tongue thrust and plunged into her mouth, consuming her, sweeping her like a whirlwind. Emma shuddered, rocking her hips faster against his as she curled her tongue around his and her hands slid along the firmness of his chest muscles. Oh, god, he felt warm and strong and so like Ben. . . .

Like Ben . . .

But different . . .

Her blood rushed. Growling low and deep, Carter pulled her flush against him and lifted her until only her toes touched the floor, holding her up by the ass as his tongue plunged and took, feasting on her mouth as though he'd been waiting in line for dinner for a long, long time.

She didn't know what happened, but suddenly he lifted her leg, grabbed one high heel and dropped it on the floor. The next followed. He curled her legs around his hips and pinned her against the wall, his massive erection nestled between her thighs.

Need gripped her by the throat. She mewled softly, grinding the tender bud of flesh between her legs against his delicious hardness.

"Tell me if you feel this, baby." His voice was gruff as he

slipped loose the two front buttons of her dress and his free hand stole through the opening to caress one lace-covered breast.

He groaned as his mouth took hers once more. Her muscles tightened reflexively as he ground his body against hers, his hand possessive as it kneaded her breast.

Stop him!

His engorged shaft rocked against her, provoking an uncontrollable fever as he squeezed and massaged her breast in a way that drove her wild with desire. Lust arrowed down to her pussy, drenching her panties.

God, he was so much like him, like Ben, and she could pretend he was there. But it wasn't him; and his mysterious, undecipherable taste proved it. The way he tasted . . .

He tasted so hot, so forbidden, so new. . . .

She could hear his breathing tear through his body, feel his erection pumping against her hungrily as his tongue wildly, savagely fucked her mouth and their hips bumped and ground desperately together. . . .

All this year's emotions—despair, this wretched sorrow— teetered on the verge of this surprising new one.

She moaned breathlessly.

Making a sound she'd never heard a man make before, Carter boosted her up higher, and she almost screamed when he yanked the fabric of her dress down and exposed one breast. He pulled down the lace, then lifted the mound until her breast bumped his lips. Without apology, he took her into his mouth. He suckled, nipped, swiped, making the sensitized pearl spring back and forth under his tongue.

A moan dredged up from her throat as she thrust her hips against his body. Her clit thrummed, taut and achy. "Carter . . ."

"Tell me. . . . Tell me, baby. You're so sexy."

Her entire body trembled from the heat, the way he drawled, "sex-saaay."

Emma thought of how she wanted to die, for the first time wanted to die but from the pleasure. Thoughts of feeling a man's thick cock inside her again made her feverish. Shaking, she pulled his face up for another kiss, for more of his hot lips . . . when the phone rang. Three rings. Then his voice came. His beautiful voice, mingled with hers.

Hey, you're calling Ben and Emma. Obviously we're either not here, or don't want to talk to you. . . .

All fell still for the next three heartbeats.

A bomb of regrets exploded inside her. Emma wrenched free and spun away, scraping his taste off her mouth with the back of her hand.

She fumbled to readjust her dress, her fingers cramped and stiff on each button.

With his lips set in a tight line, Carter wiped the back of his hand across his mouth, too. He laughed. Mocking himself. "Well, that sure puts a damper on things, don't it?"

Had he just fondled her?

Had they just kissed like . . . like horny Neanderthals?

In all her life, Emma had kissed only one man like this. *One.* And the thought that she'd just doubled her number appalled her. The way she'd responded!

They were both still panting, and Emma was acutely aware of the hot flush rising up her cheeks. Her clitoris continued tingling like a living, breathing thing. A hungry thing. A lonely thing. God, a hateful thing!

"Hell, at least we both know what your real problem is, princess." Chest heaving, Carter stared at her in a way that made her insides feel wild. His eyes burned with something beyond the physical, beyond anything her stunned mind could understand right now. "You need a man. You desperately need a man."

Angry at the heat pulsing between her thighs, Emma gritted her teeth against the sensation, her voice breaking. "What I need is for you to take me to that club, Carter."

"What is it you want to do there, for god's sake?" He swung away and started pacing, and Emma bit down on her puffy lips, still tasting his kiss on her mouth and hating that it aroused her.

"I want to hurt a little," she admitted. "I think I want . . . to be told what to do. To be told to stop punishing myself like this, to let go."

He threw her a sharp glance from the center of the room, then raked his eyes across the length of her body, taking in her breasts, her hips, her lips. "By who?" A hint of self-loathing crept into his voice.

"By—you."

He went rigid, then he murmured "sumfabitch" and shut his eyes and seemed to count to ten. At his sides, his hands made white-knuckled fists. "Me. Why me?"

"Because I trust you. I want you to tell me—to order me, to stop feeling like this."

Eyes tightly sealed, Carter puffed his cheeks with air as he considered, then let it out slowly. "Doesn't work that way,

Em." Shaking his rumpled head, he scraped a hand across his mouth again and stalked in her direction. "Pampered little girls don't take kindly to being spanked, trust me."

She thrust her chin out, holding her ground, trembling with lingering arousal. "I'm not a little girl, and I need someone to help me."

"Considering you're a nurse, seems awfully weird for you to be looking for pain for yourself."

"I'm just trying to cope!"

"Where do you think all the spanking and the ordering leads to, Emma?"

She blinked.

Standing threateningly close, Carter leaned over, leveling his gaze with hers, his jaw set into a belligerent angle. "What do you figure a woman and a man playing the slave and the master end up doin'?"

Oh, god, he was kissably close, his lips still moist and glistening pink from her lip gloss, and she could barely hold her shit together and not lean over and—

He caught her arm and squeezed it in his big hand, his breath a warm and fragrant blast on her face. "They end up sweaty, baby. Bare-butt naked most of the time. And they end up wanting *more*. Why the hell would you want to do this? Ain't you suffering enough, Emma?"

God, how could she explain it to him? She thought he'd understand, but maybe Carter frequented the Club in the pursuit of pleasure. Emma wanted . . . pain. "I want it to . . . stop hurting inside. If it hurts outside, then maybe . . ."

"I got news for you." His eyes flicked to her lips, then came back up with a flare of annoyance. "It won't stop hurting. Ever. I know you. I know what you felt for him. And the way you loved him ain't never gonna stop."

He smacked her ass, and she squeaked as she watched his broad back retreat. *What was that for?*

"Does this mean we're going?" she called after him.

He yanked open the door. "No, pumpkin. That spank was just my hand straying."

Chapter Three

Chase her; comfort her.

The words vibrated through Ben Newcastle, forcing him to move, keep heading down the highway. Emma's car had long faded in the distance after she'd bolted out of the bar—and for the past half hour, Ben had cursed himself ten times over for being a fool.

Rain had started falling, but it didn't touch him and instead drizzled past his shoulders, his head. Would've been nice to feel the raindrops. Hell, it would've been nice to instantly materialize home.

In this alternate state, he suspected that if he thought hard enough, concentrated enough, he could appear back at the house in an instant. But he wasn't certain how to do this yet. He'd never strayed from the things he'd done when living. Sometimes, even knowing he would pass through a door, he found himself trying to use the doorknob. And now, rather than float or fly or simply appear somewhere, he stalked the ground like a phantom, like the undead, like a lost soul.

Why the hell had he done what he did? Playing that song? *I love her! I need to remind her!* Remind her—god, yes! Remind her of everything. Of how good they were together, even when they were bad. Especially when they were bad. Heat spread through him at the memory of their nights together, enhanced by his need for her.

A sensation like arousal overflowed him at the thought of one day feeling her again, here, in heaven, *somewhere*, and it made him tremble inside. He sucked in a breath, but his lungs didn't fill—he knew they wouldn't. But he felt a warm sensation among his middle, in his center, inviting him, urging him, to follow Emma. She'd looked so sexy today . . . like the old Emma . . . his sweet, ripe Emma. . . .

Every step he took was marked by a thought, by a memory, a reminder.

He forced his legs to work faster and exhilaration swept through him as he passed the graveyard. He didn't stop there, but instead turned north and continued, driven by the memories trickling into his mind, hurting him, arousing him, making him smile.

Dammit, Emma, don't you give up on me yet. . . .

He stopped in front of his house. Their house. A lovely little redbrick thing sitting on four acres of land and crammed on all sides with cedars and oak trees.

The front door had never looked so imposing.

He concentrated at first, then managed to go through it. A sliver of anticipation shot down his spine as he materialized inside. *Home.*

All was quiet.

He took the staircase two steps at a time and then paused at the bedroom door, uncertain all of a sudden, for there was an occupant behind it; he was sure. A girl. Not a girl, a woman. His woman.

He filtered into their bedroom and saw her cuddled in the chair by his desk, his *Doctor of the Heart* book on her lap. Long time ago, Emma had thought it would be a boring read, had scrunched up her nose at him when he'd suggested she take a look at it. She'd said that only a cardiologist would find that book entertaining. Now she was reading it, holding it in her lap. God in heaven, he was in torment.

"*I'm sorry,*" Ben said raggedly. He knew she couldn't hear him, but he always expected her to when he spoke to her.

"*I'm sorry, Emma.*"

He stepped into the darkness, approaching her slowly. The hair he'd always thought of as brown, which pissed off Emma because "It's not just brown, Ben!" fell to cover her smooth cheeks.

He set a hand on those lovely tresses—not brown, no, he could see that now, see that it was dark and shimmering like brandy—and he was shaken by the tactile memory of those long glossy strands that framed her face like ribbons.

"*I didn't mean to make you cry, Em. All I wanted was for you to remember—I don't want you to forget me. I need you to remember me.*"

She shifted to her side, her long lashes forming a crescent moon against her cheekbones.

Ben could almost smell her, could feel her body heat like a living being could feel the sunlight. She was every season of the year to him now—she was fall, winter, summer, and spring, night and day, light and dark, life and death and this hell that was between them.

He noticed that she was dreaming something naughty, blazed with silent arousal.

What had excited her? Was she dreaming of him?

He tried tangling his fingers through her hair but had grown accustomed to the failure, the impotence, and settled for the memory of feeling it slip through his fingers like petals. *"If you remember me, I can still be with you. I still feel close to you."*

He burned to feel her, touch her like a man touched the woman he loved and show her she was wanted. He hadn't seen her caress herself, not once, in all this time. Never had he seen her even want to try. He knew she needed it, knew she was sexual and playful and that she burned to release her emotions all bottled up inside.

So did Ben.

To stand there, sit there, lie there, every day for who knew how long, and watch her suffer in silence, was purgatory.

Emma had lost her thirst for life. Her innate instinct to love and laugh and sing. The plants she'd nursed in the backyard had grown weeds now. And even though she continued caring for her nursing clients with the same dedication as before, she'd lost her passion for her job to the point that he feared she'd become an automaton.

Someone, dammit, someone needed to take care of *her.*

There were moments when Ben craved to show her he'd remained, was watching over her. Would she be frightened?

Tonight he'd made her cry because he'd managed to play

their song. And she'd *remembered* dancing to it in Ben's arms. And now he realized he'd been wrong to play it, wrong to believe it would bring her happiness.

He reached for her cheek, assailed by a memory of softness. "*Emma . . .*" he said hoarsely.

Her large expressive eyes fluttered open, and for a moment, it was as if she saw him, as if those dilated pupils could see beyond thin air, and see that Ben was standing there. Her hands reached out to grasp him, grasp nothing. "Ben."

As her lips softly formed his name, he noticed they were swelled and red. As if someone had kissed them or she'd licked them a thousand times with the sweet velvet of her tongue. A soul-searing arousal gripped him, and because he could find no physical relief for it, he feared that he'd explode.

What had aroused her?

Tentatively, he moved his hand, succeeding in creating a slight breeze. Her shirt hitched up, revealing a bit of creamy belly flesh. His mouth watered.

He moved his hand again, the breeze stronger, taking the T-shirt higher, stoking his hunger. *Show me my breasts. I want to see my breasts. . . .*

Emma shifted on the chair and parted her legs. Jesus!

Ben knelt before her like a starved rabid dog, cupped her thighs in his hands, remembered how silky smooth her skin felt. He peered in between her legs, and when he saw the delicate moist spot at the front of her panties, his mouth could've watered. "*My sweet baby—are you having hot, sweaty dreams about me?*"

He sensed her yearning, her heat. *Look up again and see me. . . .*

His hands ghosted across her body. He took advantage of the movements he created and dragged the fabric of her T-shirt upward as much as he could. Starved eyes took in her navel and prayed for more. For her breasts, *god, he craved to suckle them like crazy.*

He wanted to lie beside her and tuck her body against his, to plunge into her warm heat as she slept.

Eyeing the firm little points that jutted through her T-shirt, he bent and opened his mouth over a small bead, creating the memory of having that hard nipple in his mouth. He needed. Needed to drink her sweet milk, to suckle the hell out of her.

He drank, pretended to, like a starved man, a vampire lost in the bliss of his feast, while cupping her globes. She moaned—and the sound wrenched through him like a penance. *To think he couldn't please her . . .*

How could he linger? Knowing he could not speak to her again? Knowing he couldn't feel her skin? Her lips?

But the emotions he felt for her were greater, greater than this punishment. Sometimes these feelings were able to spark up fire, the wind. Now tiny lights crackled in the bedroom fireplace as he suckled from that juicy round breast, his hand stroking downward—downward—

Just knowing that he stroked her wet pussy made him summon the sensation of wetness. The slick sounds of his fingers sliding through her flesh.

She arched in the chair, yanking her own T-shirt up over her head.

"That's it. Ahh, god, now move your panties. Move them for me."

He waited in expectation until her fingers trailed

downward. One of her hands stroked a mouthwatering peach-colored nipple, her eyes closed in concentration, and the other hand inched toward the sheer black panty she wore. The thong was so sleek it bit delicately into her puckered labia.

Arousal stormed through him as she feathered a hand over her sex. The wind kicked up outside. Sparks glittered in the fireplace. His cock was hard as a lance, erect and quivering.

And her hand . . .

Going lower . . .

Inside her panties . . .

"Inside, Emma, plunge it hard inside you."

She moaned as her middle finger entered.

Ben fell against her, trying to grab her, groaning when he failed, at last settling his kneeling form between her thighs. He watched. His eyes an inch from that lucky wicked finger, ahh, Christ, she was moaning like crazy.

He was moved to suckle her pussy, to lash out his tongue, over and over, and feel shudders rack him as he imagined her juice flowing into his mouth. He'd give anything for this. Anything.

"Do you moan for your man?" he rasped against her moving hand. He pinched her nipples and almost swore she'd felt it when she let out a soft cry. *"Do you?"*

His need drove him to make humping motions as he watched her part her panties farther and inserted a second finger into her moist channel. She penetrated herself, deeply, and Ben was going mad.

He'd always been crazy about her but this was different. Now his senses were sharp as a tack, relentless, everything fiercer, more intense. When he reached for his cock, he felt pinpricks of awareness rush through him, pinpricks of fire.

He could feel her desire almost as if it were his, could feel the ravaging *pleasure* of those plunging fingers. . . .

He could make out every detail of her slim, curved body, and what she'd revealed was the kind of sin that made a man say *no* to heaven. Her folds—she splayed them open as her fingers withdrew. Her thumb rolled her clit slowly in enticing circles.

Ben stroked himself, imagining it was her hot pussy clutching his hardness. He imagined his slit leaking . . . his fist squeezing . . . her cunt clenching . . .

Ecstasy knifed through him.

"Emma, baby, you don't even know . . . do not know . . . what I would give. . . ."

He tried to grasp her nipples again, her breasts, as he arched over to kiss her. *"For this."* He licked into her mouth, craving her taste more than anything. *"To feel you."*

They seemed to moan together. In ecstasy. In pain. In passion.

But release eluded him. It eluded Emma. Though she moaned and tried and tried, she couldn't reach the pinnacle.

So she stopped.

With an angry huff, she grabbed her T-shirt—one that Ben's parents had sent him years ago that said THIS IS THE ONLY SHIRT I DIDN'T LOSE IN LAS VEGAS, put it back on, and swept past him.

Ben shuddered when her body went through his.

Emma slid under the covers, pounded her pillow three times, and then turned to stare at the pillow on Ben's side. She was panting, still aroused, without release.

Ben watched her flushed face, feeling desperate, in need. Dead.

Her eyelids fluttered shut, and her voice rang out loud and clear in the quiet of the bedroom. "Are you here, Ben?"

"Holy God, yes. Yes! I'm here." He leapt into bed beside her and lay down facing her. He fell still when she reached out. He could almost feel her hand against his jaw when the tips of her fingers caressed his pillow.

She was silent for a long, long while, her fingertips gently stroking, her short peach-colored nails grazing a spot by his temple. "I want you to be here. I want to see you so bad," she whispered.

"Baby, look at me. Try!"

"And hear you." Shining brown eyes slid open and gazed straight at him, into the stark white pillow, searing him with longing. "I miss you so much."

He tried to envelop her in his arms, setting his face against hers. *"Try and you'll hear me—you'll hear me tell you that I love you, that I'll never go anywhere without you."*

"I need to see your face."

"Hell, Em, it doesn't matter as long I can see yours."

Shifting to her back, she stared up at the ceiling. "If you're here . . . let me see you, Ben. Let me feel you. If you're here, then . . . I'm sorry I kissed him."

"Kissed who?"

She clenched her eyes shut and sighed, dragging his pillow to her stomach and clutching it to her breast as she went to sleep.

"Kissed who?"

Chapter Four

W hat in the hell was a man supposed to do with a lady fixed on getting ass-whipped?

Simmering with pent-up desire and a shitload of frustration, Carter shut the door behind him and ensconced himself in his messy office.

Outside, his staff of eight busily cleaned the tables and readied themselves for noontime, when the Silver Fox opened. Carter figured he had stuff to do that bosses usually did, checks to write to suppliers, restocking lists to run through, but he just wasn't in the mood. No shocker there. Since the same thing happened *yesterday*, too.

He eyed the place Emma had graced with her pretty feminine presence less than seventy-two hours ago and pushed a frustrated hand through his hair. His old guitar leaned against the pitifully small bookcase. It seemed to say, *Play me! You can't play her but you can play me!*

On impulse, Carter grabbed the instrument, sat down with it, and slowly stroked the wood and the strings.

A picture of him and Ben, water rafting, sat on the desk. He grabbed it and folded it facedown, his chest tight with remorse; then he leaned back with his guitar, narrow-eyed, and surveyed the rest of his desk. It was a respectable desk, one that Carter's dad sure had never had, but behind it Carter felt as unhappy as a dog chained to a tree.

He plucked the strings of his guitar, but he felt so danged blue, he knew no song sad enough. Sighing, he set it back down against the side of the desk, then rubbed his face in his hands.

I'll have your promise on that, Carter. Promise that you'll take care of her.

It had been two years ago, when he and Ben had had that I-love-you-man conversation in this very bar. They'd been so damned drunk he doubted Ben remembered, wherever he was. But Carter did.

He remembered Ben adamant, slurring his words, saying, "All I'm saying is if I step outside this instant and get run over by a damned imbecile and die, you're going to take care of Emma. She's a little handful, I know, but she needs a keeper."

"I sometimes irritate her, man, she wouldn't want—"

"Just promise me, asshole. Promise me you won't let her break."

So Carter had.

Now, three days had gone by after that damned incident of the kiss, and Carter, a big good-for-nothing wuss, hadn't stopped over to see her. Did he plan to avoid her for another three months? Did he expect her to stop by his bar again and admit that she missed him?

Emma didn't know that most every day of those three months, Carter had driven by her house with his music flaring on the speakers of his F150 truck, so just in case she was screaming or weeping, he wouldn't hear her.

She didn't know that some evenings he'd found himself lingering by her door with a strange sensation in his stomach, expecting to find her lying on the floor with a rainbow of pills scattered around her if he dared open the door. Unlike Ben's death, which had been the worst kind of accident, Emma's death would be *his* fault. Damn. Or maybe Ben's death was his fault, too.

Carter had said some things the night of his accident. Now he racked his brain to remember his exact words. And his exact words had been—

Hell, he didn't want to remember his exact words.

Okay, so he'd said those things to Ben. Who'd have figured they'd have such an effect? Ben and Emma were the poster couple for happily ever after. Heck, Emma was so wild about Ben and Ben about her, one viewed them as a single unit, both of them together. Why had Carter delighted in giving that unit a hit and a small crack that night? Because he was a jerk—why else? And because Ben had asked him a direct question, and Carter had thought it right to give a direct answer.

Did he have a hard-on for his woman?

Hell yes. Yes, he did.

Two hours later he'd received the phone call.

And then the next day had gone by as though Carter

Bates, Nintendo DS expert, so-so guitar player, proud Silver Fox owner, and reckless bastard, had made up the story in his twisted, sick mind.

He'd driven to the funeral, reeking of vodka from the night before and smelling of the kind of guilt that wouldn't wash off no matter what soap he bathed with. Because right before the crash, Ben had been in Carter's bar. Not drunk, hell no, but he had been there. Just stopping by. Saying he was marrying her. Saying he needed to know the truth—if Carter had a hard-on for his woman.

What had *possessed* Carter to admit to the truth? Did he think Ben would invite him to their bedroom? Did he think Ben would say, "Well, why didn't you say so, buddy! All best friends share!"

Heck, he'd clearly been three beers past drunk.

Ben had, point of fact, nodded grimly and with his iciest tone said, "Don't ever let me catch you looking at her again," and then he'd shoved him back and stormed out of the Silver Fox like he'd be dead before he ever returned.

Now Carter had a goddamned ache in his chest he needed his good ole doc to prescribe something for. He wanted to go to his grave and tell him *Get over here from wherever you are, you bastard, and finish what you started with me. I got a mighty fine uppercut here waiting for you!*

He wanted to embrace utter and complete recklessness. Do the kind of fool dog thing that would irk Ben to no end and would yank him right out of surgery and send him storming to Carter's to slap some sense into him. But then he figured he could tie himself to a tree during a tornado and Ben wouldn't be returning.

Heck, he could curse him from here to Alaska, because really, *what kind of dude died and missed out on a freaking lifetime with Emma!*

Ben still wouldn't come.

So now Emma had to lean on Carter.

Even at the funeral, she'd reached out one little hand and held on to his like it was all that kept her grounded to this sorry world, and before he'd known what was happening, Emma Wilkins had been leaning on him.

And what had he done? He'd kissed that rosy-tinted, wet dream of a mouth of hers. *Damn, he was such a douche bag.*

A royal douche.

'Cause now he had a mind to do something more.

Like fuck her.

Tie her. Spank her.

Gritting his teeth, he swiped the picture across his desk and heard it smash against the wall, then crash onto the floor. She wanted the Club. Said she wanted pain. Needed to cope.

Hell if Carter didn't know the kinds of things Emma really needed.

He rammed his cell phone into his jeans and stormed out of the office. "Going out," he growled as he crossed the bar. He felt his cock lengthen in his jeans, ready for action. For plunging. Conquering. Spreading his goddamned seed all over Emma.

"Something up your butt, boss?"

He glared at Wooly. "Back to work, Wools, or you'll be sorry for yours."

He climbed into his truck, turned on the ignition, and

sped off. His head near exploded with possibilities as he drove. Possibilities that made his cock pulse hot and hard—feel loaded.

She'd look so pretty spread-eagled over the cross.

So what if he felt like a traitor to Ben?

If Emma wanted the Club, then Carter would give her the Club.

He knew just what to do with her emotions, where to channel them, morph them, unleash them. Not something Ben would've approved. Not if it involved her naked, moaning, crying out for Carter. But what the hell.

This was his chance.

Burning with impatience, he caught up with her outside one of her patient's homes. A bit sickening, how Carter knew all her rounds by memory. Maybe she needed to add him to her patient list, too.

Wednesdays she visited six homes: changed dressings, IVs, did all her nursey stuff. He parked his truck under a big Texas ash tree, behind her Honda Civic, then leaned on the tree's rough trunk and waited.

When she came down the steps, she seemed thoughtful and preoccupied. She wore her hair back and carried a big black bag like a good little doctor. And she was wearing scrubs.

Carter's temperature hitched up ten thousand degrees. Dang, that was hot. The naughty cowboy inside him wanted her to check his heart rate. The naughty rancher wanted to tie her up and take her to the rodeo. "Hey, prin—" Carter paused, concern flooding through him, for Emma was as pale as a sun-dried sheet. "Emma, what's wrong? You look as if you've seen a ghost."

"Mrs. Oliver just said the most bizarre thing, and I . . . I just don't know what to make of it."

Frowning, he planted a hand on the tree trunk. "I swear nurses gossip more than hairstylists do. What'd she say?"

"That a man was standing behind me while I checked her dialysis machine."

"What man?"

"A man. She said . . . she said he was looking at me like he wanted to eat me. That he was tall and dark-haired and . . . that he looked lonely."

Carter almost choked. Ben? Feeling his skin crawl, he twisted his neck to the left, then to the right, and plunged a hand through his hair. "Hell, Em, don't get any weirder on me. Sick people say stupid things all the time. Heck, even Wooly does, and he's healthy as a mustang."

"But Mrs. Oliver's cancer has metastasized. She's *dying*. And dying people sometimes see—"

"Stop, hell, please stop. You ain't doing this to yourself, princess. Not in front of me."

"But what if he's here! What if he's a ghost!"

"Emma, Jesus, are you registering what you're sayin'?"

Her face crumpled. "You're right, it's . . . crazy thinking." As though chastised, she rubbed her arms with the palms of her hands and gazed across the front lawn of the quaint home. "It's just that Ben and I . . ." She shook her cocoa tresses, struggling internally. "I can't explain the bond we had. He . . . he sensed things I felt, and vice versa. When he died . . ."

"You aren't dead, Emma. Sure as hell feels that way to you sometimes, but you're not."

She cocked her head and glinted at him through the sun's glare. "I know I'm not. For some reason looking at you reminds me of that—but sometimes I swear I can still *feel* him."

Carter didn't get to hear the last; his mind clamped to her first words like a bear trap. The admission affected him so powerfully he felt a tremble rush through his spine. He made her feel stuff when she looked at him? He? Carter Bates?

"Anyway." She sighed, and came into the shadow of the tree. "What are you doing here, Carter?"

Attempting to lighten the mood, a single finger came up. "You get one guess."

She wrinkled her nose. "How about *I was in the neighborhood and I thought I'd stop by . . . ?*"

A rumbling chuckle rose up his chest. "Ahh, princess, for someone who wants to believe in angry black-haired ghosts who want to eat her, you lack imagination, you do."

As her lips formed a smile, his gaze locked on that pretty pink mouth. A mouth that had been sweet and hot and had last been kissed by Carter. Just looking at it was like a call to arms to his dick. His balls drew tight and high. He dropped his voice. "You still fixin' on getting spanked, sugar?"

He saw her startled look but plowed on, so damned hot by the thought of smacking her little tush he'd go off if a breeze touched him.

"How about Saturday? That a good day to get ass-whupped?"

She stared with a combination of concern and excitement, her lips softly parted. It struck him that it may have been a mistake to ask, a mistake to imagine she had really meant it—

She ducked her dark glossy head for a second, then raised her chin with a smile. "He asked you to, didn't he?"

The warm sadness in her voice ripped at him. "Who asked me?"

He knew who the fuck she meant but thought it a good idea for Emma to say the word out loud. Because Carter should hear it—as a reminder. A reminder of who she'd belonged to first. And always would.

"Ben," she said, and as usual, she *loved* the word as she spoke it. "He told you to watch over me, didn't he? It's why you don't want to take me there."

Carter ached to hold her. He knew she was fighting to survive, to be all right. She didn't gaze up at him with those huge seductive eyes on purpose.

A prick of unease slid down his spine. On impulse, he glanced behind his shoulders, then muttered, "Yeah." He scanned the streets, but no one was watching, no angry dead man come out of his grave. "But I ain't doing this for Ben."

He took her elbow gently in his hand and drew her close. Their eyes met, and he willed her to see the desperate possessiveness in his gaze, the heat swimming through his veins.

"Saturday's for me, princess."

Back home after her daily rounds, a strange hum of awareness flitted through Emma's body. Restlessly she paced the first floor. Kicked her shoes off. Poured herself a glass of wine. Sat down on the couch.

And groaned in unexpected arousal.

Her clit tingled under her panties. Her nipples ached under her bra. She drained the glass of wine and thought of spreading her legs open, reaching into her scrubs, under her panties, and . . . No!

She didn't want to want Carter. She'd never responded to him like this before. But then maybe before, Emma had been overwhelmed with love for another man. A man she desired above all others. Now her lonesome body didn't care about love. Emma didn't need love to feel desire for Carter, to notice how his smile lit up his eyes. And his hair glistened in the sunlight. And his beautiful, taut face could grace a Marlboro ad. Carter a shirtless, sexy and rugged mountaineer.

Her pussy rippled with anticipation, infuriating her. She'd been juiced up in her scrubs all day, just imagining what he would do to her this weekend. Spank her.

"What do you figure a woman and a man playing the slave and the master end up doin'?"

Her sex muscles clenched at the mere reminder. How annoying!

She hadn't expected to feel what she'd felt at the sight of Carter today, negligently leaning against that tree. What she'd felt at the sight of his slow grin, hearing his smoky voice, had been indescribable. Like awakening. Gaining eyes for the first time. And ears. And scents.

He didn't remind her of Ben. Not really. They were different—each sexy in his own way. But he made her want to forget. Made her want to feel. Where everything had failed to reach for two years, Carter had succeeded with a single look at her. With that unexpected kiss . . .

How about Saturday? That a good day to get ass-whupped?

She couldn't help but smile at the memory, then a wealth of reservations assailed her as she wondered what he'd do. What if she wanted more? Became addicted, like she knew some people playing with BDSM did? And what did she know about this anyway? What if Ben could . . . see her? He'd be . . . he'd be hurt, wouldn't he? Outraged?

A perverse part of her kept *waiting* for him to materialize, take action. Stop her. Tell her there was no need. He was here!

Saturday.

Emma had said Saturday was fine. But was it fine? Would *she* be fine?

She'd imagined seeing Ben a couple of nights ago, a tangible shadow in the darkness of her bedroom, looking down at her with a face ravaged with need.

Shaking her head at herself, at the desperate measures a mind would go to for self-preservation, she flipped open her cell phone and began to scroll down to Carter's contact number. He'd assure her it would be all right—he wouldn't do anything she didn't want him to. Right?

But as she scanned the contacts, she halted on Ben's.

For some ungodly reason, she dialed, and voice mail picked up, in his voice. Her eyes widened. Her breath caught. Her eyes sprung tears. *Leave a message. Beep.*

She remained mute, and long after the machine had stopped recording, she hung up, her hands trembling. She should've said something. Hah. Like he'd listen, wherever he was. But if the hospital had not cancelled his number, she should've said something. Like, I love you. Or maybe, she should've said some sort of . . . prayer. Not to God, because she knew he didn't listen. A prayer to Ben who was gone. Something like,

> *Come back to me, Ben.*
> *As a stupid dog if you have to*
> *As a pain so I never forget for one second that I lost you*
> *As any form or shape or size—*

Oh, god, what was she thinking?

She flung her cell phone to the wall and heard its satisfying crash, then covered her face in her hands. "I'm such a shit."

A slight breeze, like a touch, ghosted over the top of her head.

Emma stiffened. A mixture of alarm and expectancy trickled through her veins. Throat closing, she pried her fingers off her face and with a deep inhale, she cracked her eyelids open. "Ben?"

She scanned their home. Her heart twisted in her chest; she felt so stupid.

"Are you here?"

She really should stop talking to herself, but couldn't.

"Are you here, Ben?"

Shadows played inside the room. Shadows of things? Of spirits? Of a man?

"When you were going to Harvard . . ." She strained to make out a silhouette by the door, by the window, the staircase. Ben? "You said even if you weren't physically with me, you'd always be with me. You promised me—you promised me. Please. If you're here now, let me see you."

A minute passed. Every second more agonizing than the last.

Her eyes strained to the point where she began to think the shadows moved. The living room window, securely latched, began to vibrate. Leaping to action, Emma scrambled to search her purse until she pulled out a penny. She could recall perfectly—even the background music—the moment a very dead Patrick Swayze had lifted up a penny to Demi Moore's incredulous eyes.

She'd cry if this happened to her now.

She'd cry if it didn't.

Dizzy with thrill, Emma balanced the penny at the tip of her finger and held it out. Her voice was pleading. "Ben, if it's you, take this penny from me. Go on, take it; let me see."

She stood there, panting, certain that if Mrs. Oliver could see Ben, then she would, too. Certain that if Patrick did it for Demi, Ben would do it for Emma.

Heart slamming in her throat, she watched the penny, afraid of hoping, afraid of moving an inch.

She didn't wait very long.

The penny slipped. It landed on the carpet on the Lincoln side up.

Tears welled in her eyes. And then she couldn't speak anymore.

Her hand had been trembling so hard she'd dropped the penny.

. . .

Damn Emma.

Ben had seen the look on her face as she offered him a penny. She'd held it out on one trembling fingertip like she'd expected it to levitate before her very eyes. How the fuck was he supposed to manage that? Hadn't it occurred to her that if he could touch something, he'd be touching *her*?

All Ben had managed, while struggling to control the wind that threatened to kick in the window, was to flick the penny off her finger.

But it hadn't been enough.

Still rankled at his helplessness, he waited out in the sunlight Saturday afternoon, sitting on the sidewalk by the road.

In the summer, crickets could usually be heard at this hour, calling to each other like bewitched lovers. But the summer had come and gone, and as winter approached, all became still when the sun began to set.

But Ben wasn't waiting for the sun to set.

He was waiting for Carter.

A hot turbulence grew in him.

Confusion and frustration. Perturbation. He'd heard them discuss the Club. Discuss the fact that Emma was fixed on being *ass-whupped*. He'd heard about *Saturday*. He'd *seen* when she'd walked out of Mrs. Oliver's house and spotted Carter outside, waiting for her.

Ben had watched. He'd listened.

His sight, like a punishment, had remained. His hearing, like a second punishment, had remained. On his best days,

Ben was grateful for them. On his worst, like that morning, what he felt was hurt.

Their words had baffled him. *Plagued* him.

Why would Emma want to get professionally spanked? Why did she crave *pain*, when pain like the kind Ben knew here was never-ending, all-consuming, nothing he'd ever wish on anyone, much less the woman he loved.

He dragged in a gust of air—then laughed mockingly at himself. He shook his head. Still, almost two years later, he forgot that he didn't breathe.

The wind picked up through the front garden, yanking on the wiry trees. Ben wasn't sure if his emotions were summoning it, or just nature.

Nature.

Was it nature's fault that Ben couldn't leave this earth without her?

He cocked his head at a distant noise and trained his eyes on the road when the slow hum of a car motor reached his ears. A truck appeared in the distance. Ben's hands made slow, deadly fists at his sides. It was Carter coming by. Damn that lowly bastard to hell.

Irritation pricked through him as he rose, and Ben pounced on him as soon as he stepped out of the truck. *"What's this I hear about clubs and spanking, dammit!"*

Carter slammed his door shut and gazed up at the house.

"If you set one hand on my woman's ass, Bates!"

Carter stood there, feet braced wide apart, watching her window for long moments. Then, the cowboy seemed to gather up his balls and went over to knock. Ben had always thought him a suave, admirable man. Now he thought

Carter walked like he was being led by his dick. Hell, Ben couldn't remember if even one of his jokes had been all that funny.

Annoyed, he materialized by the front door and stood between it and Carter, pointing his finger. *"Listen to me very well, you hardheaded imbecile. The last thing Emma needs right now is more pain. She's had enough of it. Now, you either do something helpful like take her out into the sunlight, or get your ass in your sad old truck and leave."*

"The cowboy can't hear you, Rambo."

Ben stiffened at that casual, almost bored-sounding remark. There weren't many people who spoke to Ben now.

And yet someone was speaking to him.

As Carter rang the doorbell, a spirit stood casually on the opposite side of the road. He was the same old man Ben had seen in the graveyard the day he'd had the fun of watching Emma and his family set his body in a coffin and send it six feet under.

Ben started for him, his forehead scrunched. The man was entirely bald-headed, like Gandhi.

Gandhi with a beard—a snow-white beard that fell to his knees with a sassy, rather feminine tip. *"You following me?"*

The man nodded.

Ben cocked an eyebrow as he continued to approach. *"Have nothing better to do?"*

The man's smile came easily. *"Not particularly."*

Sensing how good, how damned good, it would feel to talk to someone, Ben joined him on his side of the sidewalk.

Every freaking day, Ben felt a hellish pull luring him back into his coffin.

Like some sort of Dracula, it called to him, called him to rest, to sleep. But he wasn't sleeping. Sure as hell not resting.

His mind was swimming with thoughts twenty-four hours of the day. Ben prowled the streets day and night. Following Emma, watching over her during the day. Lurking around the streets, like a monster, during the night.

Always, in the sooty blanket of night, hope simmered inside him. Hope of seeing something, finding something. He didn't know what, but *something*.

He'd encountered wizards this way, at the witching hour when the moon was high. He'd seen strange animals that lurked in the dark, beings without even a name. Could only Ben see them? Or could his new friend see them, too?

"You won't find what you're looking for here," the old man said, signaling toward the house. Ben spun around to watch Carter driving off with Emma.

Frustration rode him hard, consuming his mind. He didn't understand what was happening. He didn't understand what Emma needed—what Carter was offering to her.

He didn't understand *shit*.

Hands fisting at his sides, he returned his attention to the spirit. *"What am I looking for?"*

Guy gazed around for a moment. In a quick sweep he seemed to take in nothing and everything. Then he offered a half smile. *"A miracle?"*

Something like hope soared within Ben, gripping him by the throat. *"You know where I can find one?"*

A miracle. Another chance. A meeting with God.

"Not a miracle—no. But I know where you can find something similar. A way back into a body."

71

A body! A beating heart, blood, working lungs—taste, voice, touch. Emma!

His heart would've been pounding. His head would be spinning. Nothing, since that night, had ever excited him until this.

But then suspicion narrowed Ben's eyes. *"Then why are you still here, man?"*

If Gandhi could have a body, why stand here in the road, invisible as the wind, and offer help?

The old man glanced at the top window of the house, Emma's window, then his depthless eyes returned to Ben. *"Nothing to come back to now. My wife has gone on and married a guy from the 'home' ten years her junior—yup, she done got herself a seventy-year-old."* He shrugged. *"Too late for me. Now I'm just waiting to leave. Entertaining myself in the meantime."*

"I'm not going until she comes with me."

"I know. And I figured that if someone here wants you as bad as you want her, like that lady you watch over, you might just be tempted to strike a deal. Maybe the price of coming back won't seem too steep to a man like you."

"Price? The price for what?"

"Life, my friend. A new life."

Without further explanation, Gandhi started down the street. When he realized Ben had remained in place, he turned at the corner and pointedly said, *"You coming?"*

Chapter Five

D*id people come when they were spanked?*
    How . . . embarrassing.

But after a restless night Emma's body was primed so bad for pain she was afraid it would end up giving her pleasure. Her soul hurt. Her nipples ached. Her pussy wept.

Maybe tomorrow morning she'd reflect on the events of this night and realize just how wrong, just how desperate, and just how much of a fool she'd been. But for this quiet night, this moonless night, Emma needed . . . Carter.

Pushing her hair back behind her ear with a quaking hand, she peered up at his profile as his truck rumbled down the highway.

Expectation hummed in her veins. *Let go*, it hummed. *Let go let go.*

She surveyed Carter's large, capable hands, and gooseflesh pricked across her skin at the knowledge that those hands would *spank* her tonight.

His eyes were on the road ahead, but she had the sense that his attention, his alertness, was homed in on her. "You nervous, princess?"

"A little."

He turned to her. "You thought about how you want to do this yet?" His clear eyes glowed eerily in the interior of the car, and they made her feel as if her heart were in her throat. "Will you just be wantin' the spanking or will you be wantin' something more?"

Her womb gripped, and a telling moistness flowed between her thighs. *Don't you dare come for him!* "I don't know, I've never done this before," she said, squirming. She tugged her skirt toward her knee.

"Just tell me how you envision it, pumpkin."

"Well, I . . . don't have a clear vision yet."

But the truth was, she did. Have many visions. Many ideas. An image sailed through her mind then, and her pulse rocketed to the roof.

Carter, naked, mouthwatering Carter, with his hands kneading her aching breasts, his large dick buried tight and hot inside her pussy, his hips rocking, his mouth taking, making her scream in ecstasy as she came . . .

Oh, god, she actually *wanted* him.

A hungry little sound escaped her, and she opened wide, pleading eyes to his narrowing ones. "Just . . . help me, please. I want the pain." *Not the rest—I don't want to want the rest!*

He took a highway exit in silence, steering comfortably with his hands, huge bronze hands she ached to feel on her body; then he took a sidelong glance at her, a glance that strayed to her breasts, made his jaw stiffen, and then was forced back to the road. "Want me to brief you on what to expect?"

God, what was happening? The searing tension between them made it impossible to breathe. The air crackled with barely restrained arousal, and their mutual glances only seemed to feed this strange, roaring new monster.

Emma nodded at his question and swallowed, feeling all kinds of warm feelings for him at the moment. Gratitude. Appreciation. *Lust.*

He'd always been the kind of guy a smart girl wouldn't trust. He was too handsome, too sarcastic, and played the bastard only too well most of the time.

The fact that Emma trusted him more than anyone now made her wonder if she was a fool. Or maybe just desperate. Or . . . horny.

No.

She trusted him because when she gazed at the entire virile package of Carter Bates, she felt a little bit alive again.

No one else made her want things like he did.

He made his truck look small, and it smelled of him, leathery and woodsy, and her body was acting up to his male scent and powerful masculinity like a wound acted to acid. Between her legs she was burning. Her nipples were tight and sensitive under her fitted cotton top and bra and her mind whirled with possibilities she hadn't considered before.

Would he touch her with those big bronzed hands that clutched the steering wheel?

Would having those hands on her make her feel good and sexy and alive again?

She'd dreamed of him, had been dreaming of this rugged, drawler of a cowboy—not only at night, but by day, too. She didn't approve of the direction her dreams were taking. They were full of primal, sexual, animal need—and the images to match it.

This morning she'd woken up thrashing over the bed as waves and waves of pleasure threatened to unleash—but didn't. Now she rode here, nervous, drowning with pent-up need, and angsting as to what to expect from him tonight. "What'll I be spanked with?"

"You choose. Paddle. Flogger. Bare hand."

Her tummy clenched. Oh, shit, he was really sexy. What was she going to do? "What do you recommend?"

A seductive glimmer appeared in his eyes, and it was accompanied by a lazy smile that made her breathless. "Go slowly. Start slow, and if you're comfy and warm and you want more, you ask for it harder."

"So I just say . . . more?"

"Yeah, baby, you just ask for it. Or you can beg."

She drew in an unsteady breath at the thought of *begging* him. "Sounds like you've gotten lots of begging." A pang of envy hit her as she spoke, but it burst into heat when he looked at her again.

"Ain't nothing wrong with a pretty woman begging a man to please her."

Her nipples poked into her bra as if to agree, and she wrapped her arms around herself and rubbed her shoulders. *Calm down, you big whore. Calm down!* "But I don't want pleasure," she stubbornly insisted. "I want—"

"Yeah yeah yeah, you'll get whupped, princess. Don't

worry. Just remember you have the power to say no. May seem like the man's in charge in this here game, but ultimately it's the woman saying yes or no."

Yes, she thought. Yes yes *yes*.

"Now you're gonna need safe words. Could be red for stop, yellow for go slower. Some just pick a word they like. Words are important for when you get into the zone and you have no idea if yes means no or no means yes. Sometimes women like to struggle. For play. So there have to be safe words where a man can know dead sure if he's overstepping the pleasure zone."

She nodded in agreement, struggling to marshal her erotic thoughts about *something more* when his forehead creased into a dark frown. "Just remember red is stop—unless you want another word."

"I'll think about it," she murmured, again fidgeting with the hem of her skirt and pulling it low.

Carter eased his truck into a crowded parking lot and started hunting for empty slots with the same concentration she figured his ancestors had used when hunting for food. "Ben?" One lone brow went up. "He ever spank you?"

"I always wanted him to, but Ben wouldn't . . . ever. No matter how I begged, he wouldn't hurt me, couldn't."

"So I'm your first."

Was that lust in his eyes? Jealousy? *Both*, a little voice whispered in her head. Her heart fluttered. "Yep."

He seemed to digest this revelation while he parked, then he shifted restlessly in his seat, clearly uncomfortable. It was as though he were pained. Then, Emma noticed.

A bulge pushed up his jeans so high and tight he almost

grazed the steering wheel with his erection. Tantalized by the sight, Emma wondered if she'd ever seen such a raging hard-on before. Her breasts pricked painfully at the thought of running her fingers over that rock-hard shaft.

"But it's just play, right?" She heard him cut off the engine. "What happens at the Club stays at the Club, that sort of thing?"

He shifted some more. "Yeah."

Just play.

So if she and Carter did something wicked and naughty . . . if she took him in her mouth or felt that huge cock penetrate her . . .

She swallowed back a moan as her pussy rippled. "Like . . . You're the master, I'm the slave. You're in charge, I need punishing. That sort of dynamic?"

Keys in hand, he twisted around and draped one sinewy arm around the back of her seat, his lips set into a belligerent line. "Not sure I'm the right man to do this."

A flicker of alarm skidded down her spine. "What do you mean you're not the right man? You're not going to spank me?"

He sighed, then raked a hand through that sun-streaked mane of his. "You have a bottom, and she's begging you to tie her up. So you tie her up. She's begging to be paddled. So you paddle her. Your dick is hard as a rock. Your dick is harder than anything you've ever felt before—you're never quite prepared for the rush it'll give you. Hearing her beg. Seeing her for the first time . . ." His voice dropped a decibel until it was no more than a whisper, a whisper that made her every cell quiver. "Control is the game, baby—but if you lose it, someone could get hurt."

She scoffed and yanked open the door. "Nobody can possibly hurt me more than Ben did when he died."

Carter was so worked up he could barely walk in his Levi's. Quietly he guided her across the moonlit parking lot and toward the large industrial building that held no sign, boasted no name on its gray exterior.

Emma's hand trembled in his grasp.

With every step on the cold asphalt, Carter felt himself continue to respond to her. He was thickening, swelling, growing large . . . larger. Ready to detonate.

The noise filtered all the way outside when the bouncer, a guy he knew, waved them inside. Hesitating for an instant, Emma turned her wide, glossy eyes up to his. The expectation in her gaze made his cock quiver at the thought of her without clothes, writhing and tossing that dark mane of hers side to side. He'd get to see her lovely figure without a stitch on them. He would hear her whimpers. Her moans. He'd hear them for *real*.

"Let's do this," he whispered in a cragged voice.

They stepped inside, blasted by the music, the scent of flesh and sweat and perfume. He'd never felt so excited over anything in his life. Feeling Emma tremble, he put his hand protectively on the small of her back as they blended into the crowd, his blood sweeping through his system in an avalanche of longing.

The Club was packed tonight—bursting to the seams with doms, subs, curious spectators, and couples hanging out by the bar. And then there was Emma, taking it all in, dressed in that black little dress that looked decadent on her, her coffee-bean hair trailing past her shoulders. She was an angel with peachy pink lips, dressed like a naughty little slut—a naughty little slut who needed disciplining.

Even from afar she was the only woman you'd look at. The whole room revolved around her. Every guy there wanted her. Maybe a few women, too. Carter had an urge to fling her over his shoulders and take her home.

Blood coursing hot and heady in his veins, he guided her through the throng and stared at her profile, at the way her little nose seemed to curve up at the tip. God. She was so pretty, her smile so pure and perfect. Who wouldn't have a thing for her? Many, many things for her.

Inside the ring, his friend Kane was whipping a girl's bottom so thoroughly her whimpers seemed to drown out the music. The next big whack made Emma smile. "She seems to like it," she said.

As will you . . .

Kane continued, easily flicking his wrist, calm and concentrated like a guy training a horse. He was entirely in control, focused, while the woman writhed and twisted on the cross.

Emma would do that for him. Writhe. Moan. Ask for it.

The thought made him break into a sweat. He knew she ached to forget the haunting night Ben died, instinctively craved human contact more than she craved air or food. Within these walls of the noisy club, it wouldn't hurt inside.

Within these walls, the pain of losing Ben would go away.

All she would know now . . . all she would remember . . . was the way Carter Bates played her tonight.

. . .

So this was the Club.

The music thrummed so loud Emma felt it inside her, reverberating in her bones. Black was the order of the day. Black lips, black nails, black tattoos, black leather. Black collars. People had those around their necks, actually. Like dogs. She was shocked, and strangely aroused.

There was magic in this hidden place, wanting and sex. A strong, muscular bald guy who walked like He-man stood inside the gothic ring with some sort of horse crop in hand. All the doms were pretty impressive. Almost as impressive in leather as Carter in his jeans.

She watched the doms—going into rooms, out of rooms, into the circle. Was that what she really needed?

No, she thought with a pang. What she really needed had died on a dark night, and she would never be in his arms again.

In the circle, a bald man was whipping a girl's bottom so fast Emma had an impulse to rub hers. The next big whack made her pussy tighten.

The man whipped her ass again, and the woman tossed her head back, her face contorted with agony and pleasure. Emma imagined how she'd feel if it were her—then realized she wanted pain so bad, she'd probably be smiling. She was also just beginning to realize how arousing, how inexplicably arousing, having a handsome man inflict controlled pain on her would be.

Having Carter behind her, working her . . .

When the session finished, the bald guy slapped his crop/whip/whatever that article of torment was into the palm of a nearby guy who was parading around the circle with a woman on a collar. It seemed to be their turn.

"C'mon, prin." Carter shouldered their way through to the back of the room, his grip warm on Emma's as he led them through the punks and the goths and the people milling around the area.

Emma didn't know all the rules, but Carter was cautious enough to stay clear of the circle and walk around the edge— where she assumed they weren't allowed in until the couples there were finished.

"I figured you'd want a bit more privacy than this," he murmured in her ear.

She nodded, her insides twisting and turning by the thought of what was to come. How many women had Carter touched?

Carter led her up a dark staircase and flicked on the light in the second room on the second floor. "This is our room."

She drew in a steadying breath as, from the door, Carter eyed her with gentle interest. "It's okay, pumpkin. I'm gonna take care of you."

She heard him quietly shut the door behind him.

"First thing you're gonna do is: you're gonna strip for me, nice and slow, 'cause nice and slow is how I like it." His timbre was gentle, coaxing almost.

A shudder raced to her extremities. She'd always thought that women wanted to sleep with Carter when he looked at them with those eyes. Now she felt feverish to imagine those eyes on her body, a body only one man, one man with striking black eyes, had seen before.

He came over and reached out for her, his voice unfamiliar to her—husky, thick as he grasped her elbow. "Need some help?"

A bolt of electricity rushed up her arm. Instinctively pulling free, Emma reached to the side of her dress with unsteady hands. "No."

He squeezed her waist in encouragement and stepped back to let her unzip. "All right, then . . . get those clothes off your sexy body."

She quickly obeyed, hearing the scrape of fabric as the dress dropped to her ankles, aware of the tension in the room, the way he watched her. She wasn't sure whether to lose the panties. The bra.

How many sexy bodies had a man like Carter seen? Would he think her breasts too small? Her nipples too little? Would he notice she'd waxed her sex? Why had she done that anyway?

His eyes were brighter than lasers, his jaw leaden. He steepled his fingers like he did when he was deep in thought and rubbed his lips with his index fingers. She'd never seen him torn like this. Never.

"Don't hide from me. Let me see," he murmured thoughtfully.

Her pussy clenched and her blood rushed. Would he like what he saw?

When she didn't continue undressing, Carter moved to the table and searched the items. He lifted a sleek black sash.

"Blindfold, Emma?"

She licked her lips and shook her head.

"What do you want, then?" He walked around, inspecting the materials laid out. "Paddle? Flogger?"

"You choose."

He hesitated, then raised his choice for her to see. "Paddle—so you get it good." He grinned. "Do you want your hands restrained?"

"Yes. Please."

The air around them pulsed with heat and arousal and magic. An image of her being fucked by Carter seared itself into her brain, and a surge of passion roared through her. She thought she'd fall; her knees could barely hold her. She couldn't wait to be led to the wooden cross in the center of the room—be tied there, played there.

"Pick a safe word," Carter said.

"I . . . the colors you mentioned or . . . ?"

"Pick a safe word."

"Ben."

His head whipped around. "Ben?"

She nodded. The not knowing what Carter would do was killing her. The wondering what would happen now. If *he* would want her. What kinds of things he'd do to her. Painful things. Pleasurable things?

"I see." He circled her, and she noticed he'd left the paddle on the table. His fingers were curled into his hands. "Why not stick to a color, something—"

Gathering her courage, Emma reached behind to unhook her bra. "Ben's my safe word."

The sight of her as she undid her bra drove him mad. His voice throbbed with desire. "Fine. Ben it is, then. Green is go, yellow caution."

Her dress was still pooled at her ankles, and when her panties and bra joined, she stepped out. His head spiraled at the sight of her—toned and firm and bare-ass, pert breasts and pink, hairless little cunt—and the blood went straight to his cock.

Her buttocks wiggled as she walked up to the large, dominating wooden cross at the room's center. "Hit me hard."

Sweat popped up on his brow, her eagerness driving him over the edge. He swallowed, clenched his teeth. "We're warming up first."

She spread-eagled herself on the cross. "No warm-up. Just hit me."

He walked to the lone chair in the room and settled himself, aware of the bulge between his thighs, perversely wanting her to see it—to feel it. "If you're sure you want this, then show me you're ready for it. Come here, pumpkin."

She didn't hesitate. Which pleased him immensely. She let him splay her over his thighs, her chest and stomach resting against his legs, her folded knees on the floor, her body perfectly positioned so he could run a splayed hand down her back.

His cock pulsed with need as he petted her. "Don't wiggle," he whispered as he stroked her smooth, lustrous skin.

He memorized the curve of her sweet rosy rear, fondling it gently, while his lungs were near bursting with the scent of her soap and arousal and shampoo. She seemed to want to converse. "Is this common practice with your subs or—"

"Shh. First things first, Emma: you don't speak here. I do."

Seeing the crimson blush that appeared on her profile,

his long fingers skimmed down her spine, stroking the mound of her buttocks. Wetness gathered in her sex. He could smell it. Sniff it. He dragged his hand up her spine, following the delicate dents, pleased when she trembled.

He stroked diligently. Selfishly. Prolonging the moment— wanting to make it last all night. This heat, this first time with Emma. Every inch of skin on her back received equal attention, causing her to moan helplessly—a soft, drawn-out sound that purred up her throat.

She liked his soft touch?

His balls drew tight against him when she moaned again, higher, louder.

"What is it that you moan for? Do you even know?" He whispered the husky words into her ear, and followed with a wet, hot lick around her earlobe. She shuddered and his shaft pulsed heatedly. His hand grasped the flesh of a full, rounded cheek. He squeezed gently, then his fingers strayed downward. His middle finger grazed her slit.

He didn't tell her she was wet, but she was. Jesus, she was. His finger returned for another pass, another graze, just a barely there touch between her plump, swollen pussy lips, a touch that might not be welcome but he had to take.

Her breathing changed, deepened, and Carter's blood coursed in torrents in his veins. He had to have her. One day. Someday. *Soon.* Holy God, he had to have all of her.

Emma couldn't mourn Ben forever, and Carter knew he wouldn't be able to see her with another man. Which was why they were here now. Why he had her exactly where he wanted her—on his goddamned lap.

He'd stuck by her all this time, had tried to shove aside the impulse to take her. At first he thought he was just making sure she was all right, but then he realized he felt a little responsible for Ben's death and may have wanted to atone somehow, and then he knew it was only because he was such a damned masochist who wanted to spend time with a woman he was nuts about but would never have—even if sometimes she had that faraway look of being present but not.

Now he had her naked body under his hands, over his lap, was hearing her moans, scenting her arousal. His instincts didn't lie, and he knew Emma wanted him. She was hot for him, and it wouldn't be long before she was begging to be fucked by him. But Holy God, the wait would feel eternal.

"A bit of warming up before the paddlin'," he murmured. One of his hands sifted through her lustrous brown hair while the other worked between her legs. His thumb slid up and down the fissure of her ass.

Emma bucked as another moan surged from within her. God, she moaned just like he'd imagined she would. Like she was helpless. Torn. Vulnerable. She rubbed her pointy nipples across his thigh, squirming over him, brushing his aching cock. A groan wrenched out of him and his thoughts scattered into nothingness. So small and pliant, so female, so unattainable for years.

"Carter," she gasped, her need summed up in that one word.

"Fuck. I swear you have the pinkest, most pert little ass these eyes have ever seen."

"It wants to be spanked," she pleaded in a whisper. "Please."

"Oh, baby, I swear all my hand wants to do is spank it. Spank it hard." He continued petting, his breathing harsh. He knew she needed the pain, but he ached to give her pleasure, too.

Oh, god, his hands were magic. *Magic.*

She could barely summon a thought, even a sound, felt so bewitched as his calloused fingers dragged over her curves.

Her eyes drifted shut as she savored the feel of the hard outline of his erection pressing against her ribs. Was he as shaken as she? Did he feel this aroused with all the women he played with?

Carter didn't want to hurt her, she knew. Was hesitant to because of Ben. Ben would've never allowed this—never. In the past, whenever Emma had cut herself or experienced any kind of pain, Ben seemed ready to move the earth to fix it.

But this tall, dark creature holding her on his lap wasn't Ben.

He was Carter.

"Carter, what are you waiting for?"

She couldn't stand more of that magic, refused to keep acknowledging it. Concerned, she glanced past her shoulder and saw that he looked tormented with arousal. Heat spiraled through her body at the realization. Sweat broke out on her flesh.

A muscle twitched in the back of his jaw, and his eyes glowed a deep fathomless blue, like a murky ocean with no end.

"Do it," she pleaded.

"God help me, Em, when I do, this sweet little ass of yours can kiss good-bye to sittin' tomorrow." His voice was rough and rusty as he placed her back in position. Suppressing a shudder, she adjusted over his lap, shaking her buttocks in a way that she hoped would tempt him, tempt a man like him to spank her. Just spank her.

A lionlike sound rumbled up his throat. "Sure this ass wants to get it, baby?"

Emma's breathing accelerated, her heart thundering in her temples. "Please."

"How hard do you want it, baby?"

He had the most erotic bedroom voice she'd ever heard. It made her feel like a bad girl, and it was frightening, nauseating because it was so true. She was bad, bad to do this.

Wretched, she waited, holding her breath in anticipation as she sensed his big hand hovering above her ass. His voice had never sounded so crowded to her, so lustful. "I asked how hard, baby?"

His other hand cupped her rib cage, and his thumb caressed the underside of her breast. She wondered how the touch would feel on her nipple, then angrily quelled the thought.

"Hard, hit me hard," she said, unable to keep her stomach from rocking against his lap. He was hot beneath her, his legs spread wide, thick and muscled. How would his bare skin feel against hers?

Marshaling her thoughts, Emma parted her thighs wide so her pussy could feel the cool air like a balm against her heat. His cock bit prominently into her stomach, and she tried not to think about it. He was a man—of course he had a cock.

She wiggled anxiously, needing something. Pain, yes, that was all she wanted. All she would allow. "Carter, please."

When she turned, his eyes had drifted shut, his breath rapid. What was wrong with him? "This is not the way of a sub," he whispered, opening his eyes, shocking her with the lustful look in them. "Subs must please their masters in order to be pleasured—they must obey—and you do neither."

Emma sat up on his lap, shivering. "Tell me what to do."

Her breasts jiggled as she faced him. His eyes followed the movement, gaze smoldering, lingering over the pink nipples, switching from one erect nipple to the other.

He clenched his jaw. "Dammit, turn around, lie still, stop wiggling!"

Chastised, Emma folded her body over his lap again, fear and anticipation quivering in every fiber of her being.

"You have a lot to learn, Emma. *A lot.*"

Her throat barely worked out the words. "Spank me."

He chuckled roughly, almost exasperatedly. "Pumpkin, I decide when you're ready for that. You must obey me in each and every way. I demand it, and that means no speaking out of turn." His hands were all pleasure on her back, running down her curves.

She couldn't breathe, suddenly feared those gentle hands, feared they'd take all of Ben's memories away from her, all of Ben's touches. One of them slipped between her ass cheeks, briefly, an inch away from her pussy. Emma's body tightened in . . . recoil? No, no, it was expectation.

He slapped her ass so fast that she jerked from the impact.

A sharp sting bolted up her spine. Emma screeched in shock, eyes watering as the feeling registered. He caught her head by the jaw and turned her, until his own face met hers a whisper away.

His jaw tight, he spoke through his teeth, and something sinful and threatening burned deep in his eyes. "I just spanked you. And because I know deep down you liked it, I will spank you again if you say please."

Emma cried, "I need it—please."

Carter's eyes fastened on her mouth, and he nodded grimly. "Spanking is one of the many, many things you need, princess. And I have a feeling it's not the thing you need most."

His next slap came with force, making her jolt and press her sex as tight as she could over his thigh as she screeched.

"More, baby?"

His thumb grazed her ass, a dominant, sure touch that made her moan, while his other hand slapped her. Slap!

She gasped in unexpected pleasure, craving something else, something harder, more painful, to override the pleasure. "It's not hurting enough, it's not, not hurting!"

His eyes flashed. "If you keep shouting, I'm going to have to gag you, Emma."

"Just try it, Carter!"

He stared at her, an odd expression on his face as another slap came. "That feel good?"

She gritted her teeth as she fought the arousal. But the ache in her core spread—built. Her body shivered uncontrollably. She shouldn't burn like this, feel her veins heat up like this.

"Admit it feels good," he cooed.

Her breasts were crushed against his hard thighs, and she was hurting with all kinds of things that weren't from the spanking. "Carter, I—"

"Admit it feels like a fucking little piece of heaven, baby."

She bolted upright and smacked one angry fist into his chest. "You're not hitting me hard—don't treat me like a doll, damn you. I don't want to fuck around. I just want the pain!"

He caught her wrist in the manacle of his. "You're not lettin' it hurt," he growled. With a put-out sigh, he set her on her feet and adjusted his cock in his pants with a frustrated yank. "You've numbed yourself, princess. Only natural that you would." He rose slowly, his face somber and annoyingly beautiful. "I've numbed myself, too, Emma—hell if I didn't . . . I'd go stark-mad crazy with the things I want and ain't never gonna have."

With predatory grace, he walked over to the corner and fingered the paddle, his face taut with desire. "Things I never told anyone about."

Her eyes ached as he walked around her, in those jeans, that shirt, that beautiful way he walked. He was the most arresting man in this club . . . in this city . . . in the world.

Unbidden, thoughts of the most carnal, decadent kind flicked through her mind. Carter telling her what to do, Carter controlling her hair, her sighs, her moans. It was the hot heat in his voice, the quiver of lust, that made her suddenly struggle to remain standing. Why couldn't he be an ogre? Old and mean and smelling of . . . pipe smoke?

"Get in the cross, Emma."

Shaking head to toe, she positioned herself in the cross, a giant wooden X. Her fingers ached to touch him, feel the dark scruff on his jaw, the wind in his hair. She felt a little mindless, frightened, rapturous, guilty of these wants and feelings.

Holding her breath, she let him restrain her. He tied the sash around her wrists, watching her chest rise and fall on each rapid breath. "Good, princess," he praised, patting her head.

He ran his hands down her arms, and she felt as though she were dreaming, floating in an ocean of desire and want.

Carter shifted behind her, their heads resting together for a moment, his forehead to the back of her head. "Yeah . . ." His hands covered her belly, and she panted when his thumbs began to climb the underside of her breasts, reaching her strained nipples pressing into the cross. Arousal vibrated in his voice. "I know what you need. Someone who won't be afraid to bring out the pain, turn it into pleasure for you." Into her ear, he whispered, "You want to get excited again, so excited you'll be begging to come. It's not just pain you want, Em. And I fucking know it."

She flushed hotly. "That's not true."

His mouth moved against her ear; then his teeth caught her earlobe and pulled slightly. "All right now. Let's party on, you and me."

He cupped her ass in his big hand and kneaded a little. She whimpered. His hand slid into the crevice, making a moan trap in her throat. "What color are we on, Emma?"

"Uh. Green."

"Good."

He cupped her bottom with his hand, retrieved it, then smacked the paddle down.

She stiffened as her body absorbed the pain, the strange pleasure that came with the sharp hit. Heat traveled through her body, from the sting, to her breasts, her sex, her lips. Her eyes drifted shut, and she was surprised to find the face she saw in the curtain of blackness. Ben. He looked so angry. So jealous.

The paddle came down with force. One time, two, stinging her cheek. She whimpered, bit her lip, strained against her binds. "More." She clenched her eyes tighter, bracing her body for the pain. She thrust her rear out. "More!"

Carter waited, and she could feel his eyes on the pussy lips visible through her open legs, and she couldn't shake the building arousal away.

He didn't move.

"Don't stop," she gasped, panicked. "Please. I really need this!"

He was silent. Then she heard him set down the paddle on the floor. She whimpered when his hand enveloped one plump cheek. Then he bent over and kissed it. Pleasure ripped through her, and she thrashed against the binds. "No! Don't. Be. Nice."

He ran his hands up her nude back. Her pussy creamed, and she could smell herself. And then she felt one finger. Just one. Probing into the wet, slick folds of her pussy.

"Carter, please, spank me." Oh, god, she wanted to explode, was melting.

But instead he inserted the finger deep inside her. She thrashed. "Oh, god."

He bent and began to eat her with his mouth, shoving his tongue into the channel first. His mouth turned fierce, voracious, kissing her hard, French-kissing her pussy. She writhed in her binds, resisting the pleasure, telling herself she wasn't here for this, hadn't hoped for this, didn't want this.

Her clit budded under the flicks of his tongue. Her cunt juiced up like a river. Carter groaned. The sound climbed up her body, destroying her resistance.

Emma writhed, closed her eyes as his tongue penetrated again and again. He drove her so wild, she felt herself climb to orgasm with each wild flick of his tongue. "No—don't. Spank me hard—just spank me, Carter! Oh, god, I'm coming!" Her protest died on a keening cry as she started coming. Violently. Like she'd never climaxed before. Writhing in her restraints, she was pushed to a one-minute orgasm by his commanding tongue.

Stillness followed.

For a moment Emma heard only his panting breaths, and her own.

She trembled.

Oh, god, she was still not satisfied, felt feverish for more.

Carter moved in front of her and gazed down at her, a fierce, lonely, hungry big man.

"Now tell me." His voice was gruff and sexy. Something wild strained in his eyes. He seemed to be fighting his control. "Which is it that you want, Emma? More pain? Or more pleasure?"

She knew what he asked. He asked if she wanted him, would like to be fucked by him. Yes, yes, oh, she wanted it so bad. "No . . . no more pleasure." She licked her lips. Why couldn't she admit it? Wanting him? Wanting to touch him and feel him? It felt so wrong, like betrayal. "I just . . . I just want to feel what I feel inside on the outside. No more pleasure!"

He seized the flogger from the table and advanced. "Then be still."

Her chest squeezed. He looked a little angry. Like a man at his very limits, hanging on by the flimsiest, most gnawed-at rope.

He returned behind her. His voice lashed through her. Commanding. Certain. "Open your legs."

She did. He smacked her with such aching force that she yelped.

"That's all you want, then?"

"Yes!"

He smacked her fast and hard, whack whack *whack*. "Stop feeling sorry for yourself. Is it people's pity you want?" *Whack*.

"No!" she gasped.

Whack whack whack. "Then stop pretending he's coming back and start taking care of yourself. What color are we on?"

"G-green."

Whack!

"Green!"

Whack!

"Start admitting what you need and be woman enough to take it."

"Oh, Carter—green."

Whack!!

"Fuck when you need to fuck, Emma. Cry when you need to cry. Hang on to me when you need a man, dammit."

"Yes, Carter, yes; oh, Carter."

"Say *Ben* now," he dared. "Hmm? Say *Ben* now—make me stop."

"No!"

The spanking intensified, tearing a whimpering groan out of her until she was weeping tears of pleasure and pain and loss and heartache. She kept saying, *Green, green, green.* Her orgasm had released something in her, something stored for too long, and now this pain, this strange pain, was beating it to death.

"Emma, say Ben," Carter said seriously. "What color are we on?"

"Green! Green, green!" But what she meant was, he's gone, he's gone, he's gone, and I'm *still* here.

He gave her three more smacks, hard ones, his body humming with desire, his eyes stinging with the soul-wrenching tears Emma shed. His cock was aching, and his chest and every muscle in his body strained tight with wanting.

He was overwhelmed with the taste of her pussy, burning in his mouth, making his tongue tingle. Emma's plump little ass glowed a bright red. Carter's body vibrated, attuned to her energy.

Inside his pants, he was so damned firm and long, he could punch holes through a wall, but he ignored it as he listened to her demands. Holy Mary Mother of God, he'd never known Emma could lose it like this. Her cries echoed in his ears.

He gave her one more. One last hit because she kept gasping "green," but she was weeping. Weeping so hard his gut knotted to an ache. He stopped then, straining for control, and dropped the instrument at his feet.

His heart was pumping in his cock. He could barely speak. "I think we're done here."

"No, please."

"You ain't thinking right. You're too far gone, you're too—" *good for this.*

His voice altered with emotion, so he shut up. She was softly crying as he undid her binds, drew her to him, and held her close. As close as he could without breaking her bones.

Calming in his arms, Emma tilted her head to speak, but he moved by accident and his lips brushed hers.

They went utterly still.

They could've kissed.

They were there.

Panting.

She was so wet, and he was so hard.

They could've kissed.

But they didn't.

He just held her, like he should've been holding her all these months, and she gasped and hung on tight. When she came back to earth, he wondered if she'd loathe him. She might loathe him or she might . . . want him. "Thank you, Carter."

"Welcome."

Never, in his whole life, had he been so turned on, felt so out of control, or wanted something so much as to feel her. He stared down at her lips as she smiled, a little tear streaming down. He wiped it with the thick pad of his thumb.

"Didn't mean to make you cry." He was so close her fragrant breath bathed his face when she spoke.

"It's a . . . good kind of crying. I swear."

"You're crashing—it's normal to."

He couldn't take his eyes off her flushed face. Had he ever held her this close? Had she ever been so vulnerable in his arms? Maybe when Ben had died, but now she was vulnerable because she'd opened in Carter's hands. She was trembling for *Carter*.

"Did the pain stop for a little bit?" he whispered, unable to keep his eyes from heading to her lips. The steady beat of his heart pumped hot, charged blood through him. He wanted her mouth. *Kiss it.*

"Yes . . ." A pulse fluttered at the base of her throat. "I've never experienced anything like this. I feel . . . lighter. Free."

Kiss that pink mouth.

"Carter . . ." She licked her lips and stared at him, stared at him in a way he'd seen before—except she'd been looking at another man then.

His chest twisted with emotion.

"When you said you wanted things . . . did you mean me?" she asked. Hell, was that *hope* in her eyes? Was that hope jumping in *his* chest?

Still out of breath, Carter rested his forehead against hers and part laughed, part groaned. "Damn, you're a silly little pumpkin." His cock hurt. His heart hurt. His balls hurt. Tenderly, he stroked her tear-filled cheek with his fingers. "I'm in love with you, Emma."

Chapter Six

⌒

It was late into the night when he heard them.

Their low whispers as they got out of the truck and started down the gravel path echoed in the darkness. They reached his ears, slowly and surely, like the lure of a poisonous mermaid or the sight of a glutton feasting before a beggar.

Arms crossed tight as the couple headed for the house, Ben leaned against a wispy, twisted oak tree and watched. Heard. Not their words yet, no. But their tones: husky. *Intimate.*

Had they been at the Club?

Pummeled with a vision of them together, Ben fisted his hands under his armpits, emotions he didn't want to feel anymore welling up inside him.

He'd seen something today when he'd followed his new friend. He'd seen something *promising*, something that he couldn't stop thinking about.

Gandhi had led him to the dirtiest part of the city, the

darkest . . . but the only place where Ben had seen hope's light.

There were possibilities for him, he'd learned. Frightening and exciting possibilities embodied in a crazy, odd witch who seemed to have extraordinary powers and could sense the dead.

Just imagining the sensation of touching Emma again, feeling her soft skin, breathing in her scent one more time, was driving him up the wall with need. He should've approached the woman, should've asked if she could help him.

But the need to see Emma, make sure she was back home, safe, had been the stronger pull.

Fuck, he really missed walking next to her like Carter did now. Missed talking. Laughing. He loathed admitting it to himself, felt like a self-pitying *idiot*, but it was true.

He missed the busy hospital, the feel of his scrubs, some stupid little things like the great *pop* of a cork flying across the room. Most of all he missed *her*. Her little bare feet against his at night. The steady breaths in his neck as she slept.

Even when she talked to him and begged for a sign of him, it was hard to believe he still existed when those lovely eyes of hers could no longer see him.

Gut twisting tight, Ben watched as they continued to approach the house. Carter and Emma. And suddenly he could hear them perfectly. "Still nothing to say to me, pumpkin? 'Bout what I said?"

Ben frowned at this deviation from the scene he imagined would play out here. The scene where Carter should say good night and Emma would go back to the house, to slip into Ben's old T-shirt and then into bed. Where she would talk to him. Where she would say, "Are you here, Ben?" And where she would cry.

But did they do that?

No. They didn't.

Ben's head rose higher, his attention fixed on Carter as his question lingered in the cold night air. His gaze shifted to Emma, who didn't seem to have a quick answer.

Interesting.

What had Carter said?

Warning bells chimed inside his head as he waited for Emma to reply. She wore a black dress and a string of pearls and her hair down. Ben wanted to run his fingers through that silky mane. He imagined unzipping that black dress, pretended to fill his hands with the weight of her breasts, remembered how he used to nibble her pearls as he buried himself inside her.

Her laugh, soft and sweet, came suddenly. It made things grip in Ben's insides. Then Carter's hands lifted to hold her pretty oval face in a way Ben ached to, his voice insistent. "Invite me in, Em. I know you want to. Come on, sugar—*invite me.*"

Shit. What in the hell was going on here?

Emma didn't look affronted, Ben noted in growing alarm. She looked delighted. Hell, her eyes shone like warmed honey and her lips slowly formed a smile.

She ducked her head, shyly. "I'm afraid of what will happen between us if I do."

Ben stared.

A second passed. Two. Maybe a thousand.

He jumped forward and stormed toward them like a

twister. *"Son of a bitch, that's my woman you're coming on to, you son of a bitch!"*

No one saw him. No one heard him.

"And?" Carter softly persisted. "Do you want something from me, Em? Something more?"

Emma tried for a veil of disinterest, but she failed and lowered her face instead. She was standing, shifting from one foot to the other, cold. Her nose was red. Her cheeks were red. Her ears were red. And in her silence Ben felt her loneliness, her despair—choking him. He'd been company and witness for months.

Feeling wrung from the inside out, he watched that bent head as she thought of an answer.

Feeling weak, Ben walked up to her, behind her, and whispered, *"Say no, Emma. You . . . Christ, just say no. You love me. You love me."*

Ben + Emma was still carved on the inside of one of the school lockers. The name *Ben* still covered her old notebooks, in a box at the top of a closet shelf. His pictures filled her frames. She still had two in her wallet, one together, and one of Ben wakeboarding in the river.

She was laboring to breathe. Ben reached out, aching to feel the lobe of her ear under his fingertip. How could she not be aware of him? How could she not be aware of his feelings, right here before her, exposed now that he had no real body to hold them in?

He lifted his hand, set his palm over her cheek, and shuddered at the tactile memory of her warm skin under his fingers. "Emma," he whispered, like he whispered when he lay beside her in bed every night, helpless, hearing her cry.

But she didn't hear him, didn't feel him. While Ben felt *her*. Smelled *her*. Heard *her*.

Carter reached out to stroke her ear, right over where Ben held his thumb. She shivered at his touch, and Ben's insides twisted in fury.

"*Hands off,*" Ben hissed.

But instead of letting go, Carter watched her closely, raised her hand in one of his, and one by one kissed her fingertips. "I can wait if you need some time."

He slid the fingers of his free hand into her hair and curled them around her nape.

"Or I can walk into your home with you, pumpkin . . . and I can make you forget you ever wanted another man." Carter's eyes glimmered in a way Ben had seen before—just not directed at Ben's girl.

Lust.

What the man offered her, in place of the moon and the stars Ben had wanted to give her, sickened him to his stomach.

She would settle for this? This stupid jerk—Ben couldn't believe he'd trusted the bastard!—begging at her doorstep, inviting her to a world of orgies and depravity, instead of what she and Ben had had—magic!

The needs, the emotions in her, were so tumultuous Ben felt them whip around him like hurricane winds. She laughed once more, this time more weakly. "See, that's the thing. I don't want to forget, I can't . . . don't want to . . . don't want to feel like I betrayed him."

Ben had never seen Carter so hungry, so fucking aroused. His eyes seemed to be already fucking her as they ventured down her body. First his gaze lingered on her lips, then down to the breasts rising beautifully under her black dress, then to her hips, back up again to those lips. "I meant what I said, Emma," he rasped out. "I care so much about you, and I want to please you, to make you feel good again."

He stroked her cheek. A shudder racked her slim frame, and his sensual words served only to intensify her struggle.

Ben wanted to strike his fists into his face.

Then Carter caressed her nape with his fingers, and Emma's next response was visceral—a tensing of her small frame that brought her somehow closer to Carter's large body. There was no denying she reacted to him, that Carter made her react, almost in the way Ben had. He couldn't believe it!

"He's sure gone, pumpkin. And I can't offer you what he did, but I can make you smile again."

Ben's insides wrenched with pain. There was nothing, nothing, he hadn't been willing to give Emma. Nothing.

A throbbing sensation pulsed around Emma's body, desire and need mingled with hunger, and Ben was ridden by frustration and anger.

"He asked me to take care of you," Carter whispered, his eyes shining down on her. As a predator, he'd sense her resolve weakening, was sporting such a damned hard-on he was probably in his mind already coming inside of her. "And you're wasting away. I can't . . . I ain't standing by and watching more of this, princess."

"I asked you to look after her if something happened to me, you son of a bitch! I didn't mean you should fuck her!"

Then Emma said, with a voice as broken as her spirit,

"Ben's dead." She raised her face, and the fierce determination in her gaze slammed Ben like a fist. *She's determined to forget me.* "Tonight, after what we did. It struck me then."

Ben staggered back. What had they done at the Club? Had Carter beaten her? Had he tied her up? Fucked her?

No one could resist that motherfucker, no one. And apparently neither could Emma!

Carter groaned, a lean, muscled arm reaching out for Emma's waist. "Just say when, pumpkin, and before you know it we're in your bedroom. And you'll remember what it's like when a man makes love to you. I need to be that man. I need to."

Ben saw Carter draw her toward him, and something horrible went through him, blinding him, sinking its claws into him.

Carter bent down.

She wouldn't kiss him.

No way would she—

His lips closed over hers. Emma moaned and flung her arms around his neck.

"No! What the fuck are you doing? No! Emma, what are you doing?" Ben flung himself at them, and fell to the ground.

They were kissing, wide-mouthed, with wild and hungry tongues, as he stood. He fisted his hands at his sides.

"Goddamn you, bastard, I'll kill *you!"*

He flung himself at a man he'd once considered his best friend, and sprawled facedown once more. He rolled to his back, gazed up at the clouded sky, and roared in fury, a roar that sent a nearby owl hooting and flying away.

Then her scent washed through his senses, sweet and feminine. Aroused. *Goddammit!*

"Christ, sugar, I've been aching to fuck you all night, put my dick inside you all night."

Shaking in Carter's arms, as though the words *fuck* and *dick* from his lips were the most powerful aphrodisiacs, Emma let him suckle her tongue and breathed, "Carter."

The pain ripped through Ben as he pushed up to his knees, and with effort, to his feet. The hot scent of her desire overwhelmed his senses until he thought he was alive again, dying, degree by degree, all over again, this time murdered by the woman he ached to live for.

His kiss demanded her surrender.

The blazing fire in his eyes, in his fingertips, in his lips, didn't promise pain, it promised pleasure. Worlds, planets, universes of pleasure. Emma kissed him back with all her might while her mind cried for her to stop, warned that this was too soon for pleasure. But her body was screaming *please*. Please!

God, he set her on fire. He was an amazing man—one to sin with, play with, come for. Yes, wow, yes. Yes, she thought as their tongues twirled, this was what she needed. She felt queasy and nervous and unsure, but she also felt feverish and needy and aroused.

She'd ached for him at the Club. Ached to know he wanted her like this.

And for the first time, she was determined to move forward and not look back. Her life was wasting. She was wasting. For twenty months, she hadn't had this, a man's touch, a man's loving. And she wanted him. God help her, she wanted Carter inside of her—no one else would do.

Tearing free in a rush, she ushered him into the house, her heart thundering in her ears. She pulled him up the stairs, into her bedroom, and kicked off her shoes. No time for second thoughts. No time to breathe.

Growling, he manacled her wrists above her head, laid her back against the closed door with his whipcord lean body pressing and grinding against hers, and fastened his mouth on hers. Fireworks exploded in her head.

She ripped her lips free with effort. "Wait, wait!"

Heart wrung in her chest, she rushed to the bed, to the picture of Ben on the nightstand. Her hands shook as she turned it facedown.

Breathing like he'd just swam ten laps across the Pacific Ocean, Carter came up behind her, his voice low and rough. Chock-full of arousal. "Don't think about him, Em." He urged her around to face him and placed a gentle finger on her lips. His eyes, electric blue, held hers.

Emma nodded. Forget Ben's fiery mouth on her nipples, suckling her tongue, the whispers in the middle of the night. She had been taken by Ben in her dreams so many times, and never once had she been able to orgasm. She woke up crying, to remember he was gone.

"I'm not thinking about him." It hurt to admit this. To admit that Ben, a permanent resident in her mind, seemed to be kicked out of there by Carter.

In silence, Carter held her. This had been a favorite moment for her at the Club. Being held for long, long minutes, cooed to and caressed while her body trembled with shock. His erection bit into her abdomen. His hunger enveloped her as he stroked her back.

He slid his hands down her arms, making her breathless. He cupped her breasts, greedily, and oh, god, she needed this. Suddenly the window shuddered as though a wind were raging outside.

Lust coursed through her veins. Unstoppable. Like that very wind.

Feeling her breaths ache, Emma turned her face to his and let her tongue snake out to lick the corner of his lips. "Let's do it." *I'm sorry, Ben*, she thought. Could he see her from heaven? Could he see what she was doing? Would he hate her? Would he remember how she'd vowed she'd never be touched, never once love anyone else, as he had vowed the same? *Oh, god, Ben, forgive me.* When she'd spoken that vow, she hadn't been lonely. She hadn't thought sometimes of dying, and how welcoming it would be. She hadn't imagined what the grief of losing Ben would be like, and the guilt of having survived him felt like.

Drawing her closer by the shoulders, Carter took her lips, lifted her around him, put her up against the wall, and shoved his erection against her, saying, "Emma."

She moaned; it felt good. Different. Good. To rub. Grind.

He grabbed the curve of her ass, molding it in his hands as his hips rubbed against her. Her body became ungovernable, her mind seizing the sensations and spinning them around. Ben kissing her lips, whispering into her ear. Ben kissing her that last time. Saying he had to go; he had to go to work. *No.* No. No, it was not Ben. Carter. And he was not saying good-bye. His chest was steel. He was hard against her, he wanted her. Every girl she knew wanted Carter, but Carter wanted *her*.

"Emma." His hands shook as he yanked her dress up to her waist. His finger plowed between their bodies, edged the lace of her panties aside, and delved deep into her channel.

She bucked and her whole body tightened. A peak approached. So soon. "I . . . ahhhh."

He pushed it down to the root and found her G-spot. Her blood rushed and her pussy clenched around his deep powerful strokes. "Oh, god."

He clamped his lips around a nipple and suckled the dress fabric into that scalding vortex of his mouth. The air spun in the room. A storm built. Inside her. Around her. His finger pumped. *Oh, Carter, yes, move it, move it!*

Wildly pitching her hips, Emma buried her nose into his silky hair, plunging her hands in there like she'd always wanted to. Woodspice assailed her nostrils and the scent excited her beyond reason.

The tension built inside her body—every muscle, every limb stretching tight. Tighter. Something crashed inside the room. Glass shattered.

Her head whipped up.

Carter's finger stopped.

From the bookshelf, all Ben's pictures tumbled to the floor. *Crash. Crash. Crash.* One by one, they shattered as they struck, joining the frame that seemed to have toppled from the nightstand.

With a soft cry of alarm, Emma shoved Carter away

like you'd shove away a lion—with a lot of fucking effort and frantic to get away from his grasp—and stumbled free. "Stop, stop! He's here. Ben! Ohmigod, Ben!"

"Jesus, you can't be serious." Carter signaled at the bedroom window—swinging open, side to side. He stalked across the carpet and slammed it shut. He locked it. "Just a little wind, pumpkin."

Emma stood there, feeling like a jerk; she hated having spoken out loud in front of Carter.

She couldn't bear to look him in the eye now.

Why did she expect any minute now Ben would come through that door? Or that he'd call and say he'd been held up? Her mind was occupied with fantasies of Carter, but it felt like her heart was waking from sleep and she couldn't adjust to the things she was feeling.

As if the void inside her was filling up again.

Filling up with warm fuzzy feelings and desire and dreams again.

Eyes burning, Emma saw all the pictures of Ben on the floor, his face handsome and dark and strong, his eyes looking at her behind the camera, his jaw tight because it exasperated him to be photographed, and she dropped to her knees and quietly picked them up.

She should tuck them in a box, she knew, but she could not. Could not move anything. His clothes were still in the drawers. His toothbrush was still in the sink. At night, she pretended he still held her. At night, she pretended he whispered things to her about their day. And at night, she talked to him and said, *Ben, don't leave me.*

Even though he'd already left.

. . .

Damn, his little nurse really needed a shot of tender loving care. A big ole Band-Aid called Carter Bates to stick where it was aching.

Carter watched her hair tumble across her face as she gathered up the shards. His cock ached and his heart clenched for this fragile little thing. He remembered when she'd sewn up his wrist. Not even for a second during all these years had he forgotten the way her touch had spread through him. Cool, gentle, almost motherly. But Carter's mama had never made his dick jump.

He hadn't felt the needle enter. He'd hardly felt the pricks. He'd been pinned down into the old vinyl booth by the mere fact that Emma sat next to him. And that she was holding his wrist. And that she was whispering in a hell of a nice voice, *This will hurt just a little.* And that her hair smelled like a basket of berries.

He wasn't sure if he should be pushing her, felt like he was invading her space, but hell, he wanted to comfort her, protect her, give her ease. Those first months after the funeral, Emma had taken too many pills, had taken mourning to a whole new freaking masochistic level.

Carter missed Ben, too. How his cynical remarks would make Carter smile, how he would be silent as a tomb when Carter wanted someone to talk to. Loyal. *Ben wouldn't do this to you, Carter.*

He swallowed, wanting to tell her he'd pick up her shards for her, but instead he went into the bathroom and grabbed two hand towels.

It might be better to go home tonight, but he didn't want to go. He'd watched for years all of the light, fleeting caresses Ben had given her, touches that noticeably aroused her, made her smile or giggle, and Carter had been quietly ensnared with jealousy. The friend. Watching. Wanting.

Now Ben wasn't here—and yet he was. He still owned her, possessed her. Carter still felt ensnared with jealousy.

Emma moved quietly, gathering the pictures in a stack. Standing with a towel in each hand, Carter could not tear his eyes off her. The deft moves of her fingers, how her hair brushed her bare shoulders and she swiped it back.

Her dress today was sexy, true, molding to her body. But it was black. Her hair was combed behind her head, a bit severely—a widow. A young, attractive widow who'd never made it to the altar. Carter noticed as she shuffled around the glass that her pink, feminine feet were bare, and he reached out to pull her back. "You'll cut yourself."

She glanced up at him, then Carter began gathering the shards between the towels, and she said, "Thank you."

"Welcome." He worked quietly, feeling her eyes on his back, wondering if those eyes would flare the first time he showed her his cock. Would she want to taste it? Kiss it? Stroke it? Feel it?

Dumping the glass in the bathroom trash, he came back out to find her watching him.

His jeans felt tight and his dick kept expanding.

Dragging in a breath, Emma set her fingers on her stomach, scanning his face as though for signs of anger. "I'm sorry, Carter. I'm such a mess and you've been so good to me."

He choked in disbelief. "Good? Fuck, Emma, I'm a son of a bitch."

Her voice was forgiving. "Don't say that."

He grabbed a handful of his hair. A shitty bar owner shouldn't have been hounding her for a year and a half, waiting for the moment when he could take her lips, when he could rip her clothes from her body and lick every inch of skin. A decent man wouldn't have lusted after his best friend's woman and if he did, he sure as heck would not admit it to the other man!

Dropping his arm, he took a step. "The problem is I don't want to be good to you; no, pumpkin, that ain't what I want. Not by a long shot. I'm a selfish motherfucker and I'll do anything to get in that bed right there with you—you hear what I'm sayin', Emma?"

She stared at him for an electrifying moment, her chest rising and falling. Was she remembering just now? His finger inside of her? Shit, the ecstasy! The feel of her pussy coating his finger like, back at the Club, it had coated his tongue.

He groaned deep in his throat. "Come here, baby."

She released a small tortured sound but instead escaped to the window, her arms around herself. She was shaking like he was. "I can't take it when you call me baby," she whispered fiercely. "When you call me sexy."

"You're the sexiest thing these eyes have ever seen."

She shivered.

He took in her bare shoulders, the slender, milky white arms he wanted curled around his neck. The pain, the desire, continued as he waited. His need was so intense, all he could think of was feeling her with his hands, his lips, his cock. When would he get there, *be* there?

He'd moved too fast, he'd moved too fast and yet to him this wait had felt eternal. Eternal.

He watched as she made sure the window was locked, and spoke out into the night. "Us doing this is . . ." She shook her head, turned to look at him. "I'm not over him, Carter, I can't . . ."

He covered the space between them in three seconds flat and pulled her close, holding her against him, scraping his jaw against the top of her head. "Shh, it's all right. I understand."

"Look, it's just that I feel like you want something from me that I can't give!"

"Only asking for a chance, pumpkin."

Her head canted back, and her eyes fell to his mouth, her gaze hungry as though she wanted him to put it on hers. And it struck him that although she was in his every fantasy, he might not be the man in hers. Could he bear to play this game? Be inside her even if she pretended he was someone else?

He squeezed her shoulders. "Want me to leave?" he asked.

She mouthed *no* while shaking her head fast, and then she pried free of his hold and headed unsteadily for the bed. "Am I really sexy to you?"

"You're sexy. You're a hell of a sexy baby."

He noticed the effects the words had on her: like she'd just felt a firecracker explode under her skin. It drove him insane. His hunter's instinct awakened to the chase as she continued to the bed, awakened to the seizing, the taking; and his pulse rocketed through his body as he prowled slowly after her.

"You want me to stay, then, sexy?" He pulled out his wallet, yanked out a foil packet that contained a condom, tossed the wallet aside and continued toward her even as she backed away, her eyes dilated with awareness. "I'm in your goddamned room, waiting to touch you, ready to fuck you, and you keep playing hard to get. I got news, baby—I like it."

She bumped against the nightstand, caught her breath when she realized it and then wedged around. She reached behind her and gripped the edge of the bed for support. "Please . . ." she said.

He lifted his hand, cupped her face possessively, and let his thumb stroke and glory in the softness of her cheek. Her eyes flicked up to his and held so much wariness he felt like a predator. "I'm not gonna hurt you—no one ever will, as long as I live." Her skin was silk under his fingers, silk. "I crave to give you pleasure, Em. I'm gonna make you let go, forget Ben for a minute, forget everything but that I'm inside you and I ain't going anywhere else."

She closed her eyes, shuddering. "I won't let myself forget him. Never. When I die, I want to feel relief, that I'll finally . . . see him again."

"Pumpkin, you ain't dying yet." He stroked her hair, his stomach heavy and tight when she didn't stop him, allowed him to massage the back of her neck. "What about now? What about bein' close to someone? Flesh and blood. That never on your mind, Em? Wanting to live a life you can look back on in satisfaction?"

He raised her hand and kissed her fingertips. Then he licked one finger. She groaned. Her lids covered most of her eyes as he made love to that slender finger that tasted of vanilla, and then he was moving his mouth to her palm, swirling his tongue around. "All that matters is that you let me in here—and now I'm spending the night here. And, baby? You ain't gonna be sleeping."

"Oh, god, that feels good," she gasped, pushing the finger that he licked deeper into his mouth so he could bite it.

Arousal swam in his veins, demanding he take her, take this woman he'd wanted, he'd been patiently waiting for.

"When you kiss me . . ." Voraciously he twirled his tongue around her fingertip in the way he wanted her to twirl her own around his dick. "When we kiss, you ain't thinking of Ben. I know you want him, but you want me, too. You came for me at the Club—you came for *me*. Carter. No one else."

Her eyes were teary.

He cupped her warm cheek. "Damn, just kiss me, Emma. Been dying for a kiss from my sexy . . . sexy . . . baby."

She did. Oh, Jesus Mary Mother of God, she opened her lips and kissed him like she was nuts about him. He groaned as a tornado of desire whipped through his body. "Now tell me you would like my hands on you—tell me now."

"I want your hands on me, Carter."

"Oh, baby, that was fucking sexy. Now, Jesus, *give me that mouth of yours again.*"

Chapter Seven

Ben simmered as he roamed the streets, prowling the darkness like an apocalypse. The natural bridge caverns were hours away on foot. They contained chambers and chambers of spectacular crystallized formations, emerald pools, and distance. Distance from Carter and Emma.

Ben thought of finding refuge there, but instead he continued into the deadliest, most obscure alleys of the city, into the very pits of hell, into places he hadn't dared venture when alive and had stayed away from dead. Until Gandhi had taken him. He'd seen ghosts get sucked in there. Disappear with little more than a shriek. G had told him they never returned.

Now he stepped willingly into that grim darkness, bringing the wind with him, the clouds and the rain, as he stalked through an area full of ramshackle houses, warehouses, tenements, and sex shops.

The images in his mind continued torturing him. Emma

pulling Carter into their bedroom. Carter fucking a finger into her pussy. Into the pussy that belonged to Ben. His eyes burned as the vision replayed itself in his mind, real enough to want to kill them. Her legs open, her ass in his hands, his finger ramming and ramming her cunt while she cried out.

Ben had been beyond furious—stuff had begun falling apart as Emma started falling apart for Carter.

Crash, crash, crash, his photographs had gone. And Emma, at last, had remembered *Ben*.

He'd been wandering the streets for an hour now, hating himself, hating Carter. But now noises from inside this small building called to him. He peered through the grimy windows, where G had said *she*—a seller of spells—lived. Dead things hung from the ceiling. Rats? A woman danced around a pot, shaking stuff, calling up her master, calling up the devil.

Ben hadn't gone to heaven. He didn't know what he'd done wrong, why he was stuck here, but this existence was *hell*, and he'd do anything to get out of it. G had told him this woman had powers, and he'd seen firsthand how she'd revived a dog smack in the middle of this very room. Was evil the source of her power? Hell, he didn't fucking care.

The woman was immersed in one of her rituals, slicing a dagger in the center of a toad's stomach, then tossing the writhing creature into the boiling pot.

This black ritual sacrificed nothing for something, and he saw people like him, ghosts, souls without bodies, waiting for their turn. To be set free? What would he do—what would he not do—for a spell like this? But he didn't want just freedom: he wanted a body.

A dead body like that trampled dog's to be called to life again.

Could she do it to humans?

He materialized inside the room, and the woman continued chanting in a low, craggy voice, whispering numbers, diabolical numbers.

"I need your services, witch."

Her eyes widened.

He moved to her right side, growling in her ear, "Can you hear me? Can you bring people back to life?"

"Back off!" she hissed.

"I need my body back, witch. I need my life back. Name your price and I will pay it."

She moved around, gathering garlic cloves and tossing them into the simmering liquid, clucking to herself, chanting her tune. *"Dame la vida, dame el amor, dame demonio el poder que deseo . . ."*

Behind him, ghosts flickered over the boiling pot, and a ray of fire took form, blazing fluorescent red light up to the ceiling.

"I've seen ghosts disappear from here—where do you send them?"

She laughed at Ben's question and shook her head, calling one of the souls into the pot. *"Ven ven ven."*

As the ghost disappeared, Ben wanted to shake her; clenched his hands around her shoulders and attempted to. "You brought a dog back. I was outside; I saw you, just a couple of hours ago. Can you do the same to me? Can you give me back my life?"

"I'm busy!" she spat, but nodded angrily. "Besides, I'd need a body to work with first."

Exhilaration swept through him. So she could do it! She could give him what he needed, desperately, fully, more than anything. Life! "The cemetery—come with me, witch. Will you summon my body, witch? From underground?"

She said nothing and stood rooted in place, but her unseeing white eye twitched as the other dilated; then she set down her bloodied knife, wiped her hands on her sullied apron, and stared off into space, cocking her head as though trying to place him. "You'll pay the price for my services?" she asked in an eerily sweet voice.

"I will! Name it. I was a rich man. I'll make sure you're compensated."

"Money. Bah!" She waved her hand, showed her grimy teeth. "I want a husband."

"A husband?" He followed her around the pot, scowling at her tangled hair as she continued dancing around. "How am I supposed to give you a husband?"

"Are you married, boy? You sound young. Clever. You will find a way to help me. I'm cursed, you see. Under this face I'm a beautiful damsel." She flung her head back laughing, and her laughter could've made even the dead rats scuttle away to escape the scraping sound.

Ben's insides cramped as he thought of Carter taking Emma. Carter, his best friend, whom he'd bumped knuckles with, who'd been the only guy he'd told "I'm marrying Emma." Taking Emma from him.

"I know just the man."

"You do?" Her grin exposed each of her rotting teeth.

"Well then. We're in business. But I'm warning you, boy"—
she went to the shelves and began plucking up vials here and
there—"if you do not deliver a willing husband within the
cycle of the moon, you'll be back in the cemetery."

Desperation made him nod his head even though the
witch couldn't see him. He didn't know how he'd do it, he
didn't even pause to wonder, he only knew that he would.
Carter, you fucking son of a bitch, don't mess with the dead. "I'll
deliver."

"He has to come willingly to me, I say."

"I'll deliver."

"And when he comes, boy, be warned that he will never
be returning."

"Done. Now get me back into my fucking body."

Carter groaned softly as they stood trembling in each other's arms in the middle of the bedroom, his forehead resting
on hers. "Now lift your dress and show me your pussy,"
he rasped, plunging his tongue into her ear in a caress that
made her moan.

Her blood rushed and her panties moistened at the
thought of getting naked after the long, heated minutes they'd spent on foreplay. Mentally she repeated to
herself that this would be just sex—not personal—just no-
strings-attached sex.

But then why was she shivering inside?

Why was she so breathless, feeling things again, overwhelming things?

Carter hiked her skirt up to her waist, then palmed her

ass between his big hands. "I said take off your panties, baby. I want to see your pretty pussy."

Quickly she removed the lace thong, and Carter stroked the bulge in his jeans with his hand as he took in the plump sex lips nestled between her thighs. "That's nice, very nice, very sexy."

Sex-saaay.

She would have buckled if he hadn't caught her by the arm.

"No faintin', pumpkin, not yet."

The calloused heels of his palms brushed her skin lightly as he unhooked her bra. His scent as he moved closer, head ducked, made her dizzy. Diz-zaaay.

Planting one kiss on each of her shoulders, he brushed her bra aside and then jerked out of his T-shirt. Emma saw a flash of bronze, the ripple of muscle, and the instant her nipples pressed against his bare chest, she thought she'd been electrocuted.

His exquisite bronzed chest, the same one that girls salivated over as they drove past him when he washed his F150, was bare against hers, was hers to touch and lick and rub. A gold cross glinted at his throat, and it made him look sinful.

"Give me your other hand." He seized her hand while she glided the other over his taut skin, and she felt him set her palm against his fly. "Got that for you, baby. Now, tell me you wanna take it out to play."

Oh, god, he was too much. Beneath her palm he was pulsing, so firm he felt like steel, stretching the denim of his jeans to the point of tearing. Her breath became ragged.

When she raised her eyes to his piercing blue ones, his

gaze was on her mouth. Lightly, he ran two fingers over her bottom lip, making her heart pound.

"Do you want me?" he asked thickly.

I'm going to faint.

"Tell me, baby, don't deny me tonight. Tell me you want my cock."

She closed her eyes, swaying on her legs.

"Do you want this big mean bastard inside you?"

There was only one truth.

"Y-yes."

Eyes wild with hunger, Carter gently cupped and squeezed her breasts, pushing out her nipples with his fingers, grazing with his teeth, scraping her with his tongue, swiping the silky wetness over and over the peak. "How bad, baby? How bad do you want it?"

"V-very bad."

He licked a line up her throat, and she grew frantic. The heat would consume her if she didn't—

It would kill her if he soon didn't—

"Carter." Her hands flew and worked frantically on the zipper of his jeans, and then she pushed the denim along with his plain cotton briefs down his narrow hips. His cock popped out. He kicked his clothes aside and Emma didn't hesitate.

She grabbed the stiff shaft and seized a handful of his hair at the same time. Her pussy rippled as she caressed with both hands, caressed his cock, his thick soft hair—delighted at the tremor of heat that coursed through his big body.

"If you get to pet my cock, baby, then I get to pet your kitty." With a concentrated frown that made his jaw look even squarer, he ran his longest finger between the inflamed lips of her labia, hairless and swollen pink, his voice gruff. "Did you shave for me . . . to eat you with my filthy mouth?"

"Yes," she admitted. She'd been hoping. Maybe planning?

"Fuck, baby, then give it to me." He forced her down on the bed and knelt between her thighs. "Open wide, sugar, this man's dying to eat your honey."

Fire swept through her when he cupped her pussy between his palms, urging it open with his thumbs as he inserted his tongue. Shocks of pleasure rushed through her as he thrust powerfully inside.

Moonlight stole through the windowpane and his skin glowed silver. He looked like a wolf in a full moon, claiming his mate with his mouth forever. His shoulders were broad, his biceps bulging, and her eyes still stung from the brief sight of his cock she'd stolen. His cock, oh, god, it had been so big. So thick. So long.

She licked her lips, a hungry sound escaping her at the thought of tasting him, of kneeling before him and draining him, but she lost her thoughts when she felt a blazing hot scrape of his thumb tease around her clitoris. She choked on her breath when his tongue plunged into her pussy again, drinking so thirstily from her cunt that she thought he'd drain all of her juice.

He came up panting and snatched up her hand, pressing it to his erection, grinding himself into her palm. "What about that, baby?" he cooed, his teeth flashing. "You want to give it a little love?"

Undone by his smile, she was instantly on her knees. Her

fingers curled instinctively around his width and her breasts hurt when she couldn't encircle him. He was so wide.

He growled, holding the back of her head and pressing his forehead to hers as though he needed to lean on her. He panted hard against her face. "Stroke me. Up and down, move your hand on me." Her hand was tight around his cock but unmoving. Carter grabbed it and forced it to slide around him, growling in pleasure. "Work me, like that, just like that—fuck, *yeah*."

He pumped against her, aroused and making noises of desire. Her nipples ached. Her pussy pooled with wetness and her heart contracted in her chest. Oh, how she wanted him.

But this was Carter.

Carter who'd fuck anything that walked. And now he was going to fuck Emma.

"Emma," he groaned, his hips moving in circles.

He plunged a hand between her legs and tested her entrance with his middle finger. "Ahh, Christ, you're so wet."

She splayed her knees wider apart and received him with a moan. Her dampness welcomed his finger, her pussy parting as he pushed inside. Emma shuddered at his slow penetration and he made a low husky sound, thrusting his cock deep into her grip.

She closed her eyes on a gasp, overwhelmed by him. So close to falling down a cliff and never being the same again. "Oh, god."

She wanted to weep, felt so bad that she hadn't felt so good in almost two years. "Please don't stop."

Her need consumed her, turbulent and fierce and unstoppable. She fought for strength, but how could she when he had proven to be her sole weakness? Her flushed cheek dropped against his shoulder as she labored to breathe. "Oh, god."

His firm hold on her wrists tightened as he pumped in a second finger. "Had about a thousand wet dreams about this." He devoured her ear with his mouth again, kissing her roughly with tongue. "'Bout you, princess."

Groaning at the utter slowness of his powerful strokes and loathing that she even wanted them, Emma grazed his throat with her teeth as she fondled him with both her hands. One cupped his heavy sac and played with the large, taut balls, and the other worked his erection rapidly up and down.

His finger hit her G-spot. "Oh, yes. Yes," she hissed as every inch of her body trembled with lust. Feelings of such raw intensity made her eyes burn with tears, her breath hitch and come out in sharp, shuddering wheezes. "Carter, stretch me wider."

He buried his face between her breasts and made a vibrant sound of hunger when he turned to suck a nipple. His fingers stretched her pussy wider. "That feel good, baby?" He bit the tip of her nipple, his cock leaking in her hand as she fondled the bulbous head. "Shit, princess, you better stop that now before I blow." Emma let out a gasp when his thumb bit into her clit and she bucked as he stroked it, sobbing in abandon.

"You like that?"

"Yes!" Dear god, yes.

He chuckled a little, then again ravaged her ear, this time using his teeth and his breath blasted into her. "You're a feisty little kitten, aren't you, now?" He pinched her clit and made her yelp. Then he dragged his lips up to her temple, murmuring against her skin, "I love feisty little kittens, always getting their little claws where they don't belong."

Emma undulated as they knelt on the bed and caressed each other, certain she was losing her mind and too witless to care.

She pressed her open mouth to his square shoulder while he tortured each one of her breasts with flicks of his tongue. She wished for his lips to kiss and sobbed violently on each breath, not even realizing her cheeks were damp because she burned so much.

She wanted to explode in a million pieces and never be the same again, felt so very weak and so very tired of feeling nothing. It was insane and suicidal and she was stopping now.

His cock glided smoothly in her grip, tantalizing her to fantasize about feeling it inside her. Her body racked in shudders. And she found herself licking his neck, French-kissing it and gasping against the flat surface at each powerful thrust of his cock.

Both his arms all of a sudden went around her, squeezing the breath out of her as he rubbed his cock against her belly. "Moan for me, baby. Don't cry. Moan for me."

"Carter."

"I fucking want you, Emma."

With a guttural sound that rumbled in his chest, he licked one tear from the tip of her chin up to the corner of her eye as he laid her back on the bed and teased her sex with the tip of his cock. "Emma. Let go. Stop thinking. Just feel me. Cry out to me. I love it when you moan—I fucking want you, baby, I want you now."

Emma stopped thinking and grabbed his face and said, "Fuck me, fuck me as hard as you want to."

"Satanás, rescata a tu hijo de su tumba, hazlo subir a la tierra, dale la vida que se le quitó!"

Ben watched the witch go round and round his tombstone. The moon shone high above the distant hills, eerie yellow in the night. Cars drove by the nearest highway and all around the cemetery the trees swayed, stirred by the wind. But Ben was solely focused on his gravesite, on the words BENJAMIN NEWCASTLE engraved on pitch-black granite. Summoning all his energy, all his wanting, and all of his emotions, good and bad, past and present, he willed himself to come forth.

A vibration seeped into him. Slow, at first, then more desperate. The ground shuddered. He felt pulled in all directions.

"Promise to serve your new master, Benjamin Newcastle."

"I promise."

"Promise to obey his commands, Benjamin Newcastle!"

"I promise."

"Promise to deliver your fee or else know a pain unlike any other, Benjamin Newcastle."

Something slammed into him—flesh, veins, bone—and his head jerked back as he roared. "I *promise*!!"

Fuck me. Fuck me as hard as you want to.

Carter felt her words reverberate in his balls.

He was burning. He gazed down at Emma, open legged and rosy-cheeked on her bed, and his chest cramped with emotion. How many nights had he envisioned, wanted her like this?

"You're so damned beautiful my jaw hurts." His fingers moved, his cock jealously twitching, wanting to feel the burning tightness of her cunt around it, too.

She arched up as he prepared her with his fingers, her breasts jiggling. "Don't . . . make me . . . wait." But she grabbed his wrist and urged his hand harder against her, taking in two fingers now and so damned wet and swollen he was sure she could take three.

"Look at you," he rasped. She'd shut her eyes and now humped his fingers as he screwed them in repeatedly, her head rolling behind her in ecstasy as she clutched the sheets. "Oh, god, oh, god, oh god!"

"Goddamn you're hot."

In a profuse sweat, he slid naked down her body, pushed in a third finger with effort, and sucked her wet nub into his mouth. She screamed, bucked, convulsed as she came with powerful contractions. He stoked her orgasm with quick merciless stabs of his fingers, his mouth and tongue devouring her little clit.

He came up and saw her face flushed, her eyes heavy. "Do it again for me." He carefully sheathed himself with a condom, then prodded his cock into her, rolling onto his side and bringing her with him. "This time come around me."

She moaned when he draped her leg around his hips, lying side by side on the bed. "Carter," she said, breathless and flustered and at the moment, at this very special moment, his. One hand was on his shoulder, her grip as hard as her voice was soft. "Is this as good for you as it is for me?"

"God, baby, this is everything to me." He stroked his cock along her pussy—still wet from her orgasm and by the way she whimpered, maybe a little too sensitive. "I'm so there already, baby. . . ."

"Tell me Ben would be okay with this, Carter, with us being together."

He pulled out, drew her closer, then pushed into her snug sheath with a groan. "Yeah, he would be."

But he was lying, lying because he couldn't stop himself, lying because he knew the truth.

She moaned, swallowing him down to the root as she shoved up her hips against his. She clutched him so tight, was trembling so bad.

Fuck me, she's so tight.

"Shh. I'm here now," he rasped as he dropped a hand on one plump ass cheek and gave it a greedy squeeze as he fucked in deeper. "I'm here now, inside you, and ain't going anywhere."

She made a tiny choking sound and tossed her head with her eyes closed. "Oh, god, what are we doing?"

He groaned and tried to hold back his orgasm. "We're

fucking," he gritted. But then he gazed into her lust-clouded eyes. Gently, he spread out her hair so it could fall across her shoulders and behind her back like a cocoa river and he whispered, "We're making love, Emma."

They were fucking slowly, savoring every stroke and push and breathing faster as their bodies moved.

"Carter Bates doesn't know how to make love," she whispered.

A sound of protest rumbled up his throat. She was wrong. So very wrong. He cradled her jaw in his hand and kissed her, his tongue plunging into her sweet mouth only once before he murmured, "Carter Bates knows how to make love only to Emma."

Her eyes flashed with emotion, and she drew his mouth back to hers and swept him into her kiss.

She was so goddamned tight, her curvy body so malleable in his hands. The tips of her breasts grazed his chest and her ass in his hand felt like heaven. He used his grip to grab her closer and stabbed in deeper, loving the sound of her helpless yelp.

"So good, baby," he murmured even as he took her lips for an urgent kiss and began to fuck her for real now. He rolled on top of her to gain leverage, pistoning into her rippling grip with unbridled, almost clumsy thrusts. He grunted at each plunge, staring down at her with wild eyes and demanding, "Come with me, come with me now."

She was as far gone as he was, gripping his shoulders until the tip of her nails bit into his skin, meeting his ramming stabs with an upward motion of her hips. "Oh, please, *please.*"

"Say *Carter*. Say my name, Emma."

"Carter!"

"Again, baby. Again." He increased his tempo, making the bed squeak.

"Carter! Carter! Carter!"

"Benjamin Newcastle, rise from the dead! *RISE FROM THE DEAD!*"

Carter twisted when she climaxed, her pussy closing around his cock and milking him. He kept pushing into her with several rough grunting sounds, his body contracting as her vagina walls squeezed around his flesh.

"Yes," he gasped as he held her body in place and gave her a series of last wild desperate thrusts.

He came with a strangled groan, his orgasm choking out the sound. He trembled, his eyes rolling back as he gripped her body under his and continued to rub into her heated channel whispering, "Shit, baby . . . oh, shit . . ."

When he collapsed he swiftly rolled to his back and brought her with him. She cuddled perfectly to his side, the fit of their bodies unbelievably right, but she went so quiet that Carter scowled.

He studied her face, wishing to know what she was thinking. Her eyes were guarded, and even as their bodies touched, he sensed distance between them. She wasn't letting him in. Only when mindless with need did Emma seem to stop thinking about . . . Ben Newcastle.

No.

Carter wouldn't give her so much as a minute, a second, to think about him any longer.

His bones cracked the second his body slammed into him, and his organs painfully screamed as he came back to life. He convulsed. Flailing, thrashing, the pain of dying had been nothing to the pain of living again. His lungs strained to work, every breath a torment. His heart kicked like someone trying to murder him from the inside. Life started rushing through his bloodstream, and it felt like acid in his veins.

He lay on the ground, bucking. An unearthly yell tore from his lungs—a yell that was heard and echoed throughout the quiet cemetery. He roared as the blades of a thousand knives cut through him, sliced through his muscles and skin and arteries.

For eternal minutes, he lay there, gasping, cursing, his face wet from tears, his ears ringing from the noise, his skin awakening to the sensation of the wind, which felt like a hundred slaps in the freezing cold, until . . .

Until the shakes receded. Slowly. So slowly. His next breath felt easier. His next heartbeat . . . stronger.

He sat up and moved his limbs, the soreness receding. Slow. So slow.

The witch was gaping at his exposed genitals. His cock hung long and heavy between his thighs, his balls gathered close to the stalk. Her voice sounded almost like an orgasm. "Better get you some clothes! Oh, my, Benny, my, you're a handsome one. Oh, stars, you're a gifted one."

Ignoring the witch, he rose, naked as a newborn, his thighs and ass and back muddied from the ground. He shook off the dirt, thinking he couldn't go home yet. Reluctance, reason, held him back. He wanted to calm down this anger first. Calm down this desire to *kill*.

With a long, haggard breath—a breath!—he glanced across the foggy cemetery, then down at his hands. His hands. Even the scar he'd gotten surfing. He'd thought living would feel amazing, but it felt . . . wrong. He felt too small in this skin, his mind whirling, creaking as it began working again.

Setting his jaw in determination, he started walking over graves—mindless of what he stepped on, mindless of anything but reaching the street.

His bare feet hit asphalt, and all of a sudden headlights glared before his unaccustomed eyes, paralyzing him. Tires squealed—a person screamed as an old Chevy rammed into Ben. He braced for the impact, expecting to buckle, but instead the hood dented, folding around his hips, his legs.

"Ay Dios Santo, Dios mio!" A Hispanic woman was hysterical behind the wheel. Ben stepped away and walked naked into darkness.

"Benny! Benny!" the witch screamed, rushing to catch him. She could've been a bat from hell, fluttering blindly toward him, almost slamming into his chest when she reached him.

He grabbed the clothes she proffered and shoved his legs into the worn denim and buttoned up the old checkered shirt. Whatever she was about to say, a warning, whatever it was, Ben didn't listen. Emma. In his place, in their home, with Carter. Emma!

He held up a hand to silence her, leaving her with her mouth parted. "I'll deliver, witch," he said.

Ten minutes later, he stepped into a bar, the first he spotted, with neon lights flaring. The music blasted so loud that every rhyme U2 spit out made the ground shudder under his feet. "Sunday Bloody Sunday," Bono rattled on.

He had no money for a drink, but then he knew, felt, sensed, that nobody would argue with him. He gazed at the bartender. The man seemed to be holding his breath, his shoulder at an awkward angle as though he was searching for something under the counter.

"Don't," Ben said, a quiet warning. The man froze. Ben approached. "A glass of whiskey and I'm gone."

The man scrambled to give him a Johnnie Walker. Slowly draining the glass, Ben slammed it down and walked on. Bono sang, "Sunday Bloody Sunday . . ."

Ben strode outside and walked for hours until the pale morning broke overhead.

And as the sunlight rose over the earth, the trees, the city, and something as insignificant as a bug, Ben headed, undeterred, in the direction he belonged.

He headed for home.

She'd just pulled the curtains open.

Fresh from bed, Emma stretched languorously, revealing a flat, creamy white stomach, a delectable belly button, and a next-to-nothing pair of lacy panties. Ben watched her from a wide branch on the oak tree outside, frowning and peering through the window like a Peeping Tom begging for a restraining order, and the bounce of her breasts under her T-shirt left him dry-mouthed and dazed as she made the bed. Her ass jiggled, and his nails bit into the tree bark when her phone trilled.

She checked the caller ID, then sucked in a breath that made her breasts grow a size or two. She answered. "Hi, Carter. . . ." Blush. "Me, too . . ." Smile. "Yeah, me, too." Smile and blush and toeing the carpet. "Well, I admit I was a bit disappointed when I woke up and you had gone . . . but I guess I can try to pay you a visit later today at the Silver Fox." Her eyes were lit like two little suns when she lifted her gaze to the window.

They eclipsed.

The color drained from her face.

She mumbled something under her breath and took a step forward, gaping straight up and out at Ben. His heart moved in his chest as their gazes held; his narrowed. Hers started. God, to finally, finally have those eyes see him again!

The phone clattered to the floor. Then, just like that, she crossed the room to the door. Her feet thudded down the hall, slowly at first, then fast as she broke into a run.

Ben swung down and watched her yank the front door open. She rushed outside in his T-shirt and barely there panties, barefoot in the cold, staring at where he stood, Ben Newcastle, the man he'd once been, feeling unlike he'd ever felt before.

"Ben?"

Her voice. He heard it so clearly. It affected him so deeply. Hot liquid need crashed through him like an avalanche. His knees weakened. He saw himself reaching for her, hauling her mouth to his mouth, crushing her against him, but a mind-boggling anger rose in him, too.

He trembled as he made a straight path to her, the grass blackening under his feet.

How could she?

He'd lived for her, and not two years into his grave she let some sonofabitch touch her?

How could she?

He advanced in her direction, seething, and Emma backed away, her eyes tearing, her lips trembling. *Take her. Make her yours, only yours. . . .*

"Ben?"

Punish her! His cock lengthened in his pants, big and thick as never before. His smile was so sharp it could've sliced someone's head off. "So you remember me."

Chapter Eight

This was no figment of her imagination. This was real. This incredible, mind-boggling thing was happening.

The shadows of dawn played with Ben's face, dusting his bronze, perfect skin golden, highlighting the strong cheekbones, the plump, sensual curve of his mouth.

Ben.

His face became hazy as her eyes watered. She had to blink, her body shuddering uncontrollably.

Love flooded her. It stole through her insides, claiming every nook and cranny inside of her, while a dormant, sated sensation awoke in her. A sensation she knew she shouldn't be feeling right now. Something fast, and dark, and overwhelming. *Lust.*

Along with shock, along with disbelief, along with a love so profound she thought it would kill her, a wave of lust so powerful Emma could barely remain on her feet, could barely rein back the impulse to launch herself at him.

Shaking, she curled her fingers into her palms, her nails digging into her skin while her nipples lengthened painfully in her blouse. "Ben," she said, her voice cracking. "It's you."

But he did not look like him, did not sound like him, as he stepped into the rising light. His scent flooded her, making her lungs ache. His strong jaw flexed as he approached, tight-jawed and gazing at her nipples as though he already savored them.

"Yes, Emma. *Me*." His voice rippled through her like a tidal wave. He made the words sound decadent—like a curse, a bad word, like someone who relished saying the word *fuck*.

He was gazing at her like an animal—like an animal studying his prey. "Come kiss me, my love."

His voice. So, so rough. So deep. Like it meant to penetrate your depths like an erection. She drank him in as she continued tremulously walking—left leg, right leg, left— and her eyes landed on the raised scar that peeked under the collar of his soiled shirt. "Oh, my god, *Ben*." Her pulse leapt as she broke into a run. "Oh, god, please tell me I'm not dreaming."

"You're not dreaming." He grabbed her, crushed her, and slammed his lips against hers.

When his hot, familiar taste invaded her senses, she thought she'd die. Her muscles melted and then her bones. She opened her mouth, so frantic for him that their tongues didn't play; they fought, they thrust, they couldn't get enough.

Ben snagged his old T-shirt in both hands and with a hard pull of his wrists—*ripped it in two*.

He snorted, as though pleased with the destruction he'd

caused, and watched as her breasts tumbled free—right there, in broad daylight, the nipples puckered wantonly for his kiss.

His eyes raked her proprietarily, and in a voice that was erotically dangerous and that made her knees knock together, he rasped, "Get inside so I can fuck you senseless."

Gripping the tatters of her T-shirt to her chest, Emma backed into the house, shaking under the heat pummeling her from the inside, somehow sensing that this Ben was not fucking around. This Ben wanted sex—and he wanted it now.

So wet, getting so wet!

She thought of demanding an explanation, forcing him to talk before they got into anything, calling Carter so she could tell him about this, but she shook under a torrent of desire. She was sinking, sinking in wet sand, couldn't move, couldn't think, couldn't breathe, she only knew she needed him—inside. *Now now now!*

"Almost two years . . ." he rasped through haggard breaths as he walked into the house with purposeful steps, his eyes glimmering under his low eyebrows. His face was leaner, more haggard, and his body had bulked up in muscle in such a way that her toes curled at the sight.

"Twenty months . . . wondering when I could have you . . . when I could touch you . . ."

His raspy voice made her mind whirl. Right and wrong, black and white, reality and fantasy—it all merged in this moment until she didn't know who or what she was, who or what she was seeing; she knew only that she needed to be entwined with this man, needed his *tongue* in her mouth, his *cock* in her hand, his *cum* in her body. . . .

The door slammed behind him, though she hadn't seen him shove or kick it closed; it seemed to follow his mental command.

"*Against the wall,* that's where I'll take you first." He yanked at his dirty cotton shirt and whipped it off his chest.

Emma's breath left her.

Oh, my god, he was a *devil.* A devil who looked like a god. *Ben!* her mind screamed. *It's Ben.* But he seemed bigger, darker, angrier. His abs were impossibly marked, marked with scars, huge scars from the accident, and with muscles. Those bulging biceps . . . more and more scars . . . muscular abs.

Want him, want him so bad! So sexy. Sexy muscled man. My man.

Eyes stinging, heart acting crazily in her chest, she stared stupidly as he started for her, torn between hugging him and slapping him. Where had he been? What was happening to her?

Shaking almost to the point of convulsion and aware of the fever breaking across her flesh, she leaned back on the wall as he'd ordered her to, her pussy rippling with moist heat. "Ben. You're . . . you're alive."

His glance was lightning, fierce with wanting. "Strip for me, I need you to strip for me—now." He sounded desperate, his hands fisting at his sides as though to keep from harming her.

Tears sprang into her eyes; she wanted to sit with him and talk for a week, wanted to stroke and pamper him, make up for not having held him when he'd been bleeding to death, she wanted to feel his body sync with hers again, she wanted everything and strangely she wanted all that *now*. "Ben, I thought I'd go crazy without you, I—"

His hands shot out, trapping both her wrists in one hand and holding them above her head. "Strip!" But as he spoke the T-shirt she'd been clutching to her chest slid from her grasp—allowing her breast tips to feel the heat of his chest so achingly near. Ben inched his taut, angry face so close that she could feel his lips move against hers as he spoke. "Later, we'll talk all you want, love, I promise. But for now, for now I need you."

He massaged her recently bared breast in such a hot, proprietary way she let out an involuntary sound of yearning. "Oh, god, am I going crazy? I'm scared."

"No," he growled, scraping his wide, masculine jaw against her cheek as he scented her, sniffed her like some . . . predator. He lightened his hold on her breasts as he rubbed his body heatedly against her smaller one. "Everything's fine. I'd never hurt you. Never."

His erection grazed her pelvis as he leaned over and took her lips in a hungry kiss, a kiss hotter than hell.

She shuddered, his touch a flame on her body, her every sensation heightened. This was no dream; a dream couldn't be this real, this heart-wrenching.

Ben was back.

Ben was back at last.

Emma.

Emma was melting in his hands, her breasts spilling out to him like a pagan offering. Her eyes were weighted with desire, her breaths misting across his face. Not enough . . . not enough to have her like this . . .

He needed to see her, every inch of her naked, where he would make damned sure every inch was reminded who it belonged to.

Even with all the marks on his chest, even with his bruised body—which looked disturbing even to him—she gazed at him hungrily. Like he was the only man in the world for her. He sensed how badly she wanted him, had been aching for him.

With a swallow, Ben reached for her panties and tugged them down her hips—making sure she didn't prevent him by locking his lips on a pink nipple and sucking it dry. Her taste . . . ahh, Christ, her taste . . .

She curled her fingers around his shoulders, her hips undulating in a suggestive move that spoke of her arousal. "Are you real?" she gasped as she threw her head back and dragged his head closer to her breast. "Are you a dream . . . ?"

He opened wider, suckling the peak deeper into his mouth, until Emma's small body shuddered against his. "No time"—*Must take Carter to the witch; must make him stay there*—"to talk." He swirled his tongue around the taut peak, growling before he seized it with his teeth. "You taste like cream."

He ran his hands along her fevered body, perspiration coating his brow as he knelt and sought the place between her legs. Her folds were moist and bright pink as his finger spread her. "Cream and limes, and I've been going berserk for cream and limes."

He inserted one finger, and Emma's fingers dug into

the wallpaper as she arched up to his hand. "Oh, Ben, I've needed you."

She lies. . . .

Another man touched her, touched what's mine.

"Say it again to me." He hunched his big shoulders and spread her thighs farther apart, keeping them open with his hand as he tasted from her pussy. "Say I'm the only one."

She choked on it, couldn't say it. But he tortured her with his tongue, because he needed to hear the words like people need to hear the marriage vows. "Am I the only one, Emma?"

A sound of frustration rose up in her throat, and she shuddered with desire when he inserted his longest finger into her tight sheath. His chest felt tight with wanting, wanting her assurance that what had happened was nothing, that it was Ben she craved, Ben she needed—he was dying for her affection, her desire, her love.

"Did you wait?" He added a second finger, his balls tightening, his hips rolling with the desperate need he had to sink himself inside her. "Did you wait for your man?"

A deep, painful pit of disappointment stabbed him when she didn't admit it. But it vanished with the warmth, the warmth that fluttered inside him for her, released by her.

She squirmed to get closer, releasing a mewling sound of pleasure. He thrust the other hand around her and between her ass cheeks, dipping low to probe the small rosette of her ass. He penetrated both her openings, his cock twitching jealously as her tight channels clamped around his fingers.

Beneath his pants, his dick was on fire.

He stood and unbuttoned his jeans, then his hand

stole through the opening to pull out the crown leaking milk through the slit. Jesus, he'd never thought he'd feel this physical sensation again.

"I want you to kiss it," he said in a rasp, unapologetic for all the things he'd want her to do, all the ways he'd want to brand her.

His need to climax felt deadly, humming through him like an electric charge demanding an outlet, and he craved to claim Emma again like a sickness. She would never know what he'd seen, the depth of his anger, his resentment—he would woo her back into his arms, where she would remain.

Her breath stopped halfway down her throat; then she knelt between his legs and pulled his jeans lower. She licked her lips hungrily at the sight of what she revealed, his big cock jutting toward her body, his chest muscles damp with sweat, glistening in the filtering sunlight, his balls gathered high along his shaft and aching.

He caressed the back of her head. "Kiss the tip."

She rubbed her cheek against him before she hungrily kissed the tip with a small, closed-lipped kiss.

The way she trembled when she kissed the tip of his dick drove him so wild, Ben growled and pumped a little, grazing her cheek. "Ahh, god, now lick it."

She licked once. Only the tip. And a tremor of need rippled through his body. He needed this. Her love had been crucial for his security. He'd taken on the world because this woman had believed in him. He needed her to believe in him again. To want him again. To love him again. He stroked her hair, watching her melt for him again, feeling her tongue flick over his slit and circle the bloated crown.

Ben grunted in pleasure and rolled his hips, his palm anchoring her head as he tried working himself into her mouth. "Suck me."

She felt his groan in her chest as much as in his, and twisted her head so he had to fight to get his cock inside her mouth. Playing with him thrilled her, made her feel chased and hunted, but he easily won. He caught her head in both hands and pushed. His cock impaled, a sound leaving her lips, and then her hands were on the hard flesh of his ass cheeks, squeezing.

Ben watched her with burning black eyes, his voice gruff. "Did you suck another man's cock?" He reached down and rolled her nipple under his thumb. "Did you suck another man's cock with that mouth?"

She closed her eyes and suckled energetically enough to make the air hiss out of him.

"I know you're a wanton—you've been fucking around, haven't you?"

She was wet enough to drown herself in desire, couldn't bear for him to stop feeding her, touching her, being here. Tentatively, she cupped his balls and kissed them. "Please." She didn't know what she begged for. Forgiveness, relief, his love, his gentleness. "I love you. . . . I was so alone. . . . Can you understand?"

He pressed her head to his cock again, pushing into her mouth, kneading her so expertly she felt a fragrant, creamy pool of desire gather between her legs. "I understand you're a female in heat and need to be fucked until you can't walk."

"And you . . . is that why you're here, Ben?"

"I'm here to take what's mine." He pulled out and carried her upstairs to the bed, and his breath fanned her ear as he licked the lobe, melting her muscles. "Emma," he said in a hoarse, proprietary voice, "take me to heaven. Get me out of this hell."

He set her on the bed, his large shoulders hunching before her, and she spread her legs open and pulled him close, looking eager and ready to do anything for him, everything. "Fuck me, Ben, please do it. Do it now."

He grabbed her knees and pushed her legs open, keeping them apart as he kissed the damp, silken fluff between her legs.

She sucked back a sob when she felt a soft, tender lick. His kiss there was so soft, so beguiling, completely unlike the hard grip on her thighs, that she was tempted to throw her head back and push her hips up to him in offering, giving what belonged to him. She succumbed, softly crying, "Please."

The word turned to a groan as he buried his face between her legs and wrapped his arms tightly around her. "I've missed. God, how I've missed you."

Gasping for air, she tunneled her hands into his hair even as he nuzzled her stomach, leaving dewy patches on her skin with his mouth. "I've missed you, too," she said brokenly, and seized the back of his head to tip it. "Ben, kiss me."

He shifted above her in a state of jealousy and determination to claim her again, his eyes wild, his teeth gritted, nudging her apart so she could feel his body between hers.

She shuddered when she felt him poised at her entry, sure that she was dreaming, not wanting to ever wake up.

She curled her legs around him, kissing his shoulder, his neck, welcoming him back home.

Emotions tore into his voice as he scraped her slit with the tip of his cock, his body straining above hers. "Say you love me, Emma," he hissed.

"I love you."

He ran his hand up her sides, feeling the generous weight of her breasts; then he grabbed his cock and guided it to her swollen entry. Waves of heat arrowed from her nipples to her aching pussy.

He wedged the tip inside—then withdrew. "Say you'll love me forever."

She rocked her hips, moaning with need. "Forever, Ben. It's always been forever."

He braced up on his arms and yelled as he impaled. It took only three thrusts. Three harsh, erratic thrusts that made them cry out together, and they both came like they'd never in their lives come before.

It was an impulse.

That was all it was. An impulse.

With his truck parked across the cemetery at noontime, Carter ambled his way over to the scattered graves near the tall, twisting evergreens. The grass across acres and acres of land lay dormant for upcoming winter, but there was a path that was not dormant.

It sliced through the center of the cemetery like a black blade, and to either side any flowers atop graves seemed to have been struck with the same end. Death.

A chill seeped into his bones when he realized it led to Ben's tombstone. The scent of smoke made his nostrils twitch. And suddenly it felt like the fog was all concentrated around his friend's grave.

With a strange creeped-out sensation in his gut, he stared at the glossy black granite for a long, long time.

What the hell was he doing here?

Maybe he wanted to make peace with his friend. Maybe to get his blessing. Hell, he just wanted to feel like it was okay for him to be with Emma now. But as he stood there, gazing at the grave of the man he'd loved like a brother, he could feel no love anymore.

He could feel anger. Regret. A truckload of fucking guilt he could not rip off his skin no matter what he did.

Promise me, asshole. Promise me you'll take care of her.

Carter braced a hand on top of the headstone and bent his head to whisper into the black granite so that it carried his message down under.

Ben could haunt her. Appear in visions to her dying patients. He could buck and rant and roll in his grave. But he couldn't do anything about it.

So Carter whispered into the name BENJAMIN NEWCASTLE, a soft, deceptively soft hiss, "She's mine now."

Emma remembered an old saying as she lay on the bed next to him—next to the living, breathing, incredibly hot Benjamin Newcastle—hours later.

"When the gods want to punish us, they listen to our prayers."

No shit they did.

Her heart bled as she watched Ben sleep, the map of scars on his chest rising evenly on each deep, slow breath. His features were harshly set even in slumber, his brow slanted into a dark scowl—as though he couldn't let down his guard.

What had happened to him?

Would he tell her when he woke up later, and reasonably explain where in the hell he'd been?

Oh, god, Ben was *home*!

He'd been home for—she checked the clock—nine whole hours.

It was barely afternoon, but she recalled that Sundays they'd been used to spending the day in bed, lazing around, reading, laughing, cuddling, napping. Today they'd done nothing except jump each other. Emma couldn't keep her hands off him. Ben seemed to be in a perennial state of arousal. He seemed almost desperate to take her, as if their days were numbered. Or as if . . .

As if he knew about Carter.

Her stomach tumbled at the breath-clogging reminder. How on earth was she going to tell him about Carter?

How on earth would Carter react when he knew about Ben?

Restless at the thought, she shifted in Ben's strong arms. No matter how many times she'd tried to snuggle, and even after succeeding in finding her place, the *exact* place she used to doze off against before, she just couldn't close her eyes. Questions tangled around her mind and they seemed to be connected to her stomach, clenching it tight.

Was Ben safe? Was he really here?

He'd taken her wildly, without restraint, three consecutive times. His dick as hard as she'd ever seen it, he'd splayed her on her knees on the bed and took her from behind, making her scream in ecstasy. He took her in the shower, standing up, setting her on his cock, pumping deeply into her. He took her with his mouth, pushing his cock into her lips while he suckled like a starved man from her pussy.

She was exhausted, she was drained, she felt heavenly, and she felt like hell. Because she couldn't stop thinking of a pair of Tahitian sea blue eyes, and how they'd look when she told him. . . .

Dear god, they'd been best friends before. Ben and Carter. The best kind of friends: the kind who spoke their thoughts freely, unapologetically counted on the other. The differences between them had always proved to be complementary. Ben was solemn; Carter loved a good laugh. Ben was a workaholic; Carter a party man. But after they learned the truth of Emma's involvement with both, how would they react to each other? Could they still be friends?

Chest tight with dread, Emma tried to wiggle away from Ben's grasp, but his heavy arm kept her anchored. He'd never let go of her; the knowledge sank in Emma with the weight of an anchor. Her tummy flipped in both excitement and a confusing little kernel of dread. If Ben didn't let go, it meant that Carter would have to.

Could Emma? Could *she* let go of Carter now?

Last night, at the Club, Emma had grown to crave not the paddle, but the man holding it to her bottom. The arms holding her afterward.

Give up Carter. . . .

Yes, yes, she had to, because Ben was *home!*

After some slight maneuvering, she successfully managed to slip out of Ben's grasp. She padded over to the bathroom to clean up, slipped into an old T-shirt, and couldn't help but wonder if Carter would be expecting her at the bar tonight. She'd said she'd try to stop by, but now . . . now it was very hard to think of anything else but wrapping her limbs all around Ben so that he never, ever, left her again.

Leaning on the doorframe, she studied him with a mixture of adoration and pain.

Endless yards of sinew and danger stretched across the bed, his hair stark and dark against the whiteness of the pillows.

His eyelids lifted—and his gaze fixed on hers.

The way his eyes had opened, fast and sharp, startled her.

She almost gasped. His voice pitched low as he sat up, its timbre dark and thick. "I love you."

Emma's heart flipped under his penetrating stare. "I love you, too."

Something passed his eyes, an expression almost resembling pain, before he masked it. He kicked off the covers and slid out of bed in a fluid move, marvelously naked and living, and went to rummage through the closet. Emma's greedy eyes raked across his muscular frame. She could be swallowed by that hard form now, engulfed completely by its strength, its maleness.

He reached into his shelves, his muscles rippling as he touched his clothes. And then he released a choked sound, like a growl, when he found everything was still there. His head hung for a minute.

"Thank you, Emma—for keeping my things where they belong." He smelled one of his shirts, and his teeth flashed in a smile, and it was perfect. The smile, the moment. "For not forgetting me."

She shook her head fast, one hand gripping the doorframe. "Ben, I'd never forget you, never."

But the words erased the grin off his face. He stopped smiling, as though the declaration mocked him in some way. The sudden pain in his expression flooded her, and her eyes began to sting.

Oh, god, Ben, how can I tell you about what I did?

Emma stifled a shudder as their gazes held, the air thick with unspoken words. Here stood the man she'd loved her entire life. A man she shared every memory with, memories of movies seen, first kisses, and love songs. But the love she'd had for him, a lifetime of love, had been different than this wild need, this passion, she felt for this new, angry, mysterious man. She recognized him, saw the love he felt for her somewhere in his stormy black eyes, but those dark eyes also frightened her. His existence, his appearance here, *frightened* her. "Where have you been, Ben?" She swallowed.

She wanted to understand. Had to. But something felt wrong and eerie, and she couldn't push the nagging feeling aside. "All this time. Where were you, Ben?" She took a step, but halted when he started to cross the room. He was still naked.

"It doesn't matter. I'm here now," he said.

Emma inhaled sharply when his cock lengthened, thickened, hardened before her eyes. She blinked several times. The thought that he wanted her again after so many sexual rounds was confounding, just as the idea that Ben could really be here was too baffling, too mysterious, to comprehend. She blew a shaky breath, then whispered, "We buried you! We . . . I saw your body."

He laughed darkly, as though amused that she'd even consider he'd been anything but dead. "Six years living together, Emma." He pushed out six fingers of his hands and pinned her on the spot with a wildly possessive stare. "And all the years before that. All our lives it's been you and me. Just you. And *me*. Would I have left willingly? Would anything have parted me from you other than death?"

Death.

The mere word increased her fear tenfold—and also her longing. Death had separated them. No, not even death had been able to. Because Ben was here again. Ben Newcastle, the guy who had danced with her at her prom, who'd lain beside her on her bed thousands of nights, the one she'd dreamed of as a little girl.

"Oh, Ben . . ." Without thinking of the impossibility of what he was saying, she flung herself at him and he clutched her to him with the conviction of a beloved jailor, one who never planned to release her ever again.

His arousal was so palpable she could see his blood rushing against his throat, his pulse jumping against her temple. He allowed her to feel the length of his need as he embraced her, nuzzled her ear and murmured, "Did you know people can still love without a heartbeat, Emma? That I still loved you without one?"

Emma drew back, and his tortured eyes mirrored her own pain so well she almost bowled over. She studied all of his scars, so many scars she'd never imagined a living person could wear them, and Ben took her hand and forced her palm flat against his chest. "Do you feel a heartbeat now?" he asked softly.

Her eyes widened in surprise. "No."

"Dammit, feel, sweetheart. Feel."

Then she felt it. "It's . . . it's so slow." Like nothing she'd ever felt before in a living human being. The heartbeat was strong, but spaced out so much, it took long, long seconds to feel one again.

"I've never seen anything like it," he admitted, gazing down at her with dark eyes. "If a patient came to see me, I wouldn't credit it, no matter how athletic he could be."

She could barely force her trembling legs to move as she stepped back. "Ben . . . you're scaring me."

"Don't be scared." He clenched his jaw and grabbed the back of her head in a rough but somehow tender way. "I'd never hurt you, never. My heart beats for you now, just for you."

His dick was bloated and marked with veins. Her pussy watered. He stood there blazing in lust and Emma trembled with the urge to believe him, to feel him inside her once again—the only time she was sure, one hundred percent sure, Ben was here with her again.

"Now it's your turn—tell me, Emma," he insisted, clenching her hair in his fists almost violently. "Tell me if you've missed me, if you still need me."

Her nipples beaded tight. God, she needed him so bad, could barely contain all her emotions in her chest. Overwhelmed to the point of weakness, she lay down quietly on the bed, her blood coursing through her. She wanted to tell him about what she'd done, confess that she'd been lonely and afraid, but she wanted to treasure this moment forever, didn't want to ruin it with fights, with betrayals, with ugly truths. "I took it . . . one day at a time," she confessed. "I didn't want to survive at first, didn't want this life . . . not without you. . . ."

He sighed, dragged a hand down his face. "You don't look so good, Em."

She smiled sadly and surveyed him. "You look like shit, too."

"Yeah, well, I don't feel so good. I don't feel so good." He lay down beside her. The mattress creaked. His cock lay flat against his abdomen—thick and hard as a pole.

Emma closed her eyes, certain that she wanted to jump him, ride him. But she knew that they had to get accustomed again first. To talking, to the comfort, to everything. *This is what you wanted.*

Ben stared up at the ceiling, immersed in his own thoughts. He stroked his cock, up and down, up and down, breathing heavily.

She spoke quietly. "I woke up every morning and wondered, Wait, what's wrong? Something's wrong. And then I remembered. That you were gone, Ben."

"At least you slept."

He was lying totally open, his thighs spread, his balls twitching, as though immersed in nightmares that aroused him.

His breathing hitched. "I ache everywhere. It's like I was run over, my legs ache, my stomach, my heart." He was talking to the ceiling, and while he was spilling it all out, Emma was sucking it all in until she felt she couldn't hold his pain in her body any longer. "It's like I couldn't say good-bye to you. I kept thinking what I'd do to be with you, what I'd do for one night with you. And now I'm here, Em. And I'm not going anywhere, I'm not."

Her cell phone rang on the nightstand, and when he lifted it and peered into the caller ID, her heart caved in on itself.

"Carter."

Her insides heated up at the name, then froze with dread when he didn't answer, didn't smile, didn't even look particularly pleased to hear Carter was still in her life.

"Has that fuck been a good friend to you?" Ben asked with a creepily soft voice.

"Yes, Ben," she said, lowering her gaze to her lap.

He tossed the phone aside, and she held her breath as the dreaded moment crept up on her. Should she speak now?

Shit, how could she, when Ben still seemed so familiar and so strange at the same time?

She knew she couldn't withhold her night with his best friend forever from him. He'd know soon. Oh, god, he'd know, and then what?

Emma reached out and linked her arms around his thick neck, not wanting to ruin this moment, not yet. His eyes blazed into her like brands as he let her pull him down over her on the bed. "Why's he calling you?" he asked, face grim.

Drawing him with her as she lay back on the pillow, Emma's mouth opened, but rather than tell him what she'd done, admit that she was crazy, that she'd come for Carter like an earthquake had seized her entire body, admit that she hadn't been able to stop herself from enjoying every second of her time with him, she set her lips on Ben's and kissed him—hard.

"Tomorrow," she whispered heatedly, stroking his beloved face. "Tomorrow we'll talk all you want, about everything. Today I want to enjoy you, Ben. I want to—god, I want to memorize you. I love you. I love you so much."

A low growl rumbled up his chest when she began crying, his cock throbbing painfully against her upper thigh. He licked her tears thirstily, scraping his tongue across her face, and then he covered her mouth with his, his sudden need so great that their emotions and resentment and jealousy and confusion were forgotten. He licked deep into her, probing every recess of her mouth. "You're mine, Em, mine. You always will be." He rubbed against her.

"Ben, I . . ." Her palms slid up the taut skin of his chest and around his shoulders as she drew him closer. "I'm afraid of losing you again. I can't lose you. Please tell me you'll love me, no matter what happens tomorrow."

"I love you—I love you, I love you, I fucking love you."

Shuddering, she parted her legs, dragged him forward between her thighs, guided his hand down.

His knuckles grazed her breast; then he closed his palm around it, the muscles of his face relaxed with arousal.

"Now show me you're mine. Love me back, Em. Love me back again," he urged.

And for the rest of the night, Emma did. . . .

The next morning, feeling deliciously sore, Emma was

fidgeting with the kitchen cupboards, determined to make Ben a special breakfast, something to commemorate this occasion. His return. The start of their new life together, the beginning of their forever.

Unfortunately, she kept thinking of Carter.

She'd turned her phone off but had briefly stolen into the bathroom and texted him before she had, for fear that he'd come over to see her if he didn't hear from her. *Something came up. Chat with u tomorrow?*

He'd answered: *Can't wait.*

Oh, god, her stomach tumbled just remembering. She was anxious to see him, too.

She didn't hear Ben pad barefoot down the stairs, but as she plucked four slices of bread he suddenly stood before her in his boxers, with that abused chest and that cruel slash across his throat that she couldn't bear to look at without wanting to take out her medicine bag.

She smiled, relieved that nope, no hallucination. He was still here. "You're awake."

He watched her from underneath drawn eyebrows, silent.

Why did he make her so nervous? He was the same man she'd always known. Wasn't he? With unsteady hands, she opened a cupboard and pulled out two plates. "I thought I'd make French toast. Are you up for it?"

He nodded and settled at the small round dining table, which served as a breakfast table, too.

She pulled out two eggs from the fridge, then silently buttered the pan before setting it on the stove. As she added the egg and the bread, she felt him watching her. When she peered back at him past her shoulder, his narrowed gaze startled her.

His voice was grave. "If you're thinking of him, I'm going to be very pissed."

Emma's heart stopped. "Who?"

He kicked the chair aside, his face inscrutable. "You know who, Em."

The eggs hissed.

Emma's eyes raked his muscular frame. What was it about him that felt different?

The way he watches you . . . without trust, without honesty . . .

"So what are your plans with him? Now that I'm back?"

The air seemed to shift after the question. A tumultuous energy tumbled all around him. There was a hunger in him, something volatile. Dangerous. Instinctively she knew Ben wouldn't hurt her, but would he hurt Carter? Could Carter even be hurt?

The pressure in her chest mounted with every second as she flipped the toast over. The hiss started up again. Surely there would be better moments, better days, to tell him about Carter. But somehow she sensed Ben, this strange, mind-boggling Ben, wouldn't rest until she did.

And how did he know?

Nervous, she watched him go up the stairs and managed to shakily get their food onto the plates without burning herself by the time he returned. Something dangled from his fingers. His eyes studied her watchfully as he handed it to her. "I bought you this—the night I didn't come home."

Disbelief gripped her as he pressed the metal into the

circle of her palm. She stroked her thumb along an old gold locket, feeling the indentations of the scrollwork.

The thought that Ben might have been somewhere else, somewhere other than dead during the past year, was pulverized with this little proof.

Speaking became difficult. "You had this the night you . . ."

"I was going to put a ring around the chain, maybe a set of pictures in the locket. From when we were . . . kids."

Her throat closed. She'd buried this locket with him.

She'd wondered and wondered if she should keep it, or leave it with him. But he'd been holding it so tight, she hadn't dared pry it away from him, had instead quietly requested it be hung around his neck.

If she'd had any doubts about whether he'd really been dead, they were ashes now. Ashes.

Still struggling to understand, Emma carried the plates to the table while the locket dangled from her wrist. How could you die for two years and . . . revive?

She felt the uncomfortable pressure of Ben's scrutiny as they sat, and it felt as heavy as a sky coming down on top of her. Instinctively she brought the locket to her chest, as though it provided protection. Like garlic against a vampire. Lord, why was she thinking of vampires?

Ben signaled at her, speaking softly, though his eyes were full of distrust and questions. "You can still hang it around your throat, put anything you want in there," he said. His soft tone was like glass rasping down her skin. Silently it said: *You betrayed me.*

Emma stifled a shudder and tucked the locket deep into

her hand, her fingers curling lovingly around it. It was difficult to speak. "I don't know what to say—I'm not sure where to begin or . . . or what exactly we're discussing here."

With her free hand, she managed to take a small bite of her French toast, but had lost her appetite and knew it would be her last.

His plate sat untouched.

"When are you planning to tell me?" he asked softly.

His chiseled face was set into a mask, but Emma wasn't fooled one bit; the ghost of knowledge in his eyes made her thigh muscles freeze.

He knew—undoubtedly. Somehow, some way, he knew about Carter.

Her chest squeezed. She didn't want to spoil this second chance, ruin it with painful truths he might not be prepared to hear and she might not be prepared to tell.

In silence, she raised the locket and hooked it around her throat. It felt heavy on her breast. Too heavy. But it seemed like the right thing to do, like an acceptance of what he seemed to want to offer her. She couldn't reject it, couldn't. "Are you asking me about Carter?" Panic rattled in her voice as she lowered her arms.

He propped his elbows on the table and leaned over. "How many times has he kissed you?"

Emma knew she stared at him like an idiot—lips parted, blanked of thoughts. He knew? Oh, god. How much did he know? How did he know?

"How many times did he make you come?" he insisted.

She saw the truth in his accusing eyes, in the set of his

features, and she wished she could never see another ounce of pain in those eyes again. Filled with determination to reach the man who had danced with her at her prom, who'd lain beside her thousands of nights, she reached out a hand and seized his big one.

"Ben . . . it was just once. Just once . . . Please understand."

She squeaked in shock when he caught and squeezed her fingers in a lightning-fast move. "Did he take you before? Did he take you while you were mine?"

His tortured eyes mirrored her own pain so well she almost bowled over.

"No!"

"Does he make you weep when he makes love to you?" he continued, teeth gritted.

She jumped to her feet, insulted and embarrassed and loathing herself with every ounce of loathing in her heart. "Stop it, please stop. It doesn't have to mean anything, that night he spent here."

He pushed his chair back, too. "You're lying—I can always tell. You start blinking just like you're blinking now."

She held her breath, caught in her own confusing feelings about both men, and Ben walked up to her and tangled his fingers into her hair. "Tell me what's going on between you two."

Her nipples beaded tight. *Sex. Glorious, mind-boggling sex. And sexy, drawling words. And incredibly hot hands. That's what's going on between us.*

Her nerves jumped when Ben grabbed her hair and pulled her head back, staring into her eyes. "I saw you kissing him. I *saw* you with him that night." His eyes blazed into her like brands. "I know how much you loved it, Emma, how wild and wanton you were for it."

Emma swallowed, her heart pounding in her ears, her knees so weak she thought she'd collapse.

"You're *mine*!" He crushed her lips, as though he couldn't resist taking one sample of what he claimed belonged to him. "How can this not be mine? Tell me," he rasped, hauling her against him.

"It's yours," she breathed, weak.

His tongue thrust and thrust and thrust into her mouth, then tangled around hers. "How can this not be mine, Emma? Explain it to me, *fuck*."

He let go.

Trembling, Emma hugged herself and followed him to the living room. "Ben."

He shook his head as he paced. "I don't even know what to do to you first."

Fuck me, love me, forgive me.

She knew they had issues to resolve, things to discuss. Like the fact that she'd been paid his life insurance—was that money to be returned? The fact that he had no job—would he go back to the hospital? But, god, she felt so volatile it seemed the only way she could stay grounded was when he was pushing into her again. Did she want him to?

"Do you still want Carter?" he demanded, spinning around.

A heartbeat passed. Then, softly, she admitted, "Well, I can't have you both, can I?"

As she wrung her hands, she watched the words strike

him like a physical blow, his large body growing rigid. His face contorted. He was hurt by this confirmation. Had been hurt by *her*. He looked like a man trying to assimilate a great big piece of news, and barely able to take it all into his mind.

Emma plopped down on the living room couch and squeezed a small pillow between her hands as she waited for him to speak. "Ben, I was lonely. I needed—"

"I know what you need," he growled.

He stared down at her, and he drew a deep breath. For a moment she thought he looked ready to shout. But then he slowly gathered his composure. "Does his petting arouse you, Emma?" he asked quietly.

She felt like crying. But then anger surfaced, and it pushed her tears back down. Where had *he* been? This wasn't her fault! She'd had to do something with her life. She'd been wasting away. She'd had to take drastic measures, try to forget she'd live her entire life without the boy she'd loved since she was a teen.

"Yes! It aroused me! Is that what you want to hear? I liked it, Ben. I needed it. I needed it so damned bad I was crying out for it! Is that what you want to hear?"

"It's the truth no matter how you goddamn phrase it. I'm not an idiot!" He picked up the bottle of whiskey he'd left in the adjoining kitchen, poured himself a full glass, and returned with it, his nostrils flaring with each fast breath. "Am I wanted here?"

Emma flung her hands up high. "Yes! Of course you are!"

He gave one sharp, somber nod, then took a long sip and drained half a glass. "Then now is not the time for romantic fantasies, but for hard realities, Emma." Dilated black eyes pinned her on the spot as he set his glass down on a side table. "Are you through with him, Em? Now that I'm back, are you through with him?"

Emma watched him approach, her heart galloping at the possessiveness in his gaze. He leaned over her on the couch and cupped her breast, his cock already fully erect, having stolen through the parting in his boxers. "He bites these. And these are mine, Emma. *Mine*."

Emma whimpered when he stroked her nipples, responding eagerly to his swiping thumbs. "He bruised these, the motherfucking bastard. Are you *through* with him?"

She shuddered in arousal, breathing in anxious chugs. "Ben, oh, god, you're killing me."

"How hard do you come for Carter? Tell me."

Ben was used to excelling, to being the top of his game, the top of his class, the top of everything. She could see he wrestled with the knowledge that she'd been with someone else and may have liked it, may have loved the exquisite touch of another man. "I don't remember."

Disbelief made him stiffen. Then Emma felt a prickle of angry excitement tighten every inch of his body. And she wondered if this challenge, this fight, aroused him. "How many times has he had you?"

"One."

Her body knotted at the admission. Because *one* had been enough to haunt her for many nights to come, she knew.

"Did he fondle your anus while he fucked you? Did he feed you his cum? How long did your orgasm last?"

"Forget about Carter!" she cried, slamming his chest and pushing him away. "I was lonely, and I needed a friend, and I needed a lover. Just . . . forget it. You're my soul mate, Ben. You're the man I love!"

But he was clearly turned on, livid and aroused, and talking of Carter aroused her, too. "Maybe you love me, Emma—but you still want him, and I can't stand that, can't stand to know he pleasures you in ways I never could."

She was silent, shaking as she tried to stand, thinking of Carter's calloused hands . . . that sexy drawl. . . . *I'm in love with you, Emma.*

Her pussy clenched. Her cheeks flamed, and she said, "Please, let's talk about this when we're calmer."

He fisted his hands at his sides. "I'll never be calm until I see you both together again, see the way you melt for him."

"Why?" she cried. "So you can hate me?"

"No, Emma. So I can please you."

Emma blinked, her jaw hanging open. "What?"

"You heard me. I want to please you—I want you to take him if you want him. Do you fucking still *want* him? Don't look so shocked. It's a simple question. Does your pussy get wet when you look at him?"

Emma buried her face in her hands, hating how wet she was getting just by talking about him now. But Ben had been through so much, so much that she knew about and so much that she feared she had still to know. She couldn't bear to see him hurting. She should lie, should stall for time, but instead she said, "Yes, god help me."

His face tightened, and in that instant Ben looked ready for sex—and murder, simultaneously. "Do you want to have him with me? All you have to do is say please and I'll give that to you."

Head to toe, Emma was trembling. "Ben . . ." He sounded so controlled—and the fury under that control, the tightly leashed rage, frightened her more than anything.

"Answer me! Do you want Carter again?"

"If I could have you both together at least once . . . I'd be living a fantasy," she admitted, because the thought of never being with Carter again, never tasting his lips, looking at him and knowing he could've been hers . . . was torture.

"So be it," Ben said, and at last marched back to his breakfast and bit wildly into his French toast.

Chapter Nine

"Hold your danged horses, I'm coming!"

Tired, sated, and sweaty after a long workout at the gym, Carter had been running a cold shower when the doorbell chimed. He charged to answer, bare-chested, bare-footed, and wearing nothing but unbuttoned jeans that slung low over his hips.

Emma stood on his doorstep. Adorable in disarray, she was dressed in loose jeans and the only-shirt-she-hadn't-lost–in-Vegas.

The instant her big brown gaze met his, the corner of his lips kicked up. "Been thinking," he said with a crooked smile. "'Bout you and me. Holding hands tonight at the Fox. Like *boyfriend* and *girlfriend*." He mocked the last words, but it gave him pleasure to say them. He'd never really had an official girlfriend before.

"You think you're my boyfriend?"

A brow flew up in mock astonishment. "Well, I sure as

hell ain't your mother." Tenderly, he chucked her chin, but she shied away from the touch.

Too late he noticed the emotions passing through her face.

Lust first. Then confusion. Followed by . . . Christ, was that dread?

A bowling ball of fear sank inside his stomach. Was this the part where she told him she couldn't do this anymore? Was this the part where she told him *it's not you; it's me . . . yadda yadda*? No.

Christ, hell, fucking no. He didn't want to *hear* this from Emma.

He found himself frowning in concern, leaning against the frame. "You okay, pumpkin? You didn't make it yesterday and sent such a short text. . . ."

"Can I come in?" she asked, uncertain.

He stepped back to let her pass, and as she brushed past him, her sexual scent made his nostrils flare. His boner thickened in his jeans. Had she been touching herself? His blood coursed hot and his mouth salivated at the thought.

"Are you alone?" she asked. Her concerned eyes scanned the inside of his home, and Carter's eyebrows furrowed. If he didn't know better, he'd think she'd escaped from jail and expected to find her parole officer in Carter's living room.

· Her lips, devoid of lipstick, looked swelled and plump. Her hair tumbled across her shoulders, lustrous but tousled. Then he noticed her eyes looked shockingly bloodshot.

His concern growing by the second, Carter ambled closer and seized her elbow firmly in his grasp. "Emma, talk to me," he murmured, his voice harsh with the force of his worry.

She remained mute, and when he reached over to pull off her T-shirt, she pushed his hands aside.

"Not plannin' to eat you up like a marshmallow yet, pumpkin," he roughly explained. "I was fixin' myself a shower but looks like you need it more."

As though she hadn't heard, Emma sailed down the hall and into his room like she belonged there; then she settled down on the bed and wrapped her hands around herself. He'd never had such a cute little ball in his bed.

"I'm going crazy." Her voice sounded rusty.

Frowning, Carter made his way to the bathroom and turned the shower switch so that the water spilled into the bone-colored tub. Letting it fill as he stepped out, he paused inside the room and puzzled as he looked at her. During the years he'd known her, he'd learned that she'd become a vegetarian a couple of years back. He'd learned that she knew her every patient's birthday and made them cards on her Saturday afternoons. Two nights ago, he'd learned her most intimate secrets and had memorized her every sigh, her every moan. But now there was a secret in her eyes, and his every instinct told him he didn't want to know it.

She wiped a lone tear. She shook down to her toes, like she had when he'd taken her too far into the sub zone.

Heart heavy in his chest, he approached her. "Come on. Into the water, Emma. You'll feel better afterward."

He scooped her up, and she didn't protest. "I don't know what's real anymore," she said, clinging to his neck. He'd been working out, was all sweaty, but she still buried her face against his throat, holding on to him. Not minding his soaked skin, she pressed her lips against his neck and breathed him in, as if his scent grounded her, anchored her.

His balls tightened with need. He wanted to kiss the Jesus out of her, see her glistening pussy lips wrapped around his cock again, hear her cry out for him. But something was wrong—something was holding her back, holding her away from him. "Come, baby."

He set her on her feet over the plush bathroom rug and briskly undressed her. Emma lunged at him, her fists ramming into his abdomen, tearing the breath out of him. She screeched like a lunatic, clawing at him, saying, "Don't call me baby or sexy, not ever, do you hear me!" until he grabbed her hair and pulled her head back, pressing his face close to hers.

"Shh. Calm down. Calm down and tell me what happened!"

He dragged her to the tub and lowered her with a splash. She was angry. He'd wanted to give her space, give her a moment to relax and let go, but the sight of her scared the living daylights out of him.

Quiet and immersed in water up to her chest, she sat unmoving, water lapping across her breasts as he knelt by her side and took an old sponge. He heard her mumble, "We shouldn't have . . . We never should've . . ."

Stopping all of a sudden, she glared up at him and splashed water into his mouth. Choking, Carter coughed it out, wiping his face. "What the hell was that for?"

She was panting with rage, her face contorted into a

scowl. Good. So long as she was angry, she was not wilting on him. Was not retreating into that gray numbness she'd found comfort in that first year.

Gently Carter lathered the sponge with soap and began to wash her. "Talk to me."

She'd gone eerily still. As though she were afraid to move and find his touch would vanish. Carter scrubbed her rigid shoulders and neck, lifting one slender arm and running the sponge down the inside, to her armpit, continuing to her breast.

It was not the moment to think of how soft they felt, but he lingered there, switching the sponge to his other hand, using it to scrub her belly, and curling a soapy hand around it. He heard her sound—a whimper—jolting his cock, making him hard as the bath tiles.

He continued to scrub her, slipping the sponge between her legs, lathering her smooth pink pussy. She sagged, then suddenly grabbed his shoulder to right herself. He looked into her eyes. Her gaze fastened to his, her eyes tumultuous, confused, as if she didn't know what she thought or felt. He saw her fighting the sensations as he himself fought to keep her from knowing those she awoke in him.

"Not there," she hissed through her teeth.

He hesitated, then withdrew, continuing onto her back. She was breathless as he set the sponge aside and lathered her with his hands, flesh to flesh. He blocked himself, tried not to think of how fragile she felt, how good, and tried to be mechanical. But he felt his chest rise harder, as if he weren't breathing enough air.

When he finished, he wrapped her in a towel, carried

her to the bed—she seemed to weigh less than his gym duffel bag—and then dried her.

"Talk to me." He lifted a glass of water to her lips. "Here."

She glared.

"Drink, Emma, or I will make you."

After she drank a few sips of water, she said, "He's back, Carter. And he's . . . different."

Her damp hair clung to her shoulders, and as she pushed it back in frustration, she went on. "Sexy different . . . Scary different."

Alarm bells clanged inside his head and his hackles rose.

"He says he's been dead—and I believe him. But he wants me to tell you . . ." Her eyes were wide and worried, and full of longing as she reached out to stroke his jaw. "To come to dinner with us. Carter, he's really jealous—I'm afraid he'll do something drastic. He's talking about sleeping together, all three—"

"Heck, pumpkin, you lost me at hello. What in the hell are you going on about?"

"Ben's back!"

Ben was back? How in God's green earth could Ben be back?

But sure as hell, when he jumped into a quick shower, changed, and followed Emma home, Carter found himself staring straight into the back of Ben's dark head, taking in his broad shoulders, his confident stance.

Benjamin Newcastle.

Alive.

She's mine now. . . .

The words he'd uttered into his grave assaulted him. Maybe, in a tiny insignificant way, they'd been a dare, and Ben had come back to haunt him. In the flesh. Holy fuck.

Carter almost collapsed under the force of his emotions. Shock. Incredulity. Confusion. And something else, something murky and indecipherable. He wasn't the kind of bastard who'd want a friend, heck anyone, dead. But this moment he felt . . . cheated.

Like he'd slain the dragon and had just been told the kiss promised by the princess couldn't be given to a lowly serf because the prince had come to claim it in his stead.

Jesus Christ, how close had he been to Emma? Close enough to believe one day she could reciprocate his feelings. Now Ben was here. *Here.* Right in this goddamned room, putting out some serious vibes.

Music. Dim lights. The man had set up the ambience for seduction. But the air that crackled around him felt strange and tumultuous and sinister. Not friendly. Definitely not familiar.

Wary, Carter watched as Ben calmly poured himself a glass of wine in the adjoining kitchen while Emma settled down on a leather couch, tugging at her Vegas T-shirt. "Come sit with me, Carter." She patted her side in invitation, leaving him puzzled and immobilized.

She seemed to want to act like all was fine and dandy, but he'd had her in his arms just moments ago. She'd been rattled, a part of her even frightened, another aroused by his nearness even if she'd been fighting it. She hadn't wanted him to touch her—and now he knew why.

She'd wanted his touch, but had felt she'd be betraying this . . . thing. This . . . Ben.

His eyes tracked the movements of the black-haired man as he headed to the living room, then took a seat and reclined in a negligent pose, his thick legs spread apart, his large frame rivaling the wingback chair. He stared directly at Carter with a look of such control Carter could almost see the rage simmering underneath.

"Bates," came a low rumble.

Carter's spine felt as stiff as a telephone pole. "Newcastle."

Silence.

The kind that deafened you in the ears, made your heart boom in your temples.

"Is that the way you greet your friends returning from the dead? No wonder no one comes back."

A chill slithered down his spine. The tenor of Ben's voice was altered. Toneless, somehow, and deeper, as though he spoke from within a damned cave.

Blood pulsing slow and heady in his veins, Carter glanced at Emma. The instinct to throw her over his shoulder like a sack and carry her to safety pummeled through him. *Protect the woman. Protect your woman.*

He clenched his hands into fists, rooted to the spot by cold hard shock. Emma fingered a necklace he'd never seen, restless. "Ben, you promised to be civil," she chided.

Ben folded his arms across his massive chest. "You don't see his teeth scattered across the floor yet, do you?" His impenetrable black gaze fell on Carter, and the flames of anger he saw there made his hackles raise.

The threat was unmistakable. Carter had a thousand

things to say, but was so confounded he could only say one: "What the fuck's going on here?"

Ben's sleek black brows went up as he leaned back. "Good question. Exactly the same one I was going to ask you."

Was this real?

Hell, was Carter even awake?

Ben looked . . . bigger. Wider. Stronger. An aura of tumult surrounded him, lashing out at Carter. He shut his eyes, then opened them, and he could still not give credit to what he saw. This wasn't like watching some magician pull out a freaking bunny from a hat. This was a dead man. A dead man was alive, in his old home, staring at Carter with an expression of pain and mistrust he'd never seen before.

Had Ben resembled his old friend, Carter would've hugged him, heck, thrown a party for him. But now there would be no parties, no friendship, and no hugging between them. Ever. Animosity leapt between them like clawed panthers. Irrevocable. Like that fateful night Ben Newcastle had shoved him because of Carter's audacity to admit the truth.

"You look like you've seen a ghost, cowboy," Ben said, imitating his drawl.

No. Hell, no. Whatever creature sat before him with quiet murder in his eyes might be alive, but that thing was not his friend Ben. "You ain't Ben Newcastle."

"Of course he's Ben. Who else could he be?" Emma said, a tremulous smile curving her mouth when she looked at the dark-haired man. Her face was lit like a promising new rainbow as she took in his image, like he was her very own walking, talking miracle. Fiction just didn't invent shit like this!

"Ask me anything," Ben dared, standing to full height.

Carter glared in open fury. Since when were they the same height? Carter had always been two inches taller. And without boots. That sumfabitch right there just wasn't Ben!

"Anything," Ben insisted, crossing to where Emma sat, draping a possessive hand across her nape. Carter's knuckles jutted out white. "Ask me what we discussed the night of my accident. What you said when I asked if you had a hard-on for Emma."

Carter chanced a glance in her direction, and though her cheeks bore two attractive pink spots, he could see the tension in her shoulders, a tension that had never before been present when she'd been in the same room as her Ben. God, he loved her. He was sick and tired of feeling guilty about it. "She knows, all right?" he said, surly. "No need to make a tango of it."

Ben's interest shifted down to Emma, his brows raised high. "How long have you known the fool's been pining over you?"

She went rigid, and so did Carter.

Holy God, just the sight of Ben looking at Emma with those hot, proprietary eyes, towering in the room looking kingly and dangerous and indestructible, sullying the only good and decent feeling Carter had ever had, just rankled him to his bones. Carter thrust his hands up. "Who in the hell *are* you?"

Ben's slow chuckle mocked him. "What did you answer? When he told you he loved you?"

The question was directed at Emma, but Carter, feeling

a little mad, a little crazy, and a little like waving a red flag at a big black bull, found himself pointing in her direction. "She may not know it yet, but that woman right there ain't in love with you anymore. She loves me."

A heartbeat passed. Ben started forward and around the small glass coffee table, slowly, as a big black scorpion. "Does she, now?"

"Heck yeah!"

"Emma?" He turned and pinned her with the look of an apocalypse. "Is he serious?"

"Step outside with me," Carter hissed, "and I'll show you serious."

For a moment Ben regarded him, looking at him up and down, up and down, as though relishing the prospect.

"Maybe later, Bates. Tonight I have other plans. Plans I'm sure you and Emma will approve."

Ben lifted his hands, palms up, and three plates flew from the kitchen and settled on the dining table. "Neat trick, isn't it?" he said to both of his stunned spectators. "One I learned during my . . . vacation."

With a wolfish smile, he flicked three fingers, and three of the four chairs in the small dinner table slid out as though an invisible butler had just appeared.

"Sit down, my love. You, too, Bates. There's a lot of catching up to do." Pretty as you fucking please, like the guy wasn't just the creepiest thing ever, Ben took a seat and indicated the other chairs.

Carter glanced over at Emma, and when she sensed his gaze, she blanked the alarm from her face and quickly rolled her eyes at Ben's high-handedness. She wanted to pretend to be okay? And Carter should feel reassured by that?

Heart pounding a vicious warning, he warily stepped forward and dropped into the seat. *Protect her; protect Emma.* Tension gripped the room as a deafening silence settled. Nobody touched their food. Emma was perched on the edge of her seat. Ben had prepared his special dish. Mushroom risotto.

Ben seemed to be enjoying their unease. His eyes glimmered in a strange mixture of mirth and menace as he surveyed Emma, then Carter.

"I watched you touching each other Saturday night. I saw you coming when Carter fingered you, Emma. I'd like for you to stop pretending you're not hard under the table, Carter. And you, Emma, I can smell how wet you are."

"That's right, buddy, she wants me now," Carter said tightly.

Emma leapt to her feet, face aflame with indignation. "When you two are finished comparing the size of your dicks . . . !" Before Ben could say anything else, she shoved her chair back and swept up the staircase, slamming the door upstairs with a big bang.

Carter had watched her pert little rear as she went up and was so hard he could penetrate anything. Would he even have her again? Was it true that she was wet right now? For who was that pussy juiced up? Ben or Carter?

"You like that ass, don't you?" came a low, vicious snarl. "You've always liked that ass."

His face whipped back to the morose-looking creature who called himself Ben. His eyes narrowed. "Who in the fuck do you think you are? Coming here after almost two fucking years? Turning her life upside down and handing out orders! Making things fly!"

With slow deliberation, the dark-haired stranger rose. "No, Carter. Who do *you* think you are?"

"I'm the man who's been taking care of her. I'm the man she needs now."

Ben surprised him by saying, "Maybe."

He even nodded.

WTF?

"But you must have noticed, she doesn't even look at you when I'm in the same room. Emma and I have loved each other since she was fourteen. Do you understand me?"

Yeah, he understood.

Carter had seen the way she looked at him, the way she would never, ever, look at Carter. He gritted his teeth. "She won't love you when she realizes you're just a bullheaded asshole now!"

"You betrayed my trust."

"You fucking died—I say death releases a man of any obligations."

"And whose fault would that be, Carter?" The accusation, frankly, ripped Carter's heart out. "Now tell me. Do you want to fuck Emma? Do you want her pretty little tongue to lick up all your cum?"

Carter blinked. The punches were coming from both left and right, and he didn't know whether to duck, or charge, or punch back. "Ben, dammit, I never approached her—I never asked to feel . . . what I goddamn feel for her. We were best friends, for Christ's sake. I never stepped over the line, never came close."

Ben met his gaze with black, tenebrous eyes, and it was almost like looking into the devil. "But now you have, Carter. And you're going to pay."

Don't let him touch her. Protect her!

"You ain't touching her," Carter warned, because, dammit, she was his now, his. Carter's.

Ben laughed darkly, a booming sound in the suddenly small and closed room. "She craves my touch, craves it as much as I crave to give it to her. You can fight me for her—but she won't choose you. She'll never choose you over me."

"You think you're my boyfriend?"

All of a sudden her words back at his place struck his mind like a full-blown cataclysm.

"We shouldn't have . . . We never should've . . ."

A thousand pangs of regret pricked across his body, each sharp as a tack. Ben was right; it just hurt to hear the words. She'd never choose Carter over Ben.

Jesus, what should he do? Accept the fact that Ben was alive and leave them to be together? Was that the way it was supposed to be?

No, hell no. This man wasn't the man for her. Not anymore.

Ben's mind had been brilliant once. He'd been a hell of a doctor, one who infused humanity into his treatments, not just medicine. One of the precious few who incorporated natural treatments to support his medicinal ones—Emma's idea, of course. But now that mind twirled in all sorts of directions, creepy directions. At the moment, the dark-haired, walking, talking menace scrutinized Carter as though trying to recall his flaws, and his expression revealed nothing of what went on in that twisted mind.

"I don't know about you," Ben said, without inflection, "but I've had enough dancing for one night. Are you going to just stand there for the rest of the evening, or are you going to go up there and fuck her with me?"

The cowboy looked flabbergasted. Struggling to assimilate. His countenance was flushed red with anger—and lust—and it pleased Ben, yes, it pleased him to see this. Ben felt hungover. Run over. And like last night's leftover. But he wouldn't stop; no, he wouldn't.

Emma wanted Carter. She wanted him *way too much*.

Enough to lie about it.

A little, she'd said.

A little his born-again ass.

Ben still had that special connection to her—the heightened senses he'd enjoyed as a ghost remained. He sensed her every want, her every need, and felt a boundless desire to give them all to her. *To become all she needs.*

Her folds had gotten drenched when Carter had entered the room tonight. A shudder had gone through her. She had longed to sit next to him so that maybe their thighs would brush and she'd be able to smell his Woodspice scent. She'd been so physically aroused by being in the same room with the cowboy she'd kept pulling at her T-shirt in her efforts to hide her erect nipples. No one had noticed but Ben—maybe not even Emma, who'd been busy struggling to tame her reactions.

Now Ben wanted what Carter had.

He thirsted to know what Carter gave her that she liked so much.

Then he would be able to give it to her himself. And they wouldn't need Carter anymore.

"Why in this sorry little world," Carter drawled out in that insultingly slow voice of his, "would I share Emma with you when I can have her all to myself?"

Ben's lips twitched in incredulity. The cowboy had guts all right—to dare him like this. But that was okay. He wanted him to. Would relish every excuse for what he'd have to do later. "Because, Bates"—he deliberately spoke to him like a nitwit—"you know she's not yours. And because you owe me."

He could see his eyes shadow with the memories—memories of what he'd said. What a lousy freaking friend he'd turned out to be. And as he watched Carter wage an internal battle, Ben realized it wouldn't be hard to deliver him to the witch after all. Only a little reminder of what a bastard friend he really was.

"So let's go upstairs and see which of us can really satisfy her," Ben said conversationally. "What do you say? Do you think she's really into the ordering around? Is that what she likes? Or is it the pain?"

Carter shook his head and paced the opposite side of the room. "I'm not discussing this with you."

Ben pressed on. "Why does she like it?"

Facing him, Carter plunged a frustrated hand through his hair. "Hell, I don't know. Do you like to sleep butt-naked?"

"What has that got to do with anything?"

"Why the hell does anyone like anything—beats the crap out of me. The point is, she likes it. She likes me."

"You're wrong."

Carter's eyes narrowed. "You coming back is wrong. Just gonna be painful for her and painful for you."

Black fury ripped through Ben's insides, sharpening his voice as he whipped out an index finger and aimed. "Don't even pretend to know what the hell I've been through, Bates."

The presumption! Ben had to curl his fingers into his hands to keep from shoving Carter out the window, or choking him. "Fuck it, are you on for a three-way or not?" he demanded, angry.

"I ain't for rent, asshole." Angrier.

Yeah, Carter's words were more a denial than an admission, but Ben could see the storms in his eyes, the torment making his entire body tremble. The certainty that he would succumb swept through him with one last good look into Carter's hungry eyes. "You'll do this. You want her too bad."

"What about what *she* wants, sick bastard?"

Ben mentally locked the front door and heard the soft *click*. Then he gestured at the stairs. "She wants this. She wants *us*."

Until you're gone, my sorry little amigo. After that, I'm going to take care of her all by myself.

Chapter Ten

Emma's hands shook as Ben tightened the silk ties around her wrists, her body splayed and spread-eagled on the bed. Tingles of anticipation raced up and down her spine as she studied his features. He'd become unreadable, so mysterious . . . sexy, dangerous.

"See, my love? I told you I'd give him to you if you wanted him," he murmured.

Emma shuddered uncontrollably. God, she didn't know what was wrong with her. She still wanted Ben. But she couldn't be close to Carter without feeling her heart jump and her blood race in her veins. When she'd seen him today, all sweaty and gorgeous, she'd wanted to die. She'd wanted to jump him. She'd wanted to be held and kissed and championed and cherished. And now she waited for him to come to her—waited for him like a sacrifice.

Anxious he'd reject her.

Anxious he wouldn't appear soon.

When was he coming up?

"I . . . I never thought you'd share," she admitted, study-ing his inscrutable profile. Why was he doing this? Why?

Ben chuckled as he checked the restraints one last time. "That's the beauty, one of the marvels, of the human mind. Isn't it? We adapt to changing circumstances, we learn to cope. The most savvy survive, and the others . . . They die, my love. Die. But it's their own stupidity that kills them most of the time."

She imagined what Carter would see when he entered— a naked woman tied to the bed, already panting. Already wet. And her cunt clenched and her nervousness increased. "Are you sure he wants to do this?"

"Of course I'm sure." Ben kneaded one sensitized breast with a rough, proprietary hand. "He'll do anything to get into that sweet little cunt of yours. I told him to be up in five." He thumbed her pussy lips as though to remind her they had been his first; then he pushed his long bronzed middle finger inside.

She gasped, and he took advantage of the sound. He ducked his head and thrust his tongue into her mouth. "You'll get cock soon, you little wanton." He searched between her legs, insinuating a second finger between the folds. "You'll get cock in every tight, wet part of your body tonight."

The unmistakable jealousy in his voice planted a tiny kernel of fear in the pit of her being. What was wrong with him? What was wrong with *her*? Was she so desperate to feel Carter again that she would do this . . . ?

Yes, you are.

He withdrew his hand and brought her moisture up to

her lips. He teased her parted mouth with his damp fingers. "Lick." When she helplessly, hungrily, lapped at the moisture, sipping the musky taste of her, he purred, "Good girl," and swept down to lick his fingers with her. The corners of their tongues brushed, need tightening her insides.

When he lowered his hand, his eyes trapped hers, stormy with lust. He scrutinized her face. "My condition is for you not to let him make you come."

Her heart stopped. "What?"

"He can't make you come, that's my condition. As long as you don't come for him, I'll allow this."

She squeezed her eyes shut. The unearthly connection she'd shared with Ben before . . . it was altered. It carried decadent things, shameful things she didn't know the source of. "You wouldn't hurt him, would you?" she breathed, suddenly concerned.

His face remained blank, but she could still see a kernel of animosity in his eyes, an animosity neither of them had tried to hide tonight. "Not if you don't *come*," Ben replied.

Fear mingled with desire. Not come for Carter. Call it off, *call it off*, she thought wildly. But Ben wanted to punish her, wanted to reassert his power over her, and what he offered was too tempting to deny.

Carter.

Emma quaked with arousal, dreaded never being able to feel Carter's hot hands or his wet mouth on her again. Staring into Ben's eyes, the pupils dilated with desire, she burned over his proposition. She burned to placate Ben, and have the old Ben back. She burned to have Carter, period.

"What if I can't . . . stop?"

He cocked a brow, then withdrew his fingers and studied her moistened pussy, which seemed to scream for something to plunge inside. "Spread a little for me."

She spread. The air felt cold against her heat—strangely heating her even more.

"Wider."

She obeyed and gripped the iron bedpost in her fists and cried out as Ben penetrated her with two fingers. He plunged them in and out, in and out. The pleasure was excruciating. She stiffened her muscles, gritted out, "How long am I supposed to hold my orgasm?"

"All night, Emma."

He thrust a third finger in, and she gnawed her lip. "I want you, too, Ben."

"Do you, baby? Do you?" He twisted all three fingers in. Her throat closed, and her head fell back in bliss.

"He'll touch your pussy. He'll lick it and he'll fuck it. But there'll be no coming for you, Emma. You don't deserve to come—not yet."

She protested deep in her throat.

"Shh. You'll get cock soon."

"I want it now—give it to me—"

He surprised her when he unfastened his pants and shoved them down only enough so his cock could pop out. He guided it to her entry and eased an inch in first, pulled back, returned with another extra inch. She squirmed and pitched her hips upward to take all of him.

"That good for my baby?"

She groaned.

"Not good enough? I know." He bent forward, to her ear.

"You need a cock in your mouth, my love. Would you like to suck his cock while I lap up all the juice in your pussy?"

She shuddered. "Yes, god. The day I first met him, I wondered . . . what it would be like if you shared me with him. I knew it was wrong and never imagined it could happen. . . ."

"But now you won't have to wonder ever again, will you, my love? Never again will you wonder about fucking another man. You'll know that it's never as good as with me, Emma, *never*." He pulled away, holding back with ruthless self-discipline.

She mewled in misery and tossed her head back. "Don't stop, shit, don't, Ben." The fever, the need, it was over-whelming.

He pinned her face with his hands and crushed her lips with his. His tongue shot into her, plunging inside over and over again, drawing out her moans. When he pulled back, she was a firecracker waiting to explode, shivering head to toe. His eyes were wild, possessive, drinking the sight of her reddened lips with greed. His voice was a deep, frightening growl. "I want to see your pussy dripping."

She was panting hard, his words making her throb to be filled up to her throat. "Ben, please."

He patted her pussy one last time, his smile dangerous. "Wait for your lover now."

She knew what he was trying to achieve. Keep her hot and wanting so that every one of Carter's touches would be agony, so that only Ben could give her relief later. She groaned. "God." But as long as Carter touched her, as long as he still wanted her . . .

He appeared at the threshold and her heart leapt when she saw him. He was wearing a navy blue sweater over his loose, faded jeans, and though there were signs of tiredness in his eyes, his face looked clean-shaven and almost boyish without his scruff.

"Carter's going to fuck you now," Ben said.

Her stomach muscles contracted.

When Carter looked at her from the doorway, splayed on the bed, her heart galloped in her rib cage. He wore that electrifying look that made her toes curl, made her feel wanted and sexy and weak. He braced a hand on the doorframe as he studied her. "You okay, sexy?"

Her skin prickled at the sound of his voice. Sex-saay. "Yes."

His eyes raked the length of her body, from the top of her head to her toes, causing gooseflesh to rise up in every inch between. "This your idea?" His voice was soft and gentle, but his eyes were not. There was rage in those eyes, and jealousy. And *lust.*

Still, she couldn't quell the rush of desire shuddering through her. "Not really."

He shut the door of the room behind him, never once glancing at Ben, who'd taken a chair in the corner of the room. "But you want this? You want him to watch us together?"

His eyes fastened to her inflamed labia between her open legs, the bright pink folds exposed in her position, and she saw him slowly run his tongue along his front teeth. Her mouth watered and moisture pooled between her thighs.

She nodded breathlessly. It wasn't being watched that

excited her; it was being touched by Carter again, and maybe by both Ben and Carter tonight.

When Carter purposely jerked out of his cable-knit sweater, Emma's sex muscles squeezed.

"Do you want to play something? What do you want, darlin'?"

God, that draaaawl. He'd called her darling now. "Just . . . you, Carter. You and Ben."

She could salivate at the sight of him in his blue jeans, his bare chest a toasty bronze. She ran several times a week and had firm, toned muscles, but his were rigid, perfectly defined, round and indented. Emma had never seen such a beautiful torso.

He came over in those jeans and that bare chest and surprised her by untying her. Her arms fell to her sides, and she sat up and instinctively rubbed her wrists.

Carter sat at the edge of the bed looking at her, silent.

Desperate to know what he was thinking, Emma curled her arms around his neck, edged closer to him, and kissed his lips. She grasped the back of his strong neck and encouraged him with a purr that was more frustrated than seductive. He didn't kiss her back. She tried rubbing his lips apart with hers, then licked at the seam, and felt him stiffen even more.

She plunged all ten fingers into his hair and crushed her breasts against his chest. "Carter," she coaxingly whispered, grasping at straws, anything that might draw him out. "Aren't you going to kiss me back?"

"What are you doing with him, Emma? This bastard ain't Ben," he growled. He was shaking as he held her shoulders.

"It's Ben," she said, with more firmness than she felt. "He's just had a traumatic experience. He needs to find his own way to cope with the pain."

He released a low, mocking laugh. "That bastard in pain? Yeah, right—like those poor rich people, huh." He glanced at Ben, then bent closer. "When you're finished with me," he hissed into her ear, "then what? Do you plan to cuddle up with Ben on your big bed and talk about what a wonderful evening y'all had?"

"No," she gasped.

He grasped her chin and tilted her head back, so his eyes could burn her with their stare. "Do I look like a fucking gigolo to you, princess?"

"No!"

"Then how do you figure this would be, Em? What do you think it will be like for *me*? Huh? Tell me. . . . Fuck." His sudden desperate kisses commenced at the top of her head, raining down her face as he tipped her head back and seized her lips with his. His mouth was firm, frantic, his tongue sliding forcefully in and out.

Frantic, she followed his tongue into his mouth with a plunge of her own and he groaned, his arms tightening reflexively around her, locking her to his hard frame until their bodies were perfectly fitted.

When he deepened the kiss, Emma forgot everything. That while they kissed someone was watching. That this kiss was supposed to prove to her that Ben made her hotter, wilder, needier. She forgot that this man wasn't the man she was living with, wasn't the man she wanted to welcome back into her life with open arms. He was the other one.

But she forgot that.

She forgot everything but Carter, his mouth, his tongue, his powerful hold on her.

When he pulled away, he dipped his head and brushed his lips across her shoulders, then up her throat and to her ear, where he huskily murmured, "Did you plan this with him? Or are you just playing along?"

His hand trailed down her abdomen, slipping in between her legs. His fingers feathered past her clit, then slid slickly across her swollen lips. She was soaked, could hear the slippery sound of his fingers on her. She gasped, "I just want you, Carter."

"How's that pussy? Is it wet?" Ben called.

Stiffening, Carter cursed under his breath, and, tossing a glance his way, gritted, "Yeah, man, it's soaked for me." Then his voice gentled, softened for Emma as he patted her pussy, kissing her lips. "It's for me, ain't it, baby?" He slid two fingers across the folds, fondling but not entering. He spoke in whispers, for her and her alone to hear. She spoke back in kind.

"Yes," she breathed.

"Torment him, Emma! Rub his dick over his jeans! Taunt him with pussy and then don't give it to him."

She ignored Ben. He was like a demon in her head, tempting her to do things her conscience would warn her against. His arousal felt like a tornado in the house, dark and deadly. She didn't understand him, continued to doubt who he was and even his reasons for returning. But none of that mattered now. . . .

Her blood coursed hot as Carter masturbated her with

strong, calloused fingers. Undone by the moisture in her pussy, he groaned and eased one finger in through the slick tissue. Emma's entire body arched, her thighs spreading apart to give him more room. "Yes," she gasped.

He made a sound of pleasure and hooked an arm around her right leg, curling it around his hips and opening her sex even farther. He pressed a thumb to her clit and slowly rolled it under the pad.

Sharp bursts of pleasure ricocheted inside her. He kept his long finger embedded inside her while he moved his thumb, scraping her sensitive clitoris. Emma pitched her hips in quick, needy circles, her nails sinking into his skin as she moaned. "Carter."

"Yeah, it's Carter." The gruff word was whispered into her ear as he withdrew his finger and eased it back in.

His slow, thorough penetration made her so weak, so frightened of the sensations in her body, she raked her hands down his arms. "Carter."

"Yeah, baby, it's me." He moved to kiss her mouth as he twisted his hand and screwed two fingers in.

Emma bucked and whimpered, "Oh, Carter."

He groaned low and deep and dragged his mouth up her face. Against her temple, he breathed, "Again." He began to pump both fingers inside her, stretching her walls, then pressed the heel of his palm against her clitoris. "Again, Emma."

Emma gasped for air, her lungs straining. Pressure built inside her, tightening her muscles, gathering force. She lowered her head and opened her mouth on his shoulder, licking his damp, salty skin. "Carter."

"You can touch his dick, Emma," Ben said from the chair.

Carter tensed—every time Ben spoke he went rigid. But Emma was too far gone already. Her leg tightened around his narrow hips as she slipped one hand into his jeans and underwear. Under her palm, she felt his heat, his hardness, and she squeezed. A hot, quick breath shuddered out of him.

Emma's rounded gaze flew up to his strained features. "Did I squeeze too hard?"

She was about to retrieve her hand when he gruffly said, "No," and kissed her cheekbones. "Touch me, baby."

He was so broad, so rigid, and as her cupped hand slid down his length she felt a dampness trickle down her skin. She reached the base and moved her fingers so she could cup the hair-roughened sac of his balls.

"Like that?" she whispered, fondling them gently. His abdomen spasmed as he let out a harsh, ragged breath.

"Yeah." He hissed it out through his teeth, then grabbed her hand and pitched his hips up against it, grinding his cock into her palm. "Just like that."

Emma shuddered wantonly. She had fantasized about stroking him, sucking him into her mouth, and suddenly she yanked his jeans down his hips, fell to her knees before him, and gobbled him up before he could even breathe.

His taste assailed her senses, threatening her with sensory overload. He intoxicated her. His salty taste, his musky scent, his smooth skin and painfully hard muscle sliding over her tongue slowly but deeply, pausing every time he hit her throat.

He caressed her hair and rocked his hips. "So sexy."

Her pussy constricted. Sex-saay. A drop of precum slid over her tongue. His cock jerked. He cursed and yanked her back, staring down at her with a tortured look in his eyes.

"Blow your load off, cowboy. Don't be shy."

Stiffening at the mocking voice, Carter raked one hand through his hair in evident frustration. "Sumfabitch," he murmured. Then he glanced back at Emma and rasped huskily, "Lie down on the bed."

She did, slowly, and was surprised that Carter remained sitting by the edge. He took in all of her in one appraising sweep of his gaze. Then his hands surrounded her ankles and meandered up the back of her legs. His touch felt like velvet on her skin, and at the silky brush of his fingers up the back of her knees, her legs threatened to liquefy.

She held her breath as he reached the bottom swell of her buttocks, pausing there, stroking the undercurve of each fleshy cheek with his thumbs as he pressed a tender kiss on her belly, just under her navel.

She gasped. He smiled then, not a wide, happy smile, but a slow, alluring one. "You're beautiful," he whispered, then braced up on his arms and kissed her nose, the corners of her mouth. "I can't take it." He moved with predatory speed, lifting her up in his arms, sweeping her to her feet. He backed with her until her buttocks hit the wall behind her. Her arms ended up pinned at her sides, his formidable weight pressing down on her.

Heart drumming, Emma stared past his shoulders at Ben, afraid he would protest that her body was now completely shielded from view by Carter's. Had it been Carter's intent? Yes, she saw the glow of triumph in his eyes. But if he'd planned to irk Ben, he hadn't succeeded.

Ben was scowling, true, but he'd pulled his cock out and had one fisted hand sliding up and down. He looked . . . wicked.

A finger curled under her chin, tilting her head up. "Look at me, not him."

The husky command in his voice, the fast jerks of his chest as he breathed, made Emma's pussy clench with a thrill at his possessiveness. She looked up into his taut features, and his blue eyes collided with hers.

His hands lowered, and then the sensitive flesh of her breasts was completely covered by his palms. He ran the pad of his thumbs across the hard pink crests. Every harsh scrape swamped her with pleasure. "I want your eyes on me. Just me, Emma, only me. Can you do that?"

"Yes." It was just a breath, she felt so weak.

His gaze fell to her lips, hungry, raw. "He's playin' us, you know this, right?" He plucked her nipples with his fingers, tugging, pinching. "But I don't mind being played so long as I'm the one fucking you instead of watching."

Emma's head fell back against the wall. "Oh, god." Her spine curved, her chest surging up to his hands like an offering.

He cradled one breast in his hand and deftly played with the little nipple while he dipped his head and brushed his warm lips across the other. Her head thrashed to the side and she whimpered when he covered the throbbing little peak with his mouth.

Sensations unfurled in her womb as he suckled, his mouth hot, damp, every suction deeper, more intense. His tongue swiped wetly, around the rigid tip, over it. He growled like an animal would when feasting, the vibration seeping into her breast, curling down to her pussy. His hunger overwhelmed her, excited her, made her pliant and complacent. Every inch of her was his to do with as he pleased. His to touch. And Emma hoped he left no inch untasted.

Making a low, purring sound, he lapped at her breast as he pulled the opposite nipple with gentle tugs of his thumb and forefinger. Emma forgot they were being watched. Forgot about Ben.

She knew exactly who was touching her. Whose body was against hers and whose thigh slipped between her legs to press up against her pussy. She knew whose mouth tormented her breast and whose touch she craved. And whose hair she gripped just now.

He moved to suckle her other nipple; the first one felt swollen and achy, and it welcomed the smoothing stroke of his thumb when it came. His mouth covered her once again, demanding, scorching her breast as he licked and suckled. Then she felt his teeth graze. Lust speared through her until it felt like pain, a vivid, flaring ache burned inside her.

Her fingers delved into his hair, clutching the back of his head as she thrust her breasts up, her pussy rippling between her legs, soaked with moisture. "Please."

His lean frame trembled as he came up and captured her lips. He fondled her breasts as he plunged his tongue inside, no longer the easygoing man she knew, but bold and rapacious. His hands lowered to her hips, clamping around her as he pulled her closer, hips rolling, scraping, grinding with force, making his hardness known to her body. "Please what, Emma?" he rasped.

He sounded wild, out of control.

His hands cupped her buttocks and ground his erection against her pelvis. "Is that what you want?" He devoured her mouth again, his passion fully unleashed, almost frightening in its intensity. "Tell me, Emma."

Emma reached out to stroke her fingers across his face. Gazing into his hot, piercing gaze, she whispered, "I want you."

He groaned and closed his eyes as if that hurt him. Emma fisted her hands in his rich, soft hair, holding his head as her mouth ventured along his jaw. Into his ear, she whispered, "Inside me, thrust inside me." Now, before something spoiled this very moment. Now, before some tragedy took the good things in her life again.

It was his turn to whisper in her ear. "Nah, baby. As soon as I fuck you, this is over for me." He traced the shell of her earlobe with his tongue as he trailed his hands up her sides. "I want you all night, pumpkin—all night writhin'."

Emma shuddered and made a tiny sound of protest. She couldn't wait, was shivering uncontrollably. Couldn't he hear the pounding of her heart? Her gaze was clouded and her skin sang to him so loudly that she thought she'd go deaf. She couldn't stand the increasing throbbing in her pussy. Then a third voice joined them.

"Tell him you love me, Em. Whisper in his ear: I love Ben."

Carter stiffened at Ben's voice, so close. He had silently

crept up. Carter cursed softly under his breath. His sun-lightened head stayed bent to hers, the harsh puffs of his breath fanning across her ear.

Emma stared into Ben's dense, lust-filled black eyes. "I love you," she whispered and brazenly grabbed the rock-hard flesh of Carter's ass and pulled him against her, causing him to grunt as his cock dug into her belly muscle. "Now ask him to fuck me, Ben. You wanted to please me, to show me who's in charge now."

She had no shame, no modesty. She did not mind begging now. She did not mind admitting to both of them, and to herself, how much she longed to have Carter inside her.

A strange look flickered in Ben's gaze, then he growled, "Do it, cowboy—fuck her."

A long moment passed before Carter drew back enough to grab the foil packet Ben handed him. Emma bit her lip as Carter unrolled the rubber and covered every inch of that juicy organ with a sleek sheen.

"Fuck her and turn her around," Ben said. "Let me see that little ass of hers."

Carter hissed out a breath and lifted her in his arms. "Wrap your legs around me," he said gruffly, and Emma quickly did as he asked.

His hands clamped down on her waist and he pushed her down on his cock. Emma gasped as he penetrated, shuddering with heat. It was glory, to feel every steely inch of flesh slide in, to feel him stretching her tissue, invading her up to her heart.

Fully seated inside her, his forehead fell to her shoulder as he gritted, "Christ!" and started moving, surging upward, nothing holding him back now, not an urge to be gentle, not his shyness, not Ben watching.

He nibbled on her shoulder, licked up her throat, grazed his teeth across her jaw as he started pumping. Emma whimpered and held on as he fucked her, pitching her hips to meet his thrusts.

He was grimacing from the pleasure, making soft, grunting noises and kissing her indiscriminately, any part of her he could reach. Emma felt each searing kiss, each lengthy thrust of his cock, like brandings on her soul. She'd never dreamed she could so willingly surrender, be so roughly, so deliciously, so quietly fucked.

He didn't speak, and it made her all the more aware of the sounds of their bodies. The sensual brush of skin, the carnal rhythm of their breathing, the pleasure-filled whimpers that tore out of her throat and the deeper, rumbling groans of his. And the slippery sounds as he slicked in and out.

It was a sexual symphony, a feast for the senses. Emma was afraid she would dissolve from the sensations.

He continued his powerful, rhythmic thrusts, pushing inside her as though he wanted to delve right up to her heart.

The intense pleasure building, the feel of his heavy, powerful thrusts and his ragged breathing all sent her mounting toward a shattering orgasm.

She faintly heard Ben say something, but she didn't understand and at this moment she did not care. Her blood thrummed, heat spreading to her extremities as her muscles started to contract. And thrust by thrust, her orgasm continued to build as Ben stroked her backside. Pleasure shot through her when Ben cupped her breasts from behind, his hot, damp lips nuzzled her nape, and the tip of his raging erection rubbed against her buttocks. Bliss surged through her, an ecstasy sweeping through her system as they held her. Ben. And Carter. Both hot, hard, sweaty, and against her.

Ben tested the ringed entrance of her ass, making her mewl when he threatened to pierce her open. But it was Carter who drowned that cry with his heated kiss. Carter, who crushed her to him as though he did not want to share, wanted her all to himself. It was him she whimpered to, him she clung to as the three of them began to fuck, him she opened her mouth against and kissed.

"Need inside you now," Ben growled low when her tight channel almost sucked him in. "Take me in."

"Not unless you let me come!" The lubricating condom, sheathing a merciless erection, parted her untested entry. Emma shuddered at his gradual penetration and Ben made a low husky sound, embedding his cock deep inside her snug channel.

She closed her eyes on a gasp, overwhelmed by them. So close to exploding. "Oh, god. Say I can come."

"Yes, come," Ben gritted, starting to pump as he squeezed her nipples between two fingers.

"Oh, god, it feels too good."

"Yes! Come, I say!"

She wanted to weep, felt so full, so overwhelmed. "Carter, come with me."

Carter kissed her on the ear, thrusted his tongue against her. "You there, princess?"

"Yes, god, yes!" Her need consumed her, turbulent and fierce and unstoppable.

She tipped her head fully to his, seeking more of his breath, his tongue. She tasted Carter in her mouth, and whimpered as Ben's cock pried her open. She felt wetter than she'd ever been, was aware of Ben pulsing at her entry, teasing her ass, teasing apart her buttocks with his hands as his cock entered and withdrew. He was making low animal-like noises. Ben. He was so aggressive. So . . . so . . . primitive.

Driven crazy, her tongue twirled crazily around Carter's tongue, her hips pumping up for more of Ben and Carter. "Oh, god."

Carter's firm hold on the back of her head tightened as he pumped deep into her pussy, losing control. "Wanna come . . ." he said, his eyes blazing and barely open.

Groaning at the utter heat of their simultaneous strokes, Emma clawed at his ass with her nails, drawing him in deeper. "I'm going to come! God, I'm going to come so hard," she hissed even as every inch of her body trembled with lust. Feelings of such raw intensity made her eyes burn with tears, her breath hitch and come out in sharp, shuddering wheezes as she suckled him hungrily, as she met Ben's thrusts with some of her own. "Carter, come inside me!"

Ben pawed at her breasts, squeezing tight, thrusting his head back in abandon as he pistoned his hips against hers. Emma let out a gasp when Carter's cock jerked in her cunt, and Ben roared as he started coming, and she bucked over him as her orgasm swept through her.

They filled her, pushed her higher, harder, faster, until her climax promised to last forever.

As it gradually ceased, she fell limp against Carter's body, buried her face in the crook of his neck until Ben shuddered behind her and dropped motionless against her back. For a few more minutes Carter held her, naked, her arms and legs around him, his cock still inside her, while she kept her face buried in his neck and basked in his musky, male scent.

She didn't want to open her eyes, for fear of what would happen. Would this be the last time she would be with him, like this, entwined and sweaty from sex? Ben stirred behind her, while Carter was deathly still, his arms possessive around her, like huge iron manacles.

"Damn me, did I hurt you?" Ben asked, wrapping his arms around her and drawing her away. "You can let go of her, Bates," he growled.

Emma wanted to shout, felt like a baby being torn from its mother as Ben yanked her away from him. She felt Carter's arms go limp around her and then Ben was laying her down on the bed. What was wrong with her? Why did her stupid eyes sting?

"Christ, you look exhausted," Ben whispered as he urged her down and pulled a cozy purple throw over her body. Emma heard the shuffle of clothes, a zipper, a snap, and she realized Carter was getting dressed.

Her heart clenched and she kept her eyes closed just to make sure none of the tears gathering there ever spilled. So this was it? A good-bye fuck?

"I better go," she heard Carter mumble. Her eyes popped open, and she turned to watch him thrust his head into his sweater and pull it down to his waist.

"Good idea," Ben said, eyeing him warily. "Now we can forget this night ever happened."

Emma panicked. She couldn't watch him go, couldn't *let* him go, not like this, as though he were nothing more to her than a fuck.

Her throat closed in on her words, but she still managed, "Y-you don't have to leave now, Carter. We can have some dinner and hang out for a while." She felt drained, vacant, loathsome.

Her eyes were wide on his somber face, pleading with him to stay. When would she see him again? At the bar, like they were just friends again? Her heart felt like shattering.

Ben glared. "I'm really not feeling the dinner thing."

Carter started for the door, but Emma jumped to her feet, clutching the throw to her chest, her knuckles white from the effort. "Carter, really, aren't you hungry? We can have a nice quiet dinner, all three of us."

His hair was mussed and when he shook his head a strand brushed his temple. She ached to smooth it back, smooth the dark lines that had appeared on his forehead. "I need to get outta here, baby." His voice was a low, prickly rasp, and he couldn't seem to bring himself to look at her.

Did he need to go because he couldn't stand this, being close to her with Ben between them? Or did he need to go because . . . he didn't care to see her again?

He left without another word.

Emma fell back on the bed and covered her face with her hands while she heard Ben dismiss him downstairs and then heard the front door close. When Ben came back, he sat beside her and pulled her to his chest. "Why the hell did he untie you—isn't that what you like for him to do to you?"

"Stop it, Ben," she said softly, and clenched her stinging eyes shut.

"Is it his dick you like? Are you thirsty for his dick? You could barely fit it in your mouth, Emma."

What *was* it about Carter? That she felt safe? Or that she once again felt so wonderfully . . . *loved*?

When she didn't speak, Ben brushed his thumbs across her eyelids. "Are you crying, Emma?"

Emma pursed her lips and shook her head. Technically, she wasn't crying just yet. But she wanted to, oh, god, she needed to. Ben had never seen her cry for another man. She wasn't much of a sentimentalist, except ever since Ben died . . . everything seemed to scrape her raw.

With some effort, he dragged her atop his lap and started stroking his fingers through the tangles in her hair. "See, you don't need him, my love. He's no good for you—his perversions will break you."

"They're just games, Ben," she admitted, curling up on his lap like a little girl. *And I like to play them with him too much. What kind of a girlfriend does that make me?*

"But life isn't games, is it?" He smoothed one hand over the top of her head, speaking in a calm, soothing voice. "Over time, all games end—and what kind of a man will you be left with?"

One who loves me? Who unties me when I'm tied? Who'll bear humiliation in order to be with me one more night? Who spanks me when I need to feel grounded?

"I'm with you now, aren't I?" she assured, to herself and to him.

She didn't want him to know the extent of her growing

obsession. Ben would do something unpredictable. She felt the latent tension in him, saw the unspoken threat in his eyes. He was acting strange, dark, demonic.

Sin had walked into her home on Ben's heels, and now Emma was disgusted with herself. She needed to get her head straight. It all seemed surreal. This. Ben, Carter. Her feelings for each were tangled in a web inside and she couldn't unstring it.

She wiped her eyes and strived for recovery, as though all was well now after two little tears. "I'm sorry, I . . . I don't know what's got into me."

Or maybe she did.

And he'd just walked out the door.

Chapter Eleven

News of Ben's reappearance spread like a plague across his bar—and all the folks wanted the dish from Carter. But he sure as hell wasn't going to serve dead meat just like that.

"Yeah, he's back, and stop looking at me like that. That's all I fucking know."

He was rankled to his bones. It was evening on Thursday and he mingled at the Silver Fox among a couple of friends, but Heidi had just pulled him aside and bombarded him with questions. Now she stared at him in that speculative, judgmental way of hers, and Carter could see sympathy shining in her eyes.

They'd passed through this subject many times before Ben died, Heidi and Carter. It was always *this* with her, or always *that*, but mostly it was just about Heidi feeling compelled to give out advice nobody wanted, least of all Carter.

"Look, I realize it's not my place to say," Heidi said as she grabbed a pool cue from the wall, "but in case you believe I haven't noticed, Carter, I'm your friend and I have noticed."

Carter cocked a brow and grabbed his stick. Heidi was a kindergarten teacher—a mighty fine one, he had no doubt. Except she seemed to forget to leave her teacher hat over at the school. "Noticed? Noticed what? What the heck are you talking about?"

"You're in love with her, you're sick with it," Heidi continued, and she spoke *sick with it* like he truly had a disease.

The accusation unleashed a shaft of fresh pain. He remembered the hell of a week he'd been having, the sleepless nights and the nightmares, nightmares about this man—this awful man—touching Emma with soiled black hands. The need to hit something was so acute he stalked to the billiard table, powdered his cue, and aimed. "Yeah, well, everyone knows you ain't got a lick of sense, Heidi," he lied.

He didn't want them all to know, he didn't want to be the joke among them, be cast as the stupid fool.

But Heidi, that damned red-haired Irish, followed him around the table like a bee you couldn't shake off your tail. "I see the way you look at her—the way you've always looked at her. Is that why you've been drinking so much? Because Ben's back with her?"

Carter aimed at the white ball, frowning fiercely. "I drink 'cause I'm the owner of the danged bar and I'll do as I damned well please." And because he'd felt so used. Used and discarded. Worthless as chicken poop.

"Oh yeah? So it pleases you to stare at her ass like you want to kiss it?"

"Heidi—go bother Wooly."

"But you're my friend and she's my friend and she's in love with Ben—you can't expect her to ever really get over a man like that. Of course she's happy that he's back. Why wouldn't she be?"

Carter fired.

The white ball hit three balls and the three plopped into their pockets. Unfortunately one of them was the eight ball. He gritted his teeth. His aim was as pathetic as his crush on the princess. But no. Crushes were for teenagers staring at their sexy English teacher's butt while she wrote the day's assignment on the board. Crushes were for people gazing across a carnival at each other who suddenly felt a little horny. Crushes weren't for a grown man. Crushes didn't last six goddamned years.

That night at their place, Ben had played Carter and Emma like marionettes. He'd teased and tantalized him for one more taste of her, and now he knew, damn he just *knew*, the bastard would dangle the apple again only to remind him he wouldn't be getting a bite.

The thought distressed him. Could Emma not see Ben was *different*?

"She's entitled to be happy," Heidi, who didn't even have a clue as to what the fuck was going on, said as she aimed, and she shook her head in the chiding way Carter remembered his own mother doing before she'd left with the Walmart cashier. "You're the sexiest guy I know, so please don't take it personally, but you're not Mr. Right for anyone, least of all Emma. She needs someone a little bit less on the sexy side and a little more on the responsible side. Someone steady. Someone who'll stay."

"You mean like Ben?" He sneered the last word. Long time ago, the word alone made Carter envision the perfect family man; now it brought to mind some sort of good-looking Freddy Krueger. On Viagra. "He was dead for two fucking years—now he's perfect? A martyr? Should I step outside and let some car have at me so I can get her respect?"

Pity emerged in her eyes again, this time carrying a little baby of compassion. "Carter, I know you love her, but—"

He slammed the stick down on the table with a glare. "Stop saying that—or Wooly'll hear and then the entire USA and Canada will know, damn you."

He remembered Emma's pale face. The pity and regret in her expression when she'd murmured, *You think you're my boyfriend.*

"I ain't in *love* with her. I ain't in love with shit," he growled.

"Keep telling that to yourself, you big bluffer!"

He glared in fury, dropped his arms at his sides, and balled them into fists. "Swear to god if you tell anyone, Heidi—"

"I won't, but you have to stop, Carter. This instant. Ben wanted to marry her, have little babies with her—for sure he'll be wanting the same now!"

He glowered. "Ben told me before he died—he told me about his plans." Plans about puppies and babies and the continuation of their perfect life together. A nurse and a doctor, perfect specimens to produce healthy, smart off-spring . . .

But now, could that big ole jealous Frankenstein have babies?

"Damn right he had plans—unlike you. Look at you! Six p.m. and already on your way to puking your guts out, you're so drunk, and you're just proving to yourself she's right to love him and not you. Emma needs a friend now. That's all she needs."

"Well, I ain't her fucking friend anymore."

Heidi stared, aghast, then butted her cue on his rib. "You slept with her! He was right—you guys were banging!"

"Who the hell said so?"

"Wooly."

"How the heck does Wooly know?"

"He's the bartender; he's the god of knowledge around here."

Carter clenched his teeth, then waved a hand. "Ahh, bite my ass. Go yodelay somewhere else, Heidi."

Things were all fucked up.

Ben sat before their home computer, simmering with frustration.

Stupidly he'd encouraged them to fuck—and he'd learned nothing except the fact that his woman trembled in the arms of another man. He'd wanted to prove to Emma that Carter was a perverse man who played perverse games, but the son of a bitch had untied her. He'd practically made love to her in front of Ben, and Emma had clung to Carter— Carter!—rather than Ben. She'd fucking cried for him afterward, even if she didn't admit it.

The rest of the week had gone on just as shittily.

Twenty-four-seven Ben was bored, horny, and pissed.

Now Ben typed into the Google search bar: *How to drive a woman wild*

And peered at the results.

Emma was withdrawn, too withdrawn, wouldn't let him tie her up and spank her like she'd let Carter. Before, she'd trembled when Ben was near her, trembled with overwhelming desire. Now, as much as she tried to hide it, as wild as his touch drove her, she trembled with a mixture of wanting and fear.

Silly girl!

Ben scanned the computer screen for a list of things to do to drive a woman wild. A sinking sensation settled in the pit of his gut as he scanned a few. There was no trick in these lists that he didn't know, nothing he hadn't tried.

Be romantic. Think flowers.

His jaw burned with embarrassment as he recalled the ones he'd brought her yesterday. She'd looked up from the kitchen to see him standing at the door, and her eyes had gone round.

"What is that? . . . Oh, my god, are those dead flowers?"

Ben had glanced down at the black sticks with the wilted black petals and suddenly he'd wanted to kill her. The feeling embarrassed him so much he then wanted to kill himself. Then he'd realized the one he wanted to kill was Carter.

He'd exploded, tossed the rose bouquet into the air, sent the flowers flying across the room first north, then south, then east and west, and then to the ground, where he'd made them burst into cinders.

Emma had stared, dumbstruck, and had said, with soft regret, "You ask me why I won't let you tie me up, why I won't let you spank me." She signaled at the lingering smoke. "This is why, Ben."

Now he heard her talking on the phone with Heidi about the stupid welcome back party she was certain would be *good for him*. What would be good for him was for her to come right now and fuck him! For her to let him reach into her and know what the devil she was thinking!

He didn't know where his violent emotions stemmed from, but they drove him mad. Whenever he went out he couldn't stare at someone without knowing they felt envy, jealousy, were greedy, were murderers, were frauds. Even Emma was a liar! A LIAR!

A little.

Heck yeah, like summers in Texas only had *a little* sun.

Like the night was only *a little* black.

And her face was only *a little* beautiful.

"I promise to tell you all about it later," she was saying upstairs, "but yes, he's back and he's fine. But would you mind checking to see if Carter would be okay with the small party being at the Fox? With all our friends?"

What fucking friends?

"They'll be so thrilled to see him again and I want to make sure they're all there."

So we can watch them all shit in their pants when they see him.

"Oh? Carter's there with you! Uh . . . okay, so could you ask him? I'd ask him myself if I could but . . . things are . . ." There was emotion in her voice, which made Ben frown. "Awkward between us. And I really want Ben to feel welcome. . . ."

I just want to get him out of the house in the hope he'll stop trying to screw me upside, downside, and sideways all the time.

"Look, just ask Carter if he minds, all right?"

And tell him to dry-clean his monkey suit so he can wed a living fossil by the end of the month. Hell, he should be dragging Carter's ass to the witch right now, but how in the hell was he to explain the bastard's disappearance to Emma? First he needed her to get tired of him, annoyed, maybe even angry. . . .

Or maybe he just had to pressure her to the point where she had to make a choice. Damn, this was all fucked up. She was supposed to forget all about Carter when Ben appeared, supposed to realize the sex was better with Ben.

Now Ben didn't want to imagine what was on her mind when her eyes got all misty and clouded, but he'd bet his new life that she was thinking about goddamned Carter Bates.

"It's okay? He said so?" Emma said, excited. "Oh, yay. You're sure? I sort of hear him saying *there's no way in hell* in the background. . . ."

Cursing that no-good pussy and yanking his attention back to the computer screen, determined to seduce her ASAP, Ben read the rest of the damned lists. In no list, no list whatsoever did it say that a surefire way to make a woman wild was by spanking the hell out of her. So why was she *a little* bit obsessed with damned Carter?

Because he was there when you weren't. He's held her; he's wiped her tears; he's made her smile—damn him!

The inbox burst open, and a blank e-mail popped into the screen.

Letters began filling the space before his eyes, typed on his very keyboard by invisible fingers.

Made a mistake . . .

Ben frowned and watched the letters continue to appear.

Price too high

You shouldn't be here

His fingers flew instinctively to take over the keyboard, and he wrote: *Who the fuck is this?* Then it struck him that it was Gandhi; it had to be his old friend.

You're dangerous

Must go back

Ben smiled a smile as thin as a blade and slowly pounded out the letters: *NEVER!*

The Silver Fox was packed Saturday.

Carter pulled his weight behind the bar, whipping up drinks, fucking up in a major way when his mind wandered to a certain brown-eyed girl, when a strange silence settled around him.

They'd arrived.

And like a humiliating middle school dance or one's first root canal, Carter would remember this day for the rest of his life.

On the calendar, right before the upcoming Veterans Day, this day could read: Return of the Poltergeist.

The cool outside breeze trickled inside, and confused whispers erupted all around him. Sighing drearily, Carter set the margarita he'd been preparing before his customer—then turned toward the doors. The temperature in the room hitched, went from cool to hellish.

They strolled inside with their hands linked together. Ben looked fit and trim in Dockers and a white polo, and the princess . . .

His mouth watered and his eyes went sore. Petite and brown-eyed, she was made to wear skirts and dresses that showed off those lean, shapely legs. A black skirt hugged her hips, and over it she wore a white blouse with lace cuffs and a V-neck collar. A shirt that fairly screamed, *Carter, get it off me!*

"Well, shoot me in the head, so it's true," Wooly gasped at his side. "Ben Newcastle ain't dead after all."

Carter could've just swallowed a bomb, his chest ached so bad. He hadn't seen her for two weeks. Had been out of his mind jealous remembering the night they'd had her together. *She'll never choose you over me.*

"So it appears," Carter muttered in resentment.

A crowd gathered around the couple, little moths drawn to the flame, little moths that mostly constituted Ben, Emma, and Carter's friends.

Lips pursed grimly, Carter groped for a wine bottle behind him. He uncorked the cabernet and took a swig until the bottle felt light in his grasp. He didn't know why or how the bastard had returned from the dead—because he *had* been dead. All Carter knew was that he would do anything to be with Emma again, to keep her. Anything meant—hell, anything. Sell his soul to the devil and that shit.

Was that what a dead guy did? A dead guy like Ben Newcastle?

And now he could make plates fly and shit?

He heard snippets of the conversation the resurrected man was having. He was telling everyone a story about a mistake, a twin brother, and amnesia. Like the rest of the folks listening to it, Wooly seemed rapt.

When Ben was finished with the anecdote, a burst of laughter erupted, and looking convinced, Wooly tossed a penny onto the bar top. "Heck, I'll buy that."

Glowering, Carter rammed the penny back into the tip bucket.

He watched Ben wind around the tables and lead Emma to the jukebox, his hand on the small of her back.

Carter stood rigid, his eyes narrowed. Ben met his gaze and smiled, a sharp slice of danger. Of warning.

Unease stirred through him as Ben bent over the jukebox, clicked a button, and "Endless Love" began. He thought himself so original, didn't he!

Suddenly, Emma spotted him watching her and waved shyly, but she was abruptly turned into Ben's arms.

No reason to feel like the roof had just collapsed over him. It was just a stupid dance.

He had been through this before a thousand times.

He'd seen them right on the dance floor.

Had witnessed the band stop playing so that the jukebox could play "your eyes! your eyes!" until his own eyes filled up with the need to shut it the hell up.

He'd seen them kiss.

But back then he hadn't splayed Emma on a cross and

paddled her sweet little arse to the color of cherries. He hadn't felt the silky wetness of her tongue, or felt the heat of her lustful gaze on him. Hell, two weeks ago, he'd watched her and Ben have sex while he plunged into her sweet depths, and it had felt like being murdered while at the same time getting the best goddamned blowjob of his life.

Now the pair was dancing together, and Carter wanted to run out with the wolves and howl.

"Dang, that's a sweet sight," Wooly said as he watched them, a fist pressed romantically to his chest, right above his heart. "Sure makes a man feel pleasure to see things go right in this world."

Narrow-eyed with hostility, Carter spoke under his breath. "See anything funny about him, Wools?"

While Wooly assessed the freak in question, Diana Ross's voice seemed to sink its powerful spurs deep into Carter's heart as she sang about *endless love.* . . .

Christ, love sounded so true and clear when this woman sang about it, about eyes—*your eyes*—and like all you had to do to know if someone cared about you was look into them. But dammit, what if those eyes looked at another man, too? Who would they love endlessly?

The other guy, moron.

"Maybe I do see somethin' different," Wooly at last admitted. "The guy looks fucking immortal." He cackled at his own genius, thrusting his hands high. "Hell, vampiric!"

Carter turned with a glare. With his beer belly, receding hairline, and silver tooth, Wooly looked like a dweeb from a bad movie. "Not funny, man."

His silver smile faded instantly. "All righty, then." He produced a rag and polished the bar.

Heidi plopped down on an empty stool, and since the cosmo she was carrying was still full, Carter realized with dread she'd come over to *talk*.

He lifted his eyebrows in warning. "Don't even go there."

Tossing back her red mane, Heidi sighed and let her shoulders sag.

Carter tipped the wine to his lips and took a long swig, then braced his free arm on the bar top and leaned over. "Yeah yeah yeah, I know they love each other and I should jump off the next plane without a parachute."

Her shrewd eyes surveyed him, then her lips pursed primly. "I wasn't going to say that."

He frowned, noticing she looked dismayed. "What, then?"

She stole a peek at the dancing couple, entwined like a rope. Her eyes were wide and interested when she turned back to Carter. "I don't think she believes she's in the right man's arms."

Ben was hard. Very, excruciatingly hard.

Which Emma found . . . alarming, considering where they were.

He kept rolling his erection against her stomach, making her palms sweat and her mind pull in all kinds of directions. Desire for him, yes, she had that in spades. But for the past two weeks every time the need arose, a strange instinctive fear followed at its heels. *I'm afraid of him.*

Shit—why?

Why was she so wary in his arms, so stiff and unrelaxed?

They'd danced to this song before, but that was *before* Ben had gained that terrifying gleam in his eyes, *before* Emma had become acutely aware that a tall Greek god with eyes straight from a Tahitian sea stood frozen behind the bar, watching them, suckling a bottle of wine like it was mother's milk to him.

Into her ear, Ben whispered, "I want to make him toss and turn in his bed every night knowing that I'm fucking you—I want him to *feel* the rage I felt when I knew he had you and not I."

Inside the ironlike circle of his arms, an unpleasant shiver flitted through her. "You can't mean that, Ben."

"Of course I do. The thought of him suffering like I did makes me hard to fuck you. Hard to do it right here, right now, right in front of the bastard."

A tiny jab of annoyance flared through her and she had to force her legs to keep moving against his. Her Ben, her old Ben, would have never considered this. Never. She felt like a possession, a trophy to him, not like a person anymore.

"Look at him, eyeing your ass like he thinks it's his," Ben said. And then he grabbed the plump flesh and squeezed.

"Ben!"

She yanked his hand back up to her waist, glaring, but now a wicked heat raced through her bloodstream because, somehow, Carter's possessive gaze had become a tangible thing on her ass.

She couldn't banish the impression that Ben danced not to enjoy Emma—not to tease her in her ear, or seduce kisses out of her. He seemed to dance only to rub it in Carter's face.

Should Emma have lied about wanting him?

No.

Because this man would still know.

Unease pricked the back of her neck at the thought.

She'd been sleeping with him, this stranger, this unpredictable and terrifyingly sexy stranger, for two weeks. He slept with his arm firmly around her, not spooning her like before, and every time she shifted, he opened his eyes. It was eerie, the way he watched her, the way he didn't take his eyes off her. He had the strength of ten men. Flowers wilted when he passed. He didn't want to call his parents and he used to love them, love the pride in their eyes, in their voices when they told everyone they met "our son's a cardiologist."

She was desperate to believe he was back, that everything would gradually return to the way they were before. But even this dance, his body holding hers, was as alien to her as a visit to the moon.

Where was he? Where was *her* Ben? The man who couldn't stand her being hurt, the unselfish doctor who'd worried about his patients more than having sleep or food of his own?

"Why won't you look at me?" His voice, deep and rough, brought her gaze to his.

"I was just thinking . . . of old times."

One sleek eyebrow rose, and it was followed by the

other. "Old times make you frown? Perhaps we have different memories."

Emma tried a small laugh, but she didn't sound as mirthful as she wanted to. "Old times make me smile, Ben. Except . . ." She paused, stealing a sidelong glance at the bar where Carter stood. "Except these aren't like old times, are they?"

Things were changing; winter had befallen their relationship; two years had carved an abyss between them. One man had left, and another had returned.

Ben didn't seem to agree, for a hot, bright light flashed in his gaze, and his hands fisted on the small of her back. "You want Carter. You . . . you're still hot for him. Aren't you?"

Her heart began drumming. "Ben, you can't pretend all three of us didn't—"

"Stop looking at him," he whispered, and spoke so softly, so deceptively softly, alarm bells clanged in her head. His nostrils slowly flared. "You're mine."

Panic gripped her by the throat and, following his example, she softened her voice to imitate his. "Don't do this here."

Exasperated, he raised a hand and scraped his palm down his face, then let it drop heavily at his side. "Dammit, why can't you stop thinking about him?"

Emma grabbed his shoulders and tried to dance, attempting to still the bubbling hysteria threatening to burst. Ben felt challenged, and would not rest until he believed he'd won. The thought filled her with dread. *Who the hell is this man?* "Ben, even if I want him, I still want *you*," she said, rubbing his hard chest.

What in the devil am I supposed to do with him?

She'd thought she couldn't live without him, but now the gods mocked her: it was difficult to imagine living *with* him, too.

"Do you know who you want more?" Ben asked, his voice hard.

Her heart wrung when she raised her eyes to his. Emotions flooded her, wanting and love and regret. Where was *he*? "This isn't fair, Ben, and you know it."

"I still need to know." He yanked her against his chest and his hands tightened convulsively on her waist. "Did I lose you, Em?"

Close to cracking at the desperation in his voice, Emma glanced around at the staring people and squirmed. She couldn't bear the speculation in all those eyes. "Please stop, we'll discuss this back home."

"Tell me."

"Not here, Ben!"

He seized her chin between thumb and forefinger and yanked her head back a bit too forcefully. "If you had to choose one of us, who would you choose?"

She groaned to herself and pushed his grip aside. *You died and I had to survive!* she wanted to say. *I can't forget who was here for two years!* But she didn't, because she hated sounding like she wasn't thrilled to have him back, because that wasn't true either. She was. She was! She had to be. This was all she'd ever wanted, all she'd thought about for nearly two years.

"Ben," she tried carefully, gathering her composure as they resumed the dance. The music pulsed in her veins, painful in her ears. *Two hearts . . . two hearts that beat as* one . . . "What's wrong with you? You've never been like this. You're so . . . different."

The pupils in his eyes dilated, and when his teeth flashed, she almost imagined they'd grown fangs, they were so very . . . white.

"I'm the man who'd walk through hell for you, Emma. That's who I am."

Fear rippled through her, unexpected. She hadn't asked for this sacrifice, wouldn't want anyone in the world to walk through hell because of *her*, and the thought that Ben meant what he said sent a fresh burst of alarm slicing through her. "But why are you trying to hurt Carter, Ben?"

She searched for clues across his face, but he looked—he looked almost triumphant when she mentioned him hurting Carter. His smile showed whiter.

"He used to be your friend! Has it occurred to you that we can't choose the people we love, that he wasn't deliberately challenging you? What's going through your mind? I don't understand!"

"Then stop fucking trying."

Her eyes flared with outrage over his snapping tone, then narrowed in fury. "You bring me flowers, but you won't explain to me why they're dead. You want to have sex with me five times a day, but you won't tell me where you slept for two years. People change. We need to get to know each other again, but have you even tried? I stopped liking mushrooms, did you know? And I stopped visiting Mr. Granger because he always squeezed my butt when I was refilling his oxygen tank. Is the fact that I slept with Carter all you care to know about me?"

The sadness in her voice seemed to reach him, and his expression morphed to one of tenderness. He stroked her cheek with his knuckles in a long, gentle swipe.

"No, that's not all I care about. I know everything about you, Emma—everything. I was here. I was . . . watching you. A ghost. A spirit. See how it sounds? I sound like a madman! But that's the truth, so that's all I can say. I came back because . . . because I couldn't let you forget me."

He grabbed her face and seemed to spear into the depths of her with his gaze.

"It took me almost two years to find a way to come here and be with you. That's all I fucking want."

"Then come back to me," she said softly, brokenly, moving closer to him, searching for her place against his chest. "Not in body, but also . . . in soul."

She tipped her head back, loathing that he looked down at her blankly.

"What are you thinking? Feeling? Have you done something wrong? You're so angry at everyone, like you hate living, but if you do—why are you back, Ben?"

Their song ended, and suddenly, it felt so final. Like she'd never get to dance it with him again, never hear it play on that old jukebox again.

He released her abruptly, said, "You'll never—ever—want him again. Mark my words," and then she watched him plunge into her purse in search of the car keys.

He tinkled them in her face before stomping across the bar and Emma watched him go, forlorn as she wrapped her arms around herself.

If Ben had come back a month ago, she wouldn't have

known Carter's exquisitely tender touch. What a closet gentleman he was. How sexy and virile. This wouldn't be so difficult, so complicated.

Ben was back—but no, he wasn't.

He teased her, being here, reminding her of what they used to have. The man he'd once been.

He and Carter hadn't spoken a word to each other all night. The crackling antagonism between the men—best friends—was *her* fault. She had an urge to fix this, like she would to put a bandage around an oozing wound, but she just didn't know what to do, and she didn't know whose wound needed more tending.

Why couldn't she capture what she and Ben had had anymore? Why couldn't her life go back to the way it had been, before Ben *died*, before she was lonely and struggling to cope?

Ben was changed, like he'd come from another world. He was too strong, too brooding, too dark now. He was stronger, more aggressive, wilder in bed, and it drove her mad with desire, the way he took her, like a demon on fire. But then she thought of Carter—

No. She had to stop this.

As long as Ben walked this world, her place was with him.

Wasn't it?

Heart heavy in her chest, she spared one last longing glance at Ben as he reached the door, and she saw him flick his wrist like he was swatting off a fly.

The room plunged into darkness.

Her pulse stopped. Screams arose. Her world spun uncontrollably with disbelief. People had been having fun. Minding their own business. How could Ben? How could he . . . ? Among the loud, panicked sounds, there was only one voice she seized with all her being. One voice she started to stumble toward.

"Emma!" Tables crashed as though they were turned over, making a path to her. "Emma!"

She sagged when Carter caught her. "I'm here! I'm all right."

His breath exploded out of his lungs as he crushed her against him, his heart pounding hard and fast against her breast. And suddenly she felt . . . safe.

Utterly.

Completely.

"I . . ." She fisted her hands on his shirt and burrowed against him. How much had he seen? Did he realize Ben had done this? What *else* could Ben do?

Shakily, against the V of his neck, she murmured, "Could you please take me home?"

Tension rode his F150 with them.

"We going to talk about it at all?" Carter's gaze strayed from the road and met hers.

And her body, oh, god, she hated that her body hummed with sensual appreciation of the sound of his voice. "He's just confused," she defended. Strange, inexplicable emotions assailed her at the thought of Ben, and she turned her face to the window.

She gazed unseeingly at the passing landscape, her stomach

muscles contracted. Ben was hurting. She ached to help him, but didn't know how. She wanted to reach him, but she didn't know how!

"He's gone through a lot, you know," she said in an off-handed tone she barely managed to pull off. "He'll take time to adjust back to being . . . normal."

The rumble of Carter's chuckle vibrated between her thighs and she hated, hated, the way it raced down her skin, too. "Hell, Emma, you've never been blind, and sure as hell you ain't stupid. The guy's—"

"Please don't insult Ben."

A growl rumbled up his throat as he tightened his hold on the steering wheel.

They reached the house within minutes, and Emma was disturbed to discover her car wasn't out in the driveway. Ben hadn't come home. Where had he gone to, so enraged?

Rattled, she stormed out of the truck and fumbled with her keys. The pull. The need building in her like a storm cloud. The attraction that kept escalating with each minute, each second. The attraction to *Carter*. This couldn't be.

This lust was causing all the conflict, stoking the turmoil inside Ben. Emma shouldn't feel weak when those stunning blue eyes looked at her, feel pricks of excitement when that drawl emerged from that thick, strong throat. . . .

Carter accompanied her to the door, walking that sexy walk and swagger. "Emma."

She finally shoved her door open. "Thanks for the ride. Good night, Carter."

"No way in hell will you dispatch me like a good little dog!"

He pushed through and followed her into the darkened foyer, and Emma dropped her keys before she started across the living room. His quiet anger pulled at hers like a magnet. She felt angry, too. She shouldn't want him anymore! She should want Ben—just Ben. And Ben should be . . . like he'd been *before*.

"Hey," he growled, catching her shoulders and spinning her around. "Hey, pumpkin."

"I'm not your pumpkin."

The blue in his eyes flashed. "Damn you." His hands squeezed her shoulders, and she wasn't sure what caused their tremor. "Damn you, Em—why are you doing this to me? Has he hurt you?"

No! No! He'd never hurt her, never. Would he?

"Why would he hurt me, Carter?" She thrust her chin out at a challenging angle. "He loves me. He's loved me his whole life—he came back for me."

Her heart clenched when he just stared at her. Moonlight was so good to him and so cruel to her eyes, stroking his handsome face with a whisper of silver, those devastatingly virile features drawn in both light and shadows.

He scanned her features, his voice low. "Then explain to me why you're so afraid of the bastard."

"I'm not—not afraid. What have *you* got against him, anyway?"

"Shh, calm down." His cupped hand slid up her arm until his thumb reached the curve where her arm met her shoulder, and he stroked her there. Softly, as though he didn't mean to touch her but did. He could've been stroking the damp, swelled lips of her pussy for the effect it had on her. Emma bit her lip and fought back a whimper. "Let go," she croaked, tugging her arm free.

Two large, powerful hands framed her face, their size dwarfing her. "I don't trust him. And good god, Emma, the jealousy is killing me—killing me."

On his breath she could smell alcohol, and it whizzed hypnotically around her head. She inhaled slowly, then released a shuddering sigh. "I'm sorry."

"Not your fault I'm a fucking fool, baby."

Emma choked and stared down at their shoes. "I told you not to call me *baby* anymore."

He groaned long and deep and closed his eyes, dropping his forehead to hers. "But you're my baby. And I go wild when I say it and you shudder—I know what it does to you when I say *baby*. Yeah, just like that. Don't fight it."

She curled her fingers around his thick wrists and attempted to remove his hands, but he resisted, his forehead still pressing down on hers, his hands squeezing her cheeks. "Carter, just go."

"I belong with you, Emma, I feel it in my bones."

She closed her eyes and took a long inhale, dragging his clean scent inside her. Her sex spasmed and a shiver feathered down her spine.

Then he moved, holding her face in his hands as he placed a soft kiss on one eyelid, then the other. Emma forgot to breathe.

A powerful tremble coursed through his body, as though he was holding back from doing something else. He continued to hold her cheeks in big hands that shook unsteadily as he kissed the tip of her nose, his lips soft and slightly moist.

Despite the haze in her head, Emma managed to pry her eyes open just as he pulled back to stare at her.

The expression on his face was one she'd never seen. It was tight, wild. Eyes that had been warm were now a deep night sky blue. "Make him go," he whispered, surveying her eyes, her lips. "Make him go and be with me."

As he caressed her face, his elbow bumped her breast, and with a soft curse, he curled his hand around its softness and stroked her. "Come live with me." His voice was husky, coaxing, and soft. "Send him away, Em. Send him away."

"Carter, I can't."

The velvety dark enveloped them, so that it was impossible to think, to breathe, to deny those silky encouragements. "I'll be all you need. Oh, baby, I promise you." Carter fondled her lovingly, like she was his treasure alone. "Soft, creamy white titties, with these delectable little peaks, will be sucked only by me."

"Carter," she said, and that was all she could manage in her breathlessness.

"You're wild for me and I know it—god, I do." He squeezed the breast so the nipple sprung to attention. "Need you, Em."

She'd never thought eyes so blue could glow like bulbs in the shadows as they homed in on her nipple like it was all for him to see.

"Need to suckle this breast here, suckle it raw."

"Carter." His aroma was too rich, too succulent.

One splayed hand pressed into the small of her back and pulled her flush against his chest, his erection unmistakable. "Don't make me stand on the sidelines, Em. I want to fight for you. I have a fucking *right* to." He was hissing now, his whisper as fierce as the passion in his eyes. "I saw the way you looked at me tonight and—fuck, baby, I know it's killing you, too. Just say the words, say you want me—"

"Shut up, just shut up!" Emma grabbed his jaw and covered his mouth with hers, desperate to feel him, kiss him, show him what his words did to her, how much she wanted him.

He tensed for less than a heartbeat. Then he was all over her, crushing her body against his, hands running up her back, down her hips, cupping her ass, pressing her hard against him as he slanted his mouth and kissed the breath out of her.

Her head spun as lust surged inside her body. Her senses whirled at the discovery of how hard he felt, his thighs, his abdomen, his chest—all pure, solid muscle against her. She remembered him, naked and aroused, and could barely keep from ripping his clothes off.

Hungry for him, for more, Emma mewed into his mouth as she kissed him back with abandon. She wanted to tear her clothes off and ride him. Feel that magnificent penis slide deep in her channel, stretching, filling, taking.

But Carter was leading, and his mouth was insatiable.

He was fucking her with his tongue. Something thrilled inside her at the blatancy of his hunger and all she wanted was to please him . . . to give to him.

One powerful arm encircled her waist while he cupped and kneaded her ass, keeping her pinned to every lean inch of him. Her body undulated to the grinding rhythm of his hips.

Through his jeans, the stiff, swelled column of his erection scraped her sensitive mound, indirectly stimulating her clit. Her pussy rippled with contractions.

She curled her hands around his nape while she kissed him back for all she was worth. Her moans were lost inside his mouth. Eagerly she swallowed the decadent groans that rumbled up his chest.

"Sweet," he rasped before he cocked his head to the other side and captured her mouth once again.

He always made her feel devoured, left no part of her unaffected, not her breasts, or her sex, not her heart. Her sex felt bloated, drenched with the juices his kiss coaxed. Heat radiated off his body and burned into her breasts.

He tore his mouth away and pushed her at arm's length, studying her.

"Carter," she breathed. She reached out and slipped her hands under the fabric of his navy shirt. Her fingers slid up the smooth, warm silk of his skin, feeling the enticing ridges of his muscles.

He made a strangled sound as he caught her wrists. "Emma," he whispered, halting her wandering hands, "you have to leave him."

The reminder of Ben made her freeze in cold, hard shock. What had she been thinking? Doing? "I can't," she said brokenly, shaking her head fast. "Oh, god, I can't—When you love someone, you love them through good and bad!"

"You don't love him anymore."

"I do! I do! Because if I don't it means my entire life was a lie, that I never really loved him!"

"Look, I know you like to fix people in pain, but it ain't your job to fix Ben anymore. Let go of him, Emma."

Emma clung to a wad of his shirt, rubbing her breasts against the massive wall of his chest in desperation. "Carter, Carter, you don't understand. He was my champion, my everything. I'm not supposed to want another man. I'm not supposed to . . . want you. Ben should be enough—more than enough."

His face hardened in anger. "And now your need to keep him here has created a monster." He tried to pry her hands away, but she tightened her hold.

"No! He's not a monster, he's not. He loves me."

"If he loved you he'd have let you go. Like I have!"

He put her aside. His words hit her mind, and spread inside her. He loved her. He let her go because he loved her. Wanted her to be happy.

But why wasn't she?

He paced. "Christ! Don't you see?" He plunged his fingers through his hair. "The guy ain't gonna let you go if you don't let *him* go. If you love him, let him go and let him keep whatever good feelings he's got left in him, Em! The guy's not . . . right. He's diabolic."

She gasped in outrage. "Carter, Ben's not evil! How can you say that? He was your friend!"

"Dammit, I just know it. Fuck, come here."

But it was he who came and enveloped her in his arms. Emma fitted her body to his, her blood coursing hot.

She slid a hand between their bodies, aching to cup him, feel him, stroke him, but before she could touch his erection he was scooping her up into his arms. "I can't do this, baby," he whispered.

"Then put me down. Stop touching me."

"In a minute." He lowered his head as he carried her upstairs, then murmured, "Emma," and captured her mouth with a groan. The sound traveled just under her skin, delicious, throaty, male. Their tongues met, tangled, rubbed in an intricate, fevered frenzy.

He broke off the contact and planted a soft, lingering kiss on her forehead, setting her down on the mattress. His voice was terse and textured. "Here you go, on the bed." It was when he drew back to pull off her ankle boots that she realized with a sinking stomach he didn't intend to stay.

Carefully, he draped the goose down comforter over her. His hands paused against her shoulders and he stared down at her with dark, troubled eyes.

Tendons in his neck moved as he swallowed. "Tell me to go."

The air crackled between them.

His neck looked thicker. Veins strained up its length, and his eyes had a wild, glassy sheen to them. The long outline of his erection was monstrously evident under the fly of his jeans. Emma wanted to sit up and rub him, press her mouth to him, do anything to entice, tell him to stay.

But he was *Carter*.

And she couldn't do this to Ben.

"Go," she said huskily, then swallowed back the bile rising up her throat at the thought of waiting for Ben . . . afraid of what he'd do . . . what his words at the bar had meant.

But Carter didn't go, his breathing a harsh, fast mimic of her own panting breaths. One warm, slightly unsteady hand brushed back the loose tendrils of hair from her face. "Gonna be all right, Em. I'll make it right if I can, I promise you."

Emma made a choked sound, unsure and a little bit afraid. She hated being helpless and afraid. Should she kick Ben out? Make a list of house rules, rules of comportment, threaten to do something if he broke them—

It would be like housetraining a stray dog. Or a . . . a rabid dog. Or a lion.

"You gonna be okay, princess?"

She bit her lip and reached to grab both of his arms, and that single movement broke his restraint.

He leaned over her and his hand plowed under the covers, around her waist, and gripped her ass. He squeezed. "Ben's going to be a very unhappy man if he knows I was here with you."

Desire exploded through her.

"Would you like him to spank you?" he demanded.

The scruff on his jaw chafed the skin of her cheeks. She kicked the comforter down to her ankles and surged up against him, rubbing heatedly.

"I asked you if you'd like Ben to spank you. Do you want him to know I fucked you in his room? Just you and me. And that you were wild riding my dick, begging me to make you come."

Emma was panting as he opened her buttons and pushed her blouse aside, then he grabbed her bra and hooked the lace material under the swells of her breasts, exposing her pointed nipples.

"Answer me or I won't suckle you like you want me to." He gazed at the pink beads, his chest heaving.

Her cunt clenched when he licked the tip of one aching breast, then the other.

"You're provoking him," he grumbled. "You want to see if he takes charge like I do, spanks your bottom bright red like you've asked me to."

"No! That's not true, you're reading me all wrong. Oh, god, just go away."

Silence met her words; then he drew back and spoke, his timbre regretful. "Do you love me, Em?"

"I said go away."

"I want you to tell me."

"I can't." She arranged her bra and blouse as best as she could, a part of her praying Carter would do something, take her in his arms, say something, but all she heard after the shuffling of feet was silence.

"I'll take care of Ben," he murmured from the threshold.

The door shut quietly behind him.

Fuck.

Carter braced one sweaty palm on the redbrick wall outside her home and slammed a fist into it.

His chest felt heavy. His eyes burned. His lungs burned. His entire body burned. He propped one shoulder on the wall and threw his head back with a frustrated, "Aaargh!"

Years. He'd been waiting years for this moment. For her to look at him like this, exactly the way she had moments ago. For her to be begging for him. Not for a spank. Not a fucking visit to the Club. Just *him*. And this is what it had come to. Honor.

Wherever Ben was, Carter couldn't take her like this, not like this. Dammit!

He ground his teeth and stared up at the roof, his eyes blurring. His features distorted as he struggled with the rage like acid on his intestines.

Stupid, scrupulous bastard.

Who else would do what he had? Who else would leave Emma? Emma wanted him. She might not love him, but she wanted him. And she was alone in her bed, with her lips moist and swollen from his kisses—and Carter was outside. Because she was confused. Because she was Ben's. Because Carter couldn't in his right mind do this to either of them.

He closed his eyes as a wash of pain took hold of him. He remembered. The purring sounds in her throat when he kissed her. The way she'd rubbed against him, lusty and willing and eager. Her taste—apples, honeyed apples. And the wild, desperate need shining in those heartbreaking brown eyes.

And Carter knew, with every nerve and fiber of his strained, tortured body, Emma had not been thinking of Ben. Just now—*just now*—she'd wanted Carter. It was *him* she'd kissed, *his* name on her lips, it was *him*. Not Ben.

Did she feel something for him? More than lust, more than need?

Christ, at this moment he could be smoothing off that flimsy skirt she wore, licking her breasts, slipping his hand between her legs to discover the pink, wet folds he knew nestled there. He could be stroking her. His face could be buried between her thighs and his mouth in that place where she was hottest. She could be crying out his name as he tongued her sweet, damp pussy into climax and kneaded her perky breasts in hands that had ached to feel them for years.

He could be inside her again. Buried inside Emma's body. A body Ben touched every day. A body whose secrets another man knew and Carter would never, ever know again.

Aww, Christ.

After tonight, Carter doubted he'd be able to even look at her. It had always been difficult. The sight of her dainty, oval-shaped face, those clear big eyes and that pert little nose felt like a chest blow. But now it would be worse. Now he would remember her mouth, her body, her smell, and the fact that she *wanted* him so bad.

"Damn."

He started for his truck, wondering what to do with Ben. He had to force her to let go of him, prove to her the man she was living with was not the man she wanted him to be.

I'll take care of Ben, he'd told her.

He not only wanted to do it for *her*. He wanted to do it for the man who'd once been Carter's friend. If he was somewhere inside this new Frankenstein, he must be very unhappy.

Outside, the chilling wind bit at his fevered skin. He tucked his hands into his jeans and hunched forward as he went around his truck.

He pulled the car door open and dropped onto his seat as he slammed it shut, fisting his hands on the steering wheel. His muscles hurt. His dick hurt. His balls hurt. He felt like *shit*.

But he'd done the right thing.

He nodded to himself. Yeah, he'd done right by her.

He always did. Dependable, easy guy Carter. That was him.

A fucking idiot!

Gritting his teeth, he turned on the ignition and was pulling onto the street when his cell phone rang, no weird tune for him, just a regular bell. One hand on the wheel, he flipped it open. "Yeah?"

"Boss? Is Emma with you?"

Wooly's voice on the other end. He forced himself to relax and sighed. "I just dropped her home, Wooly."

"Everyone wants to talk to her."

An image of her when he left, on the bed with that look of need, made his gut twist painfully inside him. "Yeah, well, she's pretty tired. Probably taking a bath." *And I couldn't keep my eyes off her, couldn't keep my hands off her, was a second away from tearing her clothes off and sinking my hard dick into her, right into warm, pliant Emma.*

Wooly's chuckle rolled on the other end of the line. "Damn, the whole bar's in a roil. Everyone wants a look at Ben, but we have no idea where he went off to either."

"Yeah? You hear about him and you immediately let me know, a'right?"

Carter slammed on the brakes when a shadow out in the road caught his attention. He blinked into the darkened street, swearing he just saw a bald-headed man by the lamppost.

Shaking his head, Carter snapped the phone shut and tossed it onto the front seat, his eyes back on the road. And Heidi's words danced in his head, teasing, tantalizing. *She doesn't believe she's in the right man's arms.*

He'd been sure Heidi would start laughing, but one look at the princess's flushed face as she danced with Ben had confirmed it was no joke.

Carter's entire evening had been centered on that moment.

The moment his stunned mind registered that Emma—Emma from his thoughts, Emma from his dreams, Emma from the pit of his very stupid heart—wanted him. Him. *Above Ben.*

He had no clue how Heidi had expected him to react—but he'd battled with his hands all night to keep from reaching out and grabbing Emma, kissing her, just . . . holding her like Ben did.

He'd had to remind himself, *tell* himself . . .

It was a game.

A game Ben was playing, with Carter and Emma as the pawns.

A game Carter was now fucking anxious to win.

She'll never choose you over me. . . .

Well, big news, buddy: you're not you.

He'd fight the motherfucking impostor for her. Expose him for the fraud he was.

He'd been friends with Ben Newcastle once. Out of that friendship, he'd try to do things quietly.

Where the fuck are you, Ben Newcastle?

You better run for cover when I find you.

He blinked when the vision of a bald man leaning against a lamppost flashed before his eyes again. Only this time, he was very clearly pointing to the south.

Chapter Twelve

$\sim$

Damn her.

         That greedy little girl. That sweet, curious little girl. She'd always been taking things that didn't belong to her. Stealing kisses from sixteen-year-olds . . .

Ben tore down the highway in Emma's Civic, plunging through the thick fog like a bulldozer. Carter didn't belong to her, Ben did.

His hands clenched on the steering wheel, and it occurred to him he could die again, driving like this, with his mind in a tumult like this. There could be a truck in the next lane, and it could pop a tire and tip again.

Ha.

Ha. Ha. HA.

Die again? When things were unresolved between him and Emma? When he would be leaving his girl to another man?

Carter was a joke to all Texan ranchers. Born a rancher,

now he owned a bar and knew cow shit about . . . well, cow shit. Never mind Ben used to admire his honesty, how he'd loved joking around with him, his sense of humor. Bastard had betrayed him.

He would not take the thing Ben most adored.

Life had been a fucking bitch to him. He wasn't supposed to die young, dammit. He was supposed to save people, be a husband to Emma. A father. Now he'd get his life back on track. Emma had loved him before, more than anything, and she would love him again. *She'd love him again.*

God, she'd looked so vulnerable in his arms just now, wanting to know him again. He didn't even know himself! Then the look on her face when she'd glanced across the bar at Carter. Jealousy stormed through him as he remembered, eating him inside.

Because now he knew.

He knew that a man had captured her attention. He knew that Carter wasn't just pining for her—*she* was pining for Carter. Had been too busy mourning Ben before to even realize it!

All that time he'd been lingering, looking at her, trying to watch over her, she'd been leaning on Carter. And she'd been falling.

To think of the ways they'd been touching each other, wanting each other, like Emma had once only wanted Ben. To think of losing her just when he'd returned—when he'd done what he had to for another chance.

Damn you, Emma, you're falling in love with him.

But not for long.

What Ben was about to do would change the rules. It

would change everything. And, Emma, oh, baby, you'll never love anyone else but Benjamin Newcastle.

He pressed the pedal deeper, gritting his teeth, and then screeched to a halt at the dead end alley only feet away from the witch's ramshackle place.

He stormed into the grim house and found her sitting at a small square dinner table, the woman's dirty tresses covering one of her beady eyes as she looked up.

"Benny!" she cried. "We were just having tea."

Ben glowered from the door, eyeing the three empty places at the table and wondering if there were ghosts there. Besides him, of course. Ghosts craving life. Craving a miracle. Maybe the poor bastards were better off dead.

"I need to talk to you," he said, and stormed into the next room where she kept her weird ritual possessions, certain that she would follow.

She did.

"I need your help. I need something. Something to remind her . . ." His chest closed. God, why? Why couldn't things be as they were before? Why couldn't he find peace anymore? "Something to make her love me—only me."

"Trouble in paradise, Benny?" she asked, patting his cheek with a prunelike hand that seemed to be oozing some kind of goo. "You know I need only one man, and you'd be more than I could have possibly asked for."

He caught her wrist before she could touch his lips and lowered it. "Dammit, I love her. I need her." He felt wounded, lonely, and betrayed, and he'd thought Emma would make it better. But right now, she was only making it worse. *Glancing longingly at Carter . . .*

"A love potion, eh?" The witch hummed a tune as she shuffled to her pot, lit up the fire, and began preparing a brew. She was humming . . . "Humpty Dumpty"?

Humpty Dumpty sat on the wall. . . .

Humpty Dumpty had a great fall. . . .

And all the king's horses and all the king's men . . .

Couldn't put Humpty together again.

After the last line her words became alien, her language shifted to Latin? Spanish? He had no clue as to what she was saying. She hissed like a she-cat, spitting with every passionate word, moving round and round like a twister. Ben peered into the eye of that twister; watched her add liquids and potions from the shelves, then patiently eyed the carcasses hanging above while the pot boiled as her chant reached a crescendo.

"Now . . ." Dipping a spoon into the grimy pool simmering in the pot, she poured the liquid into two vials and corked them shut. "It's a bit tricky. Usually drinking love potions in a waxing moon will ensure success, but there's no waxing moon soon and I sense your urgency, Benny boy. So—I made two."

"Two," he repeated, taking the vials in his hand and eyeing the bubbling liquid.

"You are to give the potion to the person you wish to attract, and to make it foolproof, you must drink one for yourself—to render yourself more attractive."

He nodded, feeling confident. With this, Emma wouldn't want Carter ever again, wouldn't so much as look at him *longingly* ever again.

She'd forget about Carter.

She'd forget everything but the good parts of her and Ben's lives, and what they could have together. Ben could be a doctor again. They could have a family.

And Carter . . .

The hag rubbed her hands in glee. "As for payment, now." Her eyes sparkled with relish.

"Payment. Right. I've been remiss. What do you want?"

She grinned a big, sickly grin. "Didn't figure you for a pinchpenny, Benny. Why did you stiffen?"

"I didn't. I asked what do you want?"

"You could always give those potions back if you're not prepared to pay."

He rammed the vials into his pants pocket. "These are mine. Name your price, witch."

"Just a kiss, Benny. And make it a good one."

Ben was sure he'd heard wrong, but when she drew closer with her white cracked lips puckered, he knew with horrifying certainty that she meant what she said.

Disbelief and disgust warred for victory inside him. "A kiss? You expect me to kiss you for this?"

Her good eye narrowed sharply. "For giving you back the love of your life? I expect more."

Ben forced himself to nod, but he could feel the muscles in his face already forming a grimace when she puckered her lips again. God, how old was she? Like a thousand and one?

"Kiss me, Benny. Real hard, boy; I'm not as fragile as I look."

Fragile? Fuck, she looked decayed. The thought of putting his mouth, the mouth he loved Emma with, even an inch away from the witch's made him want to retch. But no.

He needed this witch, and he'd pay what she asked for. He'd gotten worse bargains than this. *Bring her a husband.* . . .

Gritting his teeth, he cupped the back of her head and bent his own, setting his lips on hers.

He held his breath. Hated every blasted second of it. The hag seemed eager to feel his lips on hers, moving her mouth a little, trying to give him tongue, but he closed his lips so tight she couldn't enter.

She screeched, like he'd bitten her or something. Reeling back, she smashed his chest and cursed him, spitting daggers at him. "You!" Her eyes went wild. "You're selfish and mean! Until you learn to put others first like you used to, you'll never be free. Never!"

Ben stalked angrily to the door, close to vomiting.

The night's cool wind blasted his face when he stormed outside and slammed the door behind him without a backward glance. He cleaned his mouth with an angry swipe of his hand. She tasted like . . . frogs. Fuck!

He spit on the ground. Behind him, the witch pulled open a cracked window. Her voice rang out across the whole neighborhood, alerting everyone within a mile. "If you don't bring my husband by the full moon, you'll get the kiss of death and find yourself back in your grave for good, you hear me? Where you belong! One kiss and *you're gone!*"

"Yeah, yeah, good evening to you, too!"

"That was practice, Benny boy! You either bring me a man that gives me what I need, or *my next kiss will send you back to the dead*—do you hear me? *You selfish, motherless corpse, you better bring me a real man next!*"

Without turning back, Ben lifted his arm and elegantly

gave her the finger, pleased that she said no more. Bitch! Things scuttled in the darkness as though running away from that disgusting old witch—or were they scuttling from him? Ben ducked into the shadows and followed the sounds into the one-way alley where he'd parked.

His grave. The thought of returning made his stomach roil, his blood chill in his veins. *Must bring Carter to the witch . . .*

He glanced above, the moon three-quarters full, and it looked like a blessing to him. By the time he saw that white, perfect circle in the sky, it would be the beginning of his new life. A life with no Carter.

Frowning at the thought of him, he was too busy working out the mechanics of bringing the cowboy to her that he didn't see the truck—

Until it slammed right into him.

Carter plowed him down with his F150 and whooped when Big Bad Ben crashed against the asphalt. Screeching to a halt, he jumped out of the truck, watching in disbelief as the man started to stand—stand like he hadn't just had an eight-thousand-pound truck trample him. For a moment he thought his eyes were shitting him. "I knew it, Holy Mama, I knew it!"

The bastard turned.

They saw each other.

Carter could almost see the smoke coming out of Ben's ears as he stomped forward. "You son of a bitch! Are you trying to kill me?"

"Ha! You're *already* dead," Carter spat, and tightened his fists at his sides, his thighs quivering from the rage. He felt like some kind of starved mutt, illegally trained for dog-fights. They fought to the death, those dogs did. Even then he was sure those mutts had more scruples than Ben did.

"Don't know what the hell you are," he gritted, "but you ain't Ben, you asshole! You're some kind of immortal freak right out of a zombie movie—and a bad one with shitty reviews."

With a roar of anger, Ben lunged, and they tackled each other to the ground, struggling. Grunting and punching, they rolled until they slammed against a crumbling brick wall.

Dust trickled down Ben's head as he grabbed Carter and pinned him down. "Stay away from Emma."

Carter rolled him onto his back and introduced his knuckles to Ben's jaw. One. Two. Three times. Watching his head fly. "Go back to where you came from, zombie."

Fingers clamped around his throat and started squeezing his windpipe, thumbs biting into his trachea. "You. Leave. Her. Alone."

Choking, he dredged up the energy to ram his knee into Ben's groin. He heard his *woof,* shoved him aside, and jumped to his feet, panting in fury. "Not very ballsy now, eh!"

"*You're going to pay for this tenfold,*" Ben barked, but the big man was hunched down, hands between his legs.

His facial features didn't even look human anymore—there was nothing benevolent there, not a vulnerable hair on his fucked-up head, and Carter doubted that his face muscles could produce anything other than that sick, murderous sneer.

His heart thundered with rage and a rush of adrenaline

pumped through his veins, tensing the muscles of his legs while every cell in his body seemed to command: protect protect protect.

Show Emma he's not the one.

A sudden yearning to be with her—in love, in lust, and in peace—pierced him like an ax. "We're going to go back home, you and I," Carter warned, his voice vehement, authoritative as he held out his index finger. "And we're going to ask her who she wants to be with once and for all. And then you're going to pack your bag and go back to hell, you fucking zombie."

Ben's grimace of pain morphed into an expression of concern. In a rush, his hand felt one of his pockets anxiously, and as though satisfied with the contents, he raised his eyes to Carter, his face black with determination. "All right! All right, let's do this!" He straightened with effort, pulling in great gusts of air. "But if she picks me, give me your word you'll do what I ask of you. You owe me, after all. . . . You *owe me*, Bates."

"Yeah yeah yeah," Carter said grumpily, but he nodded.

The bastard had gone at him with his truck! What the hell for? Intent on proving that Ben was some kind of immortal demon? Or intent on killing him?

You're the one who needs to make your goddamned will and testament, backstabber!

Ben had felt the darkness spread through him, engulf him so powerfully his fists had ached to kill him. End

Carter's miserable life once and for all. Ben could kill him with three punches, with an invisible hand, but he'd stopped himself with ruthless self-discipline. *If you kill him, you have no one to take to the witch, and you die.*

He was aware of his strength.

Of things dying when he touched them.

Those nights spent sweating and without sexual release, he'd fantasized of taking Emma, but the dreams always turned into a nightmare. . . . His touch made her breath fade. . . . Her heart halted in his hand. . . . Her last gasp was his name, the name of her murderer. . . .

No. Never! He'd be a normal man again, he'd be loved and admired again.

Now—with his unnatural speed and strength—he ran for Emma. Determined to get there before Carter did. Horny to fuck her. To make her his entirely—*damn her.*

By the time Carter ignited his stupid truck Ben would be a tenth of the way home. Minutes later, he stormed inside, using his powers to lock the windows and doors behind him, trapping Emma inside with him. By the time Carter arrived, he and Emma would have taken the drink!

He tore up the stairs, and found her sitting at the desk, staring bleakly at his books.

"I overreacted at the bar and I'm sorry," he said, inhaling sharply and willing his breath to calm.

He'd immediately burst out with an apology because he knew her. He knew she'd give him crap about leaving her at the bar. About taking the car, about acting like a jealous idiot. And so he'd beat her to the punch and denied her her little rant. Determined, he pulled her up against him and covered her lips with his. But her mouth was unresponsive, immobile, and a dagger of pain sliced through him.

"Come, darling," he coaxed. "I want to toast with you."

With an angry frown and a wary expression, she followed him down the stairs. She wanted to mope? She could mope after she drank—except then she'd be begging for him to take her and love her and pamper her like before.

"Ben, this isn't work—" she began.

"I know we have to talk, darling. First things first."

He poured the vials into two glasses. Heard banging on the door. *Bang bang bang!* Emma, startled, glanced toward the door as Ben gallantly poured them something to drink. Something magical, which would drive her wild with lust for Ben and Ben alone.

He smiled at the tantalizing thought. "Don't open," he commanded when she made to.

She paused, eyes wide as he handed her a small half-filled champagne glass, but Carter continued pounding like a madman outside.

"Emma!" Carter barked.

With a huff of annoyance directed at Ben like *he* was the one pounding at the door, Emma went to unlock the door, carrying her flute with her. Ben went after her, grabbed her, kissed her again, kissed her to piss Carter off. When he tore his lips off hers, he glanced with satisfaction past her shoulders at the pissed man on the porch and said, "Well, well, look who's come to visit. It's Carter, honey."

Carter stepped inside, his eyes riveted on Emma. "Whatever you do, don't drink it."

. . .

Desire reverberated in her heart when she found Carter's broad frame covering the doorway.

Emma breathed unsteadily; poor Carter looked beat up. She took in the glossy, tousled, sun-streaked hair. The piercing blue eyes under two brutal slashes for eyebrows, holding her gaze. The navy shirt stretched taut around broad, square shoulders, and the jeans that were tight on his muscled thighs and bunched around his ankles. Blood streaked along the corner of his lips. And the finality in his stance, the warning in his gaze, seemed to slowly sink into her brain and paralyzed her.

For a moment, Ben stared too. At her. As though whatever he saw in her eyes made him want to kill a dog or something.

Carter stalked toward her with pantherlike grace. "Don't drink it, Emma."

With a nearly imperceptible move of his hand, Ben slammed the front door behind Carter. "Now you're not leaving." His lethal whisper sent a prick of unease down her spine.

"Emma, that thing is poisoned or some shit. You should've seen the alley I found him in. Don't drink it, baby."

With a hip propped against the back of a couch in a nonchalant pose, Ben threw his head back and released a bark of laughter. He lifted the glass in a mock toast. "I assure you, there's no poison in this drink." His eyes brimmed with challenge, and he tipped the glass to his smiling lips and drank, swiftly draining it.

Puzzled, Emma glanced down at the strange, murky

liquid. What was it? It smelled like . . . She lifted it to sniff the pungent scent but Carter yanked it from her grasp and downed it in one gulp.

"Carter!" she gasped, her hand still raised—her grasp tingling empty.

Ben's expression turned to pure rage. "Jesus Christ fuck, man!" he thundered.

Emma blinked, staring at Carter, afraid that he'd change right before her eyes, change like Ben had. The floor reeled under her feet as she tried to stay calm. Where were these fears coming from? Had Ben really been changed or was he hiding somewhere underneath all that rage? What if the drink did have something in it? "Carter, are you all right? I wasn't going to drink it!" she said in disbelief.

"Why in the hell did you drink that, you *idiot*?"

"My god, what's going on?" Emma stepped in between the men, holding them back with both arms. "What's gotten into you two?"

Ben poked a blunt finger into her ribs and growled, "You."

Carter seized the palm she'd planted on his chest and covered it with his own, squeezing. "Emma, you and I are leaving. Right now."

But Emma didn't move, felt like she was standing before a fork in the road, a huge fork, and she was a stupid little girl without the balls or the courage to choose. A stupid little girl who wrongly felt a little thrill when two boys argued over her.

"You want Emma?" Ben said. "She's going to have to tell me to leave her the hell alone—and we both know she won't do that."

Oh, was she so predictable?

But no. Carter seemed to think more of her, to *expect* more of her. His eyes glimmered on her face. He stretched out his other hand, palm up, and her fingers tingled with the urge to take it. To squeeze it. "Emma, come with me," he whispered, his voice soft but commanding.

"*Guys*," Emma said breathlessly, regarding one man, then the other, feeling a wicked heat bubbling in her veins. They were fighting for her, they wanted her, and it made her feel special, beautiful, hot. God, this was all so convoluted and mixed up. "Stop! Ben, Carter—we were *best friends*. Maybe, if we played nice for just a mom—"

"No," Carter said at the same moment Ben said, "All right."

Emma cocked her eyebrow at Carter, then at Ben. "Maybe you two would like to iron out your issues?"

She headed toward the front door, intending to wait outside, but Ben caught and spun her around, his voice suddenly so businesslike and doctorly it seemed to brook no argument.

"Hold up. You're not leaving, darling. We're going to calm down, and go upstairs, and settle things *my* way. In bed."

She blinked, then rolled her eyes. "Stop using sex to get your way, Ben." But her vagina disagreed, felt hot and clenched wetly at the prospect of feeling them again. One last time, the three of them . . .

Ben's grin was lethal as he took her by the arm and led her up the stairs. "Carter's coming too. The only way we're settling our issues is right in this bedroom." He paused by the door before pushing it open. "Get into bed, Emma, this very second."

Okay, this was not good.

Sex never resolved anything, did it?

Look at where they were now!

Say no, say no, say no, Emma Wilkins. . . .

But her nipples pricked wantonly. Her cunt continued getting juiced.

"Once, I didn't have a body, love," Ben confided, oozing sexual encouragement. "And guess what I learned? We communicate through these bodies better than with any fucking words. Now get in bed, woman—we want you."

Woman?

Since when did Ben call her *woman*?

The memory of their time together in this very same bedroom made her mouth water and her pulse leap, but she stood her ground. "No, Ben."

"Hate agreeing with ole Frankenstein here, but he's right, princess."

Carter's slow voice flitted through her. He wanted this?

A fever, wicked and hot, began to pump through her bloodstream as she looked into his face. Gorgeous hardboned face, chiseled to perfection, looking at her with those eyes. He nodded somberly. Her pulse hitched even higher.

He wanted this to happen.

She should say no. Definitely no. But a full, inflamed sensation built between her thighs. And she didn't. She couldn't.

A sense of inevitability overcame her, the impending decision she had to make looming ahead, the trying to right her feelings when they were all over the place demanding her attention—but lust washed over like a tide, taking away her castles in the sand. All that mattered now was . . .

feeling. Desire. One last time . . . maybe one last time . . . with one of them.

The air felt static as she nervously wandered into the bedroom, backing away as the men moved toward her with wicked purpose. Both looked . . . lustful. Hungry.

Oh, god, the instant she'd entered, the decision had been made.

She waited, anticipating, unsure, and then the back of her knees hit the bed and her legs gave. Her hands clenched on the comforter. "What are you going to do?" she asked in a little voice.

Ben's voice was dangerously, threateningly direct as he crossed the room and produced a blindfold from the nightstand. "You're going to play with us. And you're going to make a decision. Tonight."

Her eyes flew to Carter's narrowed blue ones. His stare struck her like an electric bolt. She felt like she had to say something to him, make him know the things he made her feel, but she couldn't.

His lazy smile stretched unexpectedly—animal-like, determined, showing a flash of strong teeth. He wanted this, too? Of course he did. They were both too . . . alpha. Couldn't be in the same room without the air crackling with their warring energies.

Her heart pounded as Ben approached. "Now you see Carter," Ben murmured as a flash of red slid around her eyes, and then she was engulfed in cool, silky twilight. "And now you don't." She panted in shock, groping at her side for Ben while her stunned eyes adjusted to the darkness. "Someone should take a hand to you two boys," she breathed. Like she was calm and normal. Like something deep in her body wasn't pulsing. Moistening.

He chuckled, cupped her hips as he buzzed his lips up her neck. "Shut up and feel . . ." he purred, and gently pulled off her sleep shirt. Her breasts spilled out, and the blood rushed to the heavy globes, puckering her nipples. "Now tell me who's touching you. We're going to determine who pleases you most. Who you instinctively react to. Carter and I want to know, don't we, Bates?"

Carter's angry drawl made her thighs water. "That's right, pumpkin. Tonight's the night." Did he just step closer? "It's either Ben"—his voice came from above her head, its timbre dropped—"or it's me."

She shuddered.

She knew Ben wanted control, felt secure if things happened on his own terms. But in this instant she craved some control, too. If she gave herself over to them she was afraid she would shatter. This wasn't a decision for her body to make, whether she preferred one man above another. And yet at the moment her body ruled her senses, every inch of her preparing for physical delight—her lungs working harder, her heart pumping faster, her flesh getting hotter.

Her body relished the prospect of being touched while her mind playfully pointed out that she could teach them a lesson. She could *play them*.

With thighs that felt like putty, she sat there and heard the rustle of clothing and then she gasped when the pad of a thumb whisked over her puckered nipple. Lean, whipcord lean and muscled. Carter. Oh, *yes*. She felt the teeth behind his moving lips against her neck, wanted to weep in delight when his strong, supple tongue swirled a path up her neck. God, Carter was touching her. She could hear both his and Ben's breaths beside her own, feel their hot bodies as they flanked hers.

Need pulsed through her in waves, making her struggle to remain focused. A thumb and forefinger seized a nipple and began to massage with sharp little pinches that shot a jolt of pleasure straight to her warmed-up cunt. Arousal rushed through her in a tidal wave.

"Who's touching you?" It was Ben asking, but ooh, it was Carter touching.

"Ben . . ." she lied, playing her own game and not the men's, having her own little fun, not yet in total helpless abandon, not until *they* were, too.

The movement stopped.

And Ben, disgruntled, grumbled, "Let's try this again, hmm."

She nodded dazedly. "Let's."

"Come here, Em, up on the bed."

He swept her up and settled her on the cool sheets, and she was keenly aware of being seen even if she couldn't see. She bit her lip and lay back against a plush pillow when nothing happened. Then a finger touched the hollow at the base of her throat and slid between her breasts, up one full globe, to trace the areola, rise up to the bead, then back to circle again. Her stomach heaved.

"Tell me who touches you now."

Ben. Oh, yes, Ben. He knew just where, just how. And

she whispered, unconsciously parting her legs and bringing her hand to her stomach, ready to touch her clit in case neither of the men did. "Carter."

There was a pause. A charged silence.

Then a hand came to cover her breast, calloused but gentle as he kneaded. Her nipple stabbed into his palm and she tossed her head back slightly, exposing the long curve of her neck. Carter's touch felt divine, and she would have recognized those gentle, hot hands on her breasts anytime, but still she gasped, "Ben."

She almost bit the inside of her cheek when the men stilled. Their haggard breaths came stronger now, their combined scents filling her nostrils.

"One more time, darling," Ben whispered. Still hoping she would get it right, she supposed. And this little power over them was heady. Made her pussy tingle for a touch.

The caresses went lower and a hand dipped to probe the wet cleft between her thighs. She felt a finger stroke her clit, circle it lightly, then slide down the folds to ease into her rippling sheath. Her wall was snug around each deep, tantalizing slide. Oh, Ben. Ben. Her body welcomed him, rocking as she mewed. Her body recognized his, even if her mind sometimes did not recognize this strange, possessive new man. A heavy awareness of him not being that man she'd loved settled over her like a cloud. Who was he?

A second finger joined the first, spreading her wider, twisting in until she was undulating in ecstasy. "Carter," she gasped. "It's Carter."

A silence. Then a hiss of a whisper in her ear. "Are you trying to fuck with my head, Emma? 'Cause it's working."

"What?" she gasped.

"You know exactly who's touching you."

"Do I?"

"Tell me now!" Ben commanded.

A large, rigid body, strong and muscled and scorching, blanketed her own. A bullet of heat rushed down her blood when a fat, warm mouth opened around the throbbing tip of one breast. She bucked up, her hands flying around a taut back, fingertips sinking into the muscles as she was suckled.

A long cock was brushing up her thigh, and she knew it was Carter's. So incredibly broad and ready to fuck her and she was so juiced up. His mouth swallowed nearly her entire breast, he was so hungry. The stimulation of his mouth was almost too much for her to stand, her muscles stiffening at the sensations pulsing through her, clenching her pussy with need. She clawed at his arms and undulated, a bit to torture him and a bit to torture Ben, a bit to torture herself as well as she gasped, "Ben."

Silence fell, but Carter did not still, as though Carter did not care whether she knew it was him; all he wanted was to suck her nipple. She closed her eyes, delirious at the tugging suction of his mouth.

"Try again, baby."

Oh, Ben, my poor tortured Ben, she thought as she moved, ran her hands up Carter's hot skin, calling, "Ben."

Carter's torso was silky smooth, damp now against hers, the muscles trembling with restraint and taut against her fingertips. On impulse she surged up and buried her lips in his shoulder, licking his sweat.

There was a second when he didn't move; then his hands

gripped her hips and aligned that enormous penis against her entrance.

Her eyes flew wide open though they saw nothing but shadows, and her spine arched as he thrust inside. *Yes!*

Ben yanked the sash from her face. She was surrounded by Carter's heat, and he was gazing down at her with the hottest eyes ever. One look at him and she could tell he wasn't much for games—wanted her to decide. Decide now. And be with him forever.

Ben's voice in her ear was lush and erotically dangerous. "Does that look like me to you, Emma?" he growled, and demanded, "Does that *feel* like me to you, darling? Get the fuck off her, Carter. We're just starting."

"Not a chance in hell." He rolled away and dragged her with him, shifting her to her side. His body spooned hers, his cock a delicious pulsation against the fissure of her ass as his big hands stroked the curves of her breasts. She was shaking in his arms.

Angry, Ben sat before her and dragged her torso against his lap, his penis so wet it leaked drop after drop mere inches from her face. He was also naked.

"Stop fucking around, Em."

She let go a breath. "Then stop toying with me."

He bent his head and buzzed her ear with his nose. "Whose touch makes you burn most?" he demanded.

This game may have started with another purpose, but she could feel their goals shifting as their arousal escalated. They wanted release, they wanted sex. Carter—behind her, so hot. Hot lips, hot hands, hot skin. She rolled her hips against him and whimpered when an overwhelming fever for him broke across her flesh. "Carter, fuck me."

Carter groaned against her nape, then spread her hair aside and kissed her. "So hot for you, pumpkin."

"Fuck me there."

"You want me to fuck you here, baby?" He teased her anus with the crown of his erection.

"Yes."

He released a guttural sound, as though undone. "Then ask for it, baby."

"Do you want to fuck me? Both of you, together?"

Ben's eyes flashed at her request, and again she saw the animal there, the lurking beast, excited and jealous. He lay down on his side before her, grabbed the base of his shaft, and pushed it into her pussy without preamble. She gasped.

Carter ran his hand up her chest, feeling the generous weight of her breasts. His cock remained a torment against the rosette of her ass—so close, but still not inside, still making her roll her hips in need. "Carter . . ."

His cock stroked up and down the small fissure and her womb clenched tight around Ben's sliding shaft as he mercilessly pounded her pussy. She wanted Carter. Inside her. Pushing her over the edge, making her dizzy with desire. "Please give it to me."

"All right, baby. I'm going to give you this."

He hitched closer with an arm across her back, pitching his hips to penetrate.

Ben watched her face as Carter opened her to his possession, and Emma marveled how eyes so black could grow even blacker; they homed in on her gasp like he'd never heard something so wicked.

"Watching him fuck you makes my cock ache." Grabbing her waist, he ducked his head and bit on her breast so the pebble elongated even more. "You're a wanton and it drives me *wild*. I want to kill him and then I want to force him to fuck you harder."

She moaned and said, "Harder, Carter."

Ben released her abruptly, pulled out of her body—so that only Carter was taking her, filling her so completely she felt swelled and ready to pop—and then Ben knelt on the bed. "Do you crave more cock, Emma?" He used a fist to pull on his own cock. "Do you crave it on your tongue?"

"Yes."

He cupped his balls in his hands and weighed them, showing her, showing her how he played with them. "I'm going to fuck your mouth now. Then I'm going to fuck it *again*."

Emma could hardly see, her eyes felt weighted. Ben never used to speak that way to her, the way he now did. It made her mind rebel, but it made her body clench here, tighten there.

She undulated in delight as Carter continued slowly pumping her from behind, and god, the sounds he made sent her galloping toward the peak. His warmth swirled around her, making her pliant. She could feel his teeth behind his lips as he nuzzled her nape, went over to tease her earlobe.

She opened her mouth wide, hungry, starved, as Ben brought his penis closer. "Feed it to me."

He peered down into her face with blazing eyes and

teased her with the tip first, brushing the bloated, plum-shaped crown against her lips.

Salt. Man. Need.

She tasted all of that on his skin. Opening wider, she drew him in, determined to run her tongue down every hot firm inch of him.

Ben reached beneath and pawed her breast. He fondled, pushed the breast up and down in his hand, rubbing the nipple in soft, languorous circles. She loved it, loved this touch—recognized some part of it. In her mind—he was her old Ben. In the midst of the firestorm, it was easy to convince herself that he was.

He whispered sexy, dirty words to her, and her heart melted with each. *Suck it, eat it, take it, take me, fuck me, eat me,* he said.

Shivering in ecstasy, her hips greedily tilted back against Carter's. *Oh, yes, yes, deeper.* Her head slid back and forth as she gobbled Ben up, biting gently at the tip of his cock until he grabbed the back of her head and pulled, making her eat more.

The men's combined sexual scents, the heady musk, flowed through her body until her every breath, every inhale, was full of them.

Goose bumps pricked across her skin when Carter slid a hand around her waist and found the bud of flesh between her legs. He gave it a pass with his thumb, and white-hot pleasure knifed through her.

She wanted to say their names, tell them how good it was, but instead she showed them how she felt with her hips, her mouth. She took every inch that Carter gave her while her tongue swiped greedily around Ben—she enjoyed suck-ing his cock, tasting him, making him growl.

Carter pinched her clit, then rolled it under the pad of his thumb in such an expert, soul-wrenching way her legs trembled as excitement swept through her, setting her bones on fire.

Oh, god! She convulsed with a keening cry. "Yeah, baby, yeah," Carter moaned against her neck. Shudders jolted through his body as her ass clamped and clenched around him, and she could feel the exact moment his warmth shot deep inside her—she almost wept.

With one last grunt, one last hard, deep plunge, Ben held her head pinned between his hands and shouted in pleasure as he flooded her.

Ben collapsed on the bed, his cock twitching hungrily as he pulled out of her wet, hot mouth. Incredible, that after a passionate session like this one, he still wanted more, his cock hard as a pole. In fact, dammit, just one glimpse at a sweaty, sated Carter and his balls began filling up with cum again. He still wanted to fuck . . . except now he wanted to ram his hard dick into the cowboy's mouth. His ass. His fucking big hand. Damn him!

Their eyes met over the top of Emma's head as she snug-gled between them, sated and relaxed as a cat after a meal. Ben's blood pooled in his groin and his mouth watered with unexpected hunger to taste Carter's dick. He'd taste like Emma, and . . . different than anything he'd ever tasted before. *Damn his fucking hide for screwing up my plan like this!*

As though reading his thoughts, Carter's gaze slitted in warning, and his eyes glimmered menacingly as he pulled

Emma closer to him and allowed her to snuggle against his side.

Son of a bitch. He thought he'd won already, thought he could take what rightfully belonged to Ben.

Ben glared at him, simmering with barely repressed anger and desire. God, he would give this man a lesson. He would teach him not to mess with Ben's property, with Ben's things, with Emma, with his damned *drink*.

He was going to fuck the guy six ways till Sunday. He was going to freaking eat him until there was no drop of cum left in his tall lean body and he was going to make him like it, and then he was going to get rid of him for good.

And there was nothing, no power on this earth, that would stop him.

Chapter Thirteen

$\mathcal{I}$

Hours later, Carter groaned as he woke aroused in a sweet-smelling bed, the smooth, long steel of his shaft sliding inside a hot, tight grip. He opened his eyes, but instead of Emma's brown ones gazing into his, he saw a pair of smoldering black ones.

Carter went utterly still. "Ben."

"It's me, Bates. And I've got you by the balls. No pun intended."

Gritting his teeth, Carter struggled to keep his hips from rolling, from pushing his cock deeper into that warm fist. No! Ben was a man, dammit. What the cow fuck was this? He fisted the sheets under his fingers as a drop of moisture leaked out of the tip of his slit. "What the hell's gotten into you?" he demanded.

Ben tightened his hold, and a shot of pleasure bolted through Carter's system. He shut his eyes, groaning in misery.

"In my hell, Carter, you were Lucifer," Ben said irritably, and continued stroking. Stroking in a way that made a man want to fuck another man. Hell, want to fuck *anything*.

"What was in it, bastard!"

Ben surveyed the drop of cum on the tip of his cock and his eyes glimmered with hunger. "What was in what?"

"In the drink!"

Ben withdrew his hand and turned to a sleeping Emma. He brushed her hair back, kissed her lips, making Carter's chest constrict with rage and jealousy; then he glanced back at him. "I don't know—magic. Something to make her love me."

The torment in his eyes pulled at Carter's compassion, while the damned poison made him burn. The fever. The need. "She loved you," Carter whispered so as not to wake her. He stroked the back of a finger along the soft curve of her cheek. "But that's over. What she feels for you now isn't love. She just can't keep her giving nature from embracing a troubled butthead like yourself."

Ben snorted in disbelief, then leapt to his feet and, naked, shouldered his way out into the hall. Carter plunged into his jeans and followed, wincing when his cock grazed the inside of his fly. Fuck!

He found Ben downstairs, in the living room, hands braced on the window as he labored to breathe. His firm muscles glowed in the moonlight that filtered in, highlighting his back, his legs, his ass. His scars screamed of unbearable pain. Damn, what had it been like for him? Dying like he had?

Cock pulsing unbearably tight in his jeans, Carter controlled his breaths in an effort to control the humiliating arousal lancing through him.

"Does it wear off?" he gritted when he couldn't control worth a shit.

"What?"

"The damned drink."

Ben was eerily still, his head down in concentration, and all of a sudden the air sent Carter flying across the room and slammed him face-front against the window. He yelled in fury and yanked his head aside so he could spit at Ben's feet—but the pressure increased. The wind was knocked out of him as he was pressed more forcefully against the window, his chest crushed against the cold glass. Ben leapt on him from behind and put his hard dick against his rear. "You're so horny you'd let me fuck you, wouldn't you, Bates?" he taunted. "How can you love her when you're so damned hot for me, huh?"

Carter clenched his jaw tight, hauling great pulls of oxygen into his lungs. But already a fever broke across his flesh, and the heat seemed to emanate from his very core. Every inch of his body seemed to scream *wanna fuck wanna fuck wanna fuck.*

Ben was shaking against him, keeping Carter trapped with his unearthly force, his immortal body. Carter loathed him. Loathed that he was aroused by him.

"I used to think I deserved her," Ben murmured in his ear. His tongue snaked out to give him a lick.

Carter groaned. Desperate reason attempted to wrestle the arousal, but the heat wouldn't be restrained. With a painful wrench, he tried getting free, his arms bulging as they pushed against a force that kept him pinned, pinned like a fly. He failed. "I used to think I didn't," he strained out.

Ben's long, hard cock ground against his jean-clad ass, sending a lightning bolt through his system. "You put me through hell, Bates," he hissed, "the worst kind of hell. I trusted you like a brother."

Sweat popped across Carter's brow as he fought him once more, but failure forced him back to stillness. His chest jerked at each breath. "Damn, Ben, she needed me. You were gone and I was all she had."

With a haggard, intoxicated sound, Ben scraped Carter's temple with his rough jaw. "But now I'm here. And she still . . ." He cursed and released his unearthly grip, only to slam Carter flatter against the window. "*Wants you!* We're supposed to be soul mates, her and me! She told me so—always."

The breath burned in Carter's lungs. He couldn't unlock his teeth, spoke in a hiss through his clamped jaw. "Maybe she wasn't supposed to be with you her entire life. Maybe you can have . . . more than one soul mate."

"I'm it!"

Ben wrenched Carter's face around at an awkward angle, crushing the left side against the glass. His jaw ached and his cock jerked hungrily. Dammit, *ouch*. "But now you've bartered your soul," he hissed, "so you're not her mate anymore and we both know it."

Ben twisted his head around a fraction more so that an agonizing blade seemed to cut down his neck. "You had to go and take the goddamned drink!" Ben cried. "You've been taking things that belong to me for months, you bastard. Now I'm going to take you!"

He reached around and plunged his hand into Carter's jeans. Hissing when he found him rock-hard, Ben stroked his erection while his hips rocked powerfully against his body. "It's so stiff, it must be for me. Is this for me, you traitor?" he demanded.

A choked sound of pleasure rumbled up Carter's throat when Ben's fingers slipped down to the balls. "I don't give a fuck who it's for, just pull the motherfucker."

Suddenly Ben planted his hands over his dark head and groaned, taking two steps back. "How hard have you fallen for her?" he demanded. "How hard?"

Carter's nuts ached in his jeans as he turned, his arms a shaking mass of muscle at his sides. "You know damned well I fell long before I should have."

His temperature hitched at the sight of Ben's nakedness.

Ben regarded him with sinister black eyes, his cock sliding inside his working fist. "But if you loved her, you wouldn't be so damned hard and hot for me right now, would you? Would you?"

Carter cursed and fell into the couch, shutting his eyes, his cock throbbing. "Son of a bitch," he hissed, and rammed his hand into his jeans and stroked.

Ben took a step. "That's right, you're about to explode just thinking about having my dick in you, aren't you?"

Carter could not stop fisting his aching cock, was rolling his hips, desperate to come. "Damn, it's not you I want."

Carter hissed as his grip tightened around his thick shaft, his strokes taking him higher . . . higher . . . close to the peak. . . . God, what was wrong with him? He couldn't stop watching Ben's hand do the same, work his big fat juicy goddamned cock. "Ahhh, god, go away!" Carter said.

With a low, angry sound, Ben stomped forward, fell on his knees, and Carter watched in horror as his dick disappeared into Ben's mouth. Holy freaking fuck! A wet, hungry tongue attacked his cock, his senses. His blood stirred and his balls squeezed with need. His cock twitched inside that feasting mouth, delighted with the attention. Out of breath, Carter instinctively pitched upward, pumping and pumping for tongue.

"Fuck, get away from me—shit, don't stop," he growled, his fingers biting into the couch leather.

Ben squeezed himself tighter. Carter could see his hand working, fast and sure, pulling at his hard dick, and the sight was so damned erotic he felt his cock jerk, starting to come.

Ahh, fuck. He bucked into that delicious motherfucking mouth and spurted inside, three shots of hot salty cum, and before he knew it he grabbed the back of Ben's head and shot him some more.

Ben's eyes rolled back as a powerful shudder overtook him. His tongue and mouth wildly licked and drank all of Carter's seed while he blew off in his fist, shooting off so powerfully the milk flew and fell over the couch with a splat.

Silence settled for three hammering heartbeats, the air so thick and coarse with their haggard breathing it was obvious that whatever demon had possessed them had not left yet.

"Touch me, you bastard," Ben rasped in the same instant Carter realized both their erections remained stiff as ever. Then in a lightning-fast move, Ben pulled him up against him and pistoned his hips until their hungered groans echoed in the room. "Yeah, man, yeah, feel that? You feel that? Touch it."

Carter clamped his teeth together, stiff against the arousal coursing through him, but a noise of ecstasy whistled through his lips when their cocks—still hard as baseball bats—grazed and their balls bumped, over and over. God, it felt good, felt sick and twisted but so *good*.

"Yeah, cowboy," Ben said in a guttural sound as he reached for the bloated organ between them, the one he'd just sucked but was still not dry, and he started yanking it.

Carter set his fists on his shoulders and wrestled with him, trying to get free, dammit, not wanting any more of this, but Ben shoved him back down on the couch and fell on top of him—a great big weight pinning him down.

"I could fuck you if you turn around. You'd like it so bad, cowboy, so damned bad."

"Son of a bitch," Carter said through gritted teeth, but Ben silenced him—his mouth clamping over his, his tongue thrusting hard.

Fuck.

Holy Jesus fuck.

They were kissing.

Carter wasn't stopping him.

Heck, he couldn't pull back his hungry tongue from wanting to shove its way down Ben's throat.

He didn't know what the hell happened, but before he knew it Ben's cock was sliding fast and needy inside Carter's closed fist, and Carter was getting the hand job of a lifetime.

Yes. Harder! Pull it harder, he thought, heck, maybe even said it aloud.

They moved so violently against the other that they could've been humping like mongrels, fighting and mating at the same time. They came in the space of a minute, first Ben, and then Carter, spurting each other's hands and abdomens as they pumped, and it seemed strange and infuriating and annoying as hell that Ben felt the need to suck on Carter's tongue one last time before he pushed himself away.

Carter sucked his tongue before he retreated, too.

What in the hell?

Quietly, a good foot apart now, Carter limp on the couch, Ben standing, they rearranged themselves, saying nothing. Hell, if Carter had his way, they would never talk of this again.

Ben wiped his mouth with the back of his hand and swiped the couch first, then his creamed stomach with a kitchen rag. "Now it's time to do what you promised," he said, calmer, and yet an unmistakable threat glimmered in his dark eyes. Carter felt dumb as a skeleton and remained just as speechless.

He watched as Ben disappeared upstairs and then reappeared dressed, his hair slicked back, his face washed. "You gave me your word you would do me a favor."

"I'm not leaving her."

"One evening of your time, Bates, and then I won't bother you again." The steely determination in his voice complemented the cold glimmer in his eyes. "You're not afraid of me, are you?" he taunted. "A big bad cowboy like yourself."

"What the hell are you proposing?"

"I'd like to show you where I've been. You do want to know how I came back, don't you?"

"Yeah, I want to know." For Emma's sake. He pushed to his feet and planted his hands on his hips. "I want her. Emma." Her roughly spoken name echoed in the silence. "I plan to prove to her you're not Ben Newcastle," Carter warned.

Only fair to give the man a heads-up. This man could go find a Morticia for himself, Carter didn't care what he did. But it was only fair the bastard knew that, one way or another, Emma was Carter's now.

Ben's smile was all danger as he fished for the car keys at the small bowl by the entrance. "So? You coming? There's someone I'd like you to meet."

Emma woke to find the bed empty. Her body was sore everywhere, every little spot. Groaning in lingering pleasure, she sat up and called, "Carter? Ben?"

No one answered.

She went to the bathroom instead, closing the door behind her. A part of her had hoped they would be gone by the time she woke up, so she could organize her thoughts, while another ached for them to be there. Both of them.

But she knew they couldn't live like this. Them, fighting. Her, feeling torn. She ran the bath water until the steam fogged the mirror nearby and the tub was filled. She slipped into the tub, sighing as the water touched her everywhere she hurt, relaxing her muscles. She closed her eyes, vowing she wouldn't think of him. When her eyes fluttered open, it was to imagine blue eyes watching her, his body leaning against the wall with a look of appraisal and his arms crossed over his chest.

She grabbed the sponge and arched up her chest to run it between her breasts. She moaned aloud, remembering how he'd bathed her. God, she knew what she felt when she saw him. She knew what she felt for Ben and it wasn't like before anymore. Desire. Longing for what they used to have. For the man he would have been. Love, but a different kind now. Tenderness. Pity.

But Carter—he made her want to live again. Be happy again. Laugh. Experiment. Tease.

Let go, Emma.

His words haunted her. Sometimes it felt like only her mind was keeping her from Carter. Sometimes it felt like she loved someone because she thought she should love him, and other times she just loved someone despite everything.

Had she summoned Ben back with her grief and her need? If she had, then tonight had been her farewell to Ben.

God, something had gone awfully wrong, awfully wrong in her life.

How on earth was she going to tell him? To admit that every day with him she realized she didn't need him like she used to. That she didn't trust him like she used to. That she didn't feel their connection anymore. That she just couldn't imagine living the rest of her life with him now.

That she was in love with another man.

Whatever supernatural force had given Ben back his life, it was bubbling with the excitement of victory as he drove deeper into the worst part of town. Carter sat relaxed at his side, not even wary. Ben smiled in satisfaction. *Enjoy your last breaths, traitor.*

"That's the place." He signaled at the ramshackle house where the witch would be waiting. Or would she? He was early . . . a week early . . . but eager to get his new life on track.

It was now or never.

With the same detachment the guy used when surveying movie posters, Carter eyed the decrepit exterior of the house now, taking in the grimy, cracked windows and the rotting door. "You were here last night," was all he said, recognizing the place.

He followed Ben out of the car and slammed the door shut.

"Let's go in, then," Ben said with a nod, politely signaling at the door.

No sooner had Carter charged inside, with Ben at his heels, than a coarse voice ruptured the silence in the house. "Benny! You brought me my husband!"

Carter gazed around the room, oblivious to the fact that they were referring to *him*. Curious as a cat, he circled the room in amused speculation before he suddenly halted, turned, and asked, "Husband?"

Confusion wrinkled the corners of his eyes. Then Ben could see the reality slowly sink into his brain. The truth seemed to wrap around him like ice, freezing him.

Accusation flared in his expression, and with every small, resuscitated cell of his once-dead body, Ben hoped the betrayal was profound. As profoundly painful as all the times Ben had watched him with Emma, watched him touch her, kiss her.

Their stares held, until the enormity of what Ben had done settled on his shoulders like a lead weight, until a cold, condemning anger burned in his friend's blue eyes.

Carter tilted his face up to the ceiling as though praying for patience; then he puffed his cheeks with air, let it out, and faced him again. When he spoke, his voice held censure, but not surprise. "You traded my life for yours. My punishment for wanting your woman."

Ben's eyes blurred from the force of his guilt. His fists trembled at his sides. "I have to do this. Dammit, I want to live my life! Either you take my place and die or I'm dead for good."

The witch, bouncy with delight, circled Carter like the cowboy was a feast for her single open eye. She raked that eye up his butt, along his muscled arms, his broad chest.

Carter indulged her scrutiny, standing motionless with his legs braced apart and his brain working behind that head of his as he stared at Ben. His face remained disturbingly inscrutable.

"What? No argument?" Ben asked.

Carter's attention flicked down to the witch, then gave a quick survey of his surroundings again before returning to her. "Carter Bates, ma'am." He shook her hand.

Ben glared, disgusted that there would be no fight, no reason to hate the bastard, to *hate him* from here to eternity. Fury trampled through his insides. "That's *it?*"

Carter met his gaze, and Ben saw no hint of fear there, no sign of the battle Ben itched to wage on the man. Only determination hardened his jaw, his eyes. "If you're damned sure one of us has to die—well, I ain't no murderer."

Chapter Fourteen

All right, so Ben wanted him dead. No newsflash there. What Carter couldn't figure out was why he had to marry this odd little gremlin. He didn't look like anyone's husband, and the only wife he'd ever imagined puttering around with was . . .

Fuck, she was probably in Ben's arms right now.

"So." He surveyed her in speculation, having never seen a woman like this one. "Just you and me now, huh?"

He lounged back in one of the small creaky chairs and watched the old gal fidget around a big, steaming black casserole. His mind worked overtime as he digested this new development, adding one and one together to get two, and so on. He mainly got down to two wee facts here. 1) Ben had bargained with this ugly little woman. 2) This woman had given Ben a second chance, in exchange for Carter.

He tried to feel indignant about all this, but instead he just felt beat up and blue. And insatiably curious. "I keep wonderin'." He sat forward and propped his elbows on his knees. "Someone like you is just born this way, or did you become a witch later on?"

She stopped stirring, her eye—yellow as a crow's foot—sparking with confusion. "Are you bored, boy?"

Carter felt his lips twitch as he signaled at himself. "Hell, look at me; I'm sitting down on a chair that hardly fits me, abandoned like the runt of the litter. Yeah, lady. I'm bored. Just making chitchat here. Not your first time chatting with a man, is it?"

Her nose colored red, like instead of blushing in the cheeks like everyone else in the world, this little figure blushed in the nose like a reindeer. "I was cursed," she admitted. "I haven't talked with a living being in . . . decades." A hint of pain crept into her voice as she continued to stir. "No one's born like this; you become it. Good choices, bad choices . . ."

"Really now? So what turned you into a witch?"

"A powerful wizard loved me. Centuries ago. And I couldn't . . . reciprocate. He cursed me. The devil embraces all curses and so now I'm his servant."

Carter whistled in slow sympathy. "Bet you wish you'd loved him well and hard now, that wizard," he said.

She surprised him with a smile, a crooked smile that showed a mouthful of cavities, and then she added a nice, rough little cackle. "Never. I'd rather stay like this, I swear."

His thumb scraped across his chin as he pondered her situation. Ben's situation. Carter's situation. A whole lot of fucked-up situations here. "Any way to undo your . . . curse?" He raised a brow. The room was beginning to smell of acid, and rotted food, and rhinoceros shit.

"Sure, boy. There are always ways out of a curse, but if the spell-caster was smart, he'd make it as impossible as possible."

"Really now." He stood and paced the area, hands linked behind his back. "What would the way out of Ben's be? I assume you cursed him?"

"Of course not. I simply made a bargain. Life doesn't come free, you know—there's always a price."

"So he owes you."

She pursed her lips. "He owes me. And he delivered—you." Her scrutiny took in Carter's rumpled head down to his booted toes. "You're special. You're used to sacrificing yourself. Taking care of people."

"You got the wrong man, lady. I'm a real sumfabitch, you know. A sumfabitch."

"Yeah yeah yeah." She studied him. "A handsome son-ofabitch."

Plopping back down on the chair, he propped his boots up on the wobbly three-legged table and stacked his hands behind his head. "Why'd you resuscitate poor ole Ben, anyways?"

"I saved him because there was hope that he could break my curse. He had a good soul; I believed he might not . . . lose it." Her lone good eye sparked in accusation, and then she primly ran her hands along the flowing old dress cling-ing to her small shoulders. "I don't go resuscitating the dead just like that. Many become . . ."

"Evil."

She nodded, displeased, and took up stirring again.

"Corrupt their soul, some shit like that?"

She nodded.

"If your curse is broken, what happens to Ben? The bastard's free as Free Willy?"

She seemed to debate whether to speak; then she continued stirring in a frenzy, her wrinkled forehead carving deeper into a frown. "He'll be free to live a normal life. All it takes is an unselfish act of love. For a man to commit himself to me, and to show me with his kiss."

Carter digested this.

So this ugly little witch was stuck in her own private hell for withholding her love from a man. And the only way out was if another man was as foolish as the wizard who'd loved her and chased after her sallow little bones. Man! It was almost funny.

"Well, I got good news and bad news. I ain't the commitment kind. But as for kissing . . ."

Her eyes widened, and the hope in them pulled at his heartstrings on many levels. Many. Mainly the level of the man that had for years loved a woman, and had hoped that one day, *one*, he'd get this same offer from her. Emma . . . God, what wouldn't he do for her? To make her happy?

"You want to kiss me?" A little squeak from the witch.

"Ain't got nothing better to do." Shifting in his seat and hooking a thumb into his jeans, he shot her one of his most wicked smiles, the one that made his eyes glimmer. "I've always wondered if, with your eyes closed, one woman's just as good as the next."

"They're not."

Of course he knew they were not. But he knew how to navigate this area. He could charm any woman. "Well heck, I don't want to take your word for it. I want to find out for myself. It would give me immense *pleasure* to investigate." Break the curse. Free Ben. Go back home and . . . and what? Watch him have a happily ever after with Emma?

Ben would owe him one now. Carter would save the day. Be the man now. The heart doctor. And Carter would allow Ben to love Emma, as long as the real Ben returned. Could work. Why not? He'd had shittier ideas before.

"Just tell me one thing. What happens to me if I kiss you and, you know, I don't really mean it?" he said. But he knew, down to his femur, it was death.

"You die."

"Instantly?" He was starting to sweat. Felt the moisture pop up in his brow, the back of his neck.

"Soon enough."

"And what happens to *you* if I manage to break this danged curse you got shackled with?"

"I die."

He almost fell over. "You die?"

That cackle again. Kind of peevish this time. "When you've been here as long as I have, death starts to look pretty darned good."

What a strange form of euthanasia, he thought. Kissing. Loving. In order to put someone out of her misery. But then maybe that's what euthanasia was all about. A wicked act done out of compassion and caring for the sufferer. Hell, someone should've shot Carter years ago.

"Okay, enough chitchat, lady, come here." He braced his legs apart and opened his arms, and she stiffened. "Aw, don't hesitate, or I'll think you don't want me. Come on, now, witch, come to daddy."

She took an eager step forward, and halted. "Willow."

"What?"

"That's my name. Willow."

"Then, Willow, get ready for the hottest goddamned kiss of your entire life."

She grinned a big waxy grin, but then her face scrunched with worry. "It won't work if you're thinking of that woman you two fools are in love with."

"Not thinking about her. Not even thinking about me." He nodded down at her, dead serious as he watched her approach. "This ain't my first rodeo, Willow. I like to take care of women. I play games, games where it excites the fuck out of me to give them what they need. And you sorely need a kiss, baby. So come on over here, sweetheart. I am gonna kiss you hard enough to make your mouth explode."

Victory was his.

He'd shown Carter Bates not to mess with Ben New-castle.

Triumph followed him home, so intoxicating he even rolled down the window of the car and stuck his head out to feel the wind. Yeah, baby, yeah.

A block away from the house, the excitement dissipated.

The guy had just stood there—without a fight?

Was the cowboy goddamned stupid? Had he not real-ized he was going to *die*?

When he pulled into the driveway, Ben's hands were damp with sweat, and his insides had gone so numb he felt dead. Weighted. Cold. Deader than dead. *Get a grip on yourself, pussy.*

With a shaky breath, he dragged his feet down the path to the front door, sparing a sidelong glance at the defunct bushes and the sooty grass. It had thrilled him in a perverse way, to have such power—such control over death.

Tonight, this same thrill had jetted through his bloodstream, his mouth dried up with the anticipation of tasting his new life again. But why the fuck did he feel so empty now? *I ain't no murderer.*

Dammit, he was such a *fuck!*

Emma wrenched the door open before Ben had covered the length of the gravel path. Her wet hair flew behind her in a tangle, her body tucked into a white drawstring robe, and her eyes . . . They widened when she saw him. Only him.

"Where have you been? It's five in the morning, Ben."

Ben took in the sight of her and just stood there, looking at her innocent face. Her eyes were half-hidden by her sleepy lids, but that didn't hide the vigilant regard with which she watched him.

"I know," was all Ben said then.

"So what in God's green earth is going on!" she exploded.

He paused at the porch and waited there, like an unwelcome suitor. Nervous. Unsure of what the hell to say that wouldn't make her hate him for the rest of his godforsaken life.

"Where's Carter?" she asked, glancing around.

Ben studied her expression. Vexation traced the corner of her lips. But no. She couldn't know, suspect, what he'd done. Because her eyes still shone on him, waiting expectantly for an answer.

Her hair. It tumbled past her shoulders, lustrous. Her

lips, such desirable lips. And her eyes . . . those big brown eyes . . .

Ben had always been proud to be the man he saw mirrored in those eyes. The man she loved. He peered into those eyes tonight, with the moon as his witness, and his spirits deflated when he realized he didn't see that man now. All he saw was an alien, a poor excuse of a creature. Not human, not alive, not dead. Desperation lived inside that creature, and anger, and despair, and loneliness. He saw death there, too. Stamped there, in his own unyielding black eyes. Like a scarlet letter forever ostracizing him from love and laughter and a normal life.

Did Emma see the same? Did she feel pity for this creature? Disgust?

If he lied to her now, would she believe his lies? Explanations he could probably give her, easily enough.

Carter's gone, he'd say.

Where? Why? She'd be confused.

He would shrug. *I don't know where he is. He just took off and left his truck behind.*

And she'd say, *Oh. Okay.*

No, not anymore. Two years ago, she'd have accepted whatever he said. And then she would've gone up to their room and curled against Ben.

Fuck!

Could he spend his new life pretending to be the man she thought he was, the one he'd been before, after he'd just *escorted his best friend to his murder?*

A hollow grew inside his gut, and he somberly shook his head and tried to step inside. "Carter's gone, Emma."

The words seemed to splash her like ice-cold water. She seemed to frost over immediately, her expression losing its warmth. She planted a hand against the doorframe, forbidding him entrance. "Ben, what have you done?"

The low, wretched sound belonged to Ben. "I didn't come back so I could watch him take you from me!"

He'd been desperate to be with her, to get back his life. Desperate enough to sacrifice his friend. What kind of man was he? He'd saved lives once. He'd been respected, admired, envied. Now he didn't envy himself, he didn't admire himself, and he sure as heck didn't respect himself. And if Emma knew . . .

He stared out at the F150 parked across the street, a truck that would not be driven by its owner again. *Carter had willingly stayed at the witch's place.* Dammit, why hadn't he done something? Why had Bates done the noble thing? The thing Ben Newcastle might have done for him— *before* he died, before he had been betrayed and had watched his life fall apart on him.

Frantic at his silence, Emma gripped his arms. "What did you do, Ben? What did you do?"

"I traded his life for mine." He saw the blank confusion in her face, so he explained. "That's why I was able to come back. I offered . . . to bring *him*."

Her expression crumpled. Tears spilled down her cheeks. Immediate. Heart-wrenching. "How could you? How could you!" When her fists pummeled his chest, Ben didn't stop her. He just stood there, absorbing it, weathering it, deserving it. "I love him, you moron! I love him like I used to love you!"

He caught her flailing wrists, his heart almost stopping. "Dammit, I wasn't supposed to die!"

"Yes, you were! You're not supposed to be here, Ben!" she cried, then smothered her face in her hands.

But the words could not be taken back, could never be taken back.

Ben's world shifted under his feet, spinning wildly all around him. In what alternate reality did Emma not love him? In what sick, fucked-up world did Emma love Carter? His hands could barely close around her small shoulders. The squeeze he gave her was weak, apologetic. "Emma, this isn't the way we were going to end. I was supposed to make you happy."

"You did, my entire life, you did! You brought me here, Ben, your work brought me here, your dreams. You introduced me to the man I could be with now. You taught me to love his humor, to admire and respect him like you did. We're over, Ben. We were over that horrible day . . . no matter how much we've both wished that it never ended. We're . . . Oh, god, our time's up, Ben. Would you kill your best friend for a few more stolen minutes? Would you?" And then, soft, so softly, "Who are you?"

A monster, a voice whispered.

Not the man she needs.

Not the man she's meant to be with now.

You're a monster.

A monster.

He'd done monstrous things. Now he'd doomed the people he loved to live in the hell he alone deserved.

Inside his very depths, right down to the last vestiges of the man he'd left behind, honor clawed its way to the surface.

Do something! Show her you're better than this! "Maybe it's not too late." With single-minded purpose, he shoved Emma back into the house, his fate determined. "Get dressed—we don't have much time."

The Civic tore through the winding streets in the middle of nowhere, Ben the spitting image of a devil on wheels.

What had he done?

He seemed to have been stripped of all decency and morality, had been reduced to some sort of beast ruled solely by instinct—survival of the fittest and all that—but something about Emma's words had connected with him. Something had reached the small hidden human inside of him. She only prayed it wasn't too late. For the real Ben to surface. For Carter, oh, god.

Out the window, the streets were still. The last shreds of the night felt alive in its hunger, like the mouth of an animal. Emma could detect no signs of life, barely a flicker of light. Her wet hair dripped across her blouse, giving her a little chill as Ben drove them deeper still into the shadiest, most decrepit part of town.

"What happened to us, Ben?" Her voice was a wispy sound in the interior of the car. "What's happened to . . . me, to you . . . ?"

Ben had avoided facing her throughout the entire ride; he seemed incapable of meeting her accusing gaze. As though he knew Emma was his judge and jury now and he refused to hear the verdict just yet.

"Death, Emma. Death happened." There was such regret in

his words the tears started spilling down her cheeks again. "Jealousy. Lies. Betrayal. Love." His voice cracked, and he inhaled raggedly. "Marriages are torn apart; families crumple . . . wars are waged. Sometimes all in the name of love."

Love? she wondered.

She envisioned the beautiful Helen of Troy, the catalyst in a brutal war and thousands of deaths. Never, ever, had Emma imagined she would be loved so hard, or wanted so much, to drive a man to harm another in his efforts to claim her again. She didn't deserve it—*no one* deserved to be loved to such a degree. Was that really love?

It wasn't, she knew it wasn't. But it was Ben's love. The remains of their poisoned, ruined love, yanked away from them before they were ready to let go. Ben's dark love . . .

With a trembling hand, Emma swiped at the remaining moisture on her cheeks. "What's going to happen to him?"

Jaw tight, he turned those petrifying, penetrating black eyes to hers—at last. "Ever heard of something called the kiss of death?"

She couldn't manage a decent breath. "That's for . . . vampires in fiction."

The laugh he released was sad, cynical, as he shook his head. "There are worse things than vampires. She said next time she'd kiss me and send me back to my grave."

"Next time? What are you talking about? Who told you this?"

"A witch—a powerful witch."

"And what does that witch want with Carter?"

Grim as a death sentence, she heard his low words: "I think she wants his soul."

Her heart vaulted and then fell so still she thought it would never beat again. "Oh, god, Ben, why?"

Ben had been willing to *kill* Carter! Sweet, sexy, unique Carter. Ben had been planning to kill him—all along. He'd let him touch Emma, had watched in morbid fascination as they got sucked into a whirlwind of emotions, all the while with the certainty that it would soon be over. Now he'd taken his old friend to this horrible . . . witch person. A *witch*. Like in some goddamned horror movie.

The rage was so great that if he hadn't been driving, and risked running over some unfortunate soul or getting them both killed, she'd be kicking and pounding his arrogant face in. But now, a little ball burned inside of her, a little ball she recognized as hope. How long had he been gone? Surely nothing would happen to Carter. He was a big strong man, a *very* big strong man. . . .

"Please forgive me."

The gentle whisper, spoken like a boy she'd grown up with would have spoken them, spun painfully around her head. She didn't know what would happen to them, and right now, it wasn't important. Whatever the outcome, she knew she would always be a part of Ben, and Ben of her. She would hurt when he hurt, and she was hurting like a bitch.

But she couldn't reply, would never, could never forgive any human being who hurt Carter.

"We're here." Jerking to a halt, the car at an awkward angle to the sidewalk, Ben pulled her out into the night and dragged her into a small house that was so deteriorated it seemed to mock every existing rule of gravity.

Emma's heart splintered when she spotted Carter across

a small, decimated room. He was gorgeous, smiling, *hers*. Then it all but tore when Ben spoke. "Stop! Stop whatever you're doing! Take me instead."

Ben's heart thundered as he tore into the room, but his words had no impact on the witch. Had no impact on Carter. An uncomfortable moment of déjà vu knifed through him, and he remembered all those days, all those nights, hanging around them like a phantom, unheard and unseen and ignored.

Ignored.

Even now, he was being ignored.

With her sole focus trained on Carter, the witch rubbed her wrinkled little hands together and asked, "Sure you're willing to do it?" She was grinning.

"Let's do it, lady," he said. He was grinning, too.

What in the hell? He was willing to die? So easily?

Shock rooted him to the spot.

A part of Ben, the corrupt one, the new one, yelled for him to let her take Carter, to leave with Emma and live happily ever after. But as the witch reached out for the smiling cowboy, Ben was struck with the realization that he'd not only die for Emma. He'd die for Carter, too.

He dragged in one last breath, then spun a startled Emma around. "I love you—I always will." Before she realized his intention, he charged forward and grabbed the witch so forcefully the little woman gasped. He dove for her mouth—his lips slammed over hers, hungrily taking her kiss. This was not the last kiss he'd wished for in his past life, not even in this life, but he took it as if it *were*.

Emma. In the distance, she was screaming. She screeched so loud the windows could've shattered as she said, *"No! Ben, no!"* But his lips moved against the puckered ones beneath his, pushing them apart. Their breaths met, their tongues touched, their energies meshed. Red-hot lightning blasted through his body. Pain exploded inside of his head, weakening him. His whole life, all of it, in rapid order, flashed before his eyes. Emma kissing him for the very first time . . .

Kissing him awkwardly, like the little girl she was.

What the hell was that for?

I just wanted to see if you knew how to do it. . . .

I do, you little minx. Do you?

He saw her with braces, with her first set of scrubs. With her hair short when she'd been in nursing school and with her hair long. He saw her in the shower, calling for a towel. He saw her unpacking their things when they'd arrived at their new home, their home in San Antone. He saw her at his funeral, strong, numb, heartbroken. He saw her kissing Carter Bates on the gravel path outside that very home. He saw her at their doorstep less than an hour ago, disappointed, crushed. He saw her now, her eyes wide and frightened when he told her he'd always love her.

And then he saw nothing.

"No!"

Lunging, Emma pulled at the witch's grimy hair with all her might. But their mouths were clamped, their eerily still bodies locked in this moment—like a sculpture that captured this sickening, disturbing display of a kiss: a gorgeous man kissing a withered old woman. A withered old woman Emma couldn't pull away from Ben.

Everything in her rebelled at the sight of that dark head bent, kissing someone else. There seemed to be no motion between them, no breath, except the one connection of their lips as the kiss continued.

"You're not taking him!" Emma curled an arm around her fragile neck and squeezed, squeezed harder, but strong arms seized her from behind and wrenched her away.

"Shh, baby, shh. It was Ben's choice. . . . Let him do what he—"

She fought. "*No! Noooo! Ben, don't you dare die again. Don't you dare!*"

Carter tightened his hold around her, his heartbeat as frantic as her own, and suddenly it all seemed to dawn on her, and she stilled.

Somewhere in the depths of her panic she heard him speak words, but she was unable to grasp them. A thousand regrets came pummeling at her, one after another.

Ben had come back to her, and they hadn't been to the movies, gone for a walk. They hadn't danced to their song, not really, the way they had before. She'd hurt him, had mistrusted him. Maybe her own fear, her own lack of faith in the possibility of his being there, had prevented her from giving him a chance.

A long time later, when Carter fell quiet, and she missed the sound of his whispers against the top of her head, Emma opened her eyes and saw him.

Saw Ben, on the ground, still as death.

She felt the pang of a million heartbreaks, the sounds of a million screams, but there was only one heart breaking, one scream, as she fell to her knees.

"Oh, god, no!" Emma scrambled toward Ben's sprawled body and jerked his torso upward, setting his head in her lap as she knelt. "Ben? Ben, please!"

She checked his heart, his pulse, his image becoming a blur when she felt nothing. Nothing. Terror swept through her when he didn't rouse. She'd seen his battered body a lifetime ago, had recognized the bloodied corpse on the table as Ben.

This felt just like it.

Then his body jerked as though with electric shock, and she caught her breath. He released a low, keening sound and bucked violently. Veins strained in his neck, tinged black. A blue hue crawled up his face.

"He's having a seizure!"

Carter charged and seized Ben's flailing wrists, effortlessly controlling his body as he thrashed.

Emma's instincts kicked in. "No! Restraining him could only hurt him."

"Well hell, little nurse, tell me what to do!"

Where Emma found the strength to move, she didn't know, but she hurried across the room, rummaged through the ungodly mess, and found a long wooden spoon. Rushing back to him, she forced the length into his mouth so that he didn't bite himself, so that his tongue wouldn't end up bruised or totally swallowed.

Choked sounds were emerging from his throat, the noise terrifying, painful to listen to. Angrily, Carter whipped around in search of the witch; a slim figure in loose garb who was now fiddling around a steaming casserole. He was about to demand her assistance when she turned.

His jaw went slack at the sight of her approaching, and Emma gaped from Ben's side. The witch was . . . beautiful. Surreal, ethereal, young. Yellow teeth had been replaced by a row of perfect white pearly ones. Her jaundiced skin was now flawless, long blond hair framing a perfectly heart-shaped face and clear green eyes.

"Carter?" Emma asked, disbelief in her voice.

He immediately scowled, up on his feet. "Ben broke your spell. Why is he yelling in pain? Don't tell me you're just gonna stand there, Willow! You said if you were uncursed, he'd be, too!"

Even the way she moved was graceful now. Every lurking shadow seemed to have been lifted from her face, and the light spilled across her face like a sun ray's blessing. But Ben was still engulfed in darkness. Thrashing. Cursed. In *pain*.

"It's his choice now . . ." she whispered, before she disappeared through the door and out into the night.

Lowering herself to the ground, Emma rested on her haunches, watching Ben, waiting.

"Ben, come back—" she said.

Abruptly she fell silent. It sounded so familiar, the plea. She'd said it so many times, in her sleep, awake, for nearly two years. She'd begged him to come back and he had. At any cost, he had. All this was *her* fault, for now he would do what no man had ever done. He'd have to die twice. Oh, god.

"I'm sorry, Ben," she whispered brokenly, then raised her lashes to Carter. Carter Bates. Friend and gentleman. Rogue and lover.

Who'd been ready to make this sacrifice, too. Her chest

swelled with gratitude and emotion. He could've died, and he'd never have known, he'd never have known how she felt about him.

For a few seconds they both stared, she and Carter, as though uncertain of what to do. Taking three slow steps, he reached out for her face, slowly, his eyes not leaving hers for an instant. He was all right. He was all right, she sang in a weird mental mantra.

She told herself she wouldn't launch herself against him. She told herself she wouldn't wrap her legs around him and kiss him like her life depended on it. She told herself, once again, that she would *not* launch herself against him. But she was already standing, and her body swayed, and when he reached out to grab her shoulders, she was flinging herself at him, as fast and hard as she could, until they smashed together and clasped each other tight. She clung to his neck and he whirled her around, then lowered her feet to the ground and bent down to kiss her.

"Ah, baby."

He kissed her thoroughly, his taste glorious in her mouth. His long, lean arms around her felt like a safe haven. It was as if she'd arrived home, where she belonged.

He pulled away and cupped her face. "Are you all right?" he said, his eyes shining with emotion. "I was worrying and worrying you'd think I left you."

"No, no. I know you wouldn't," she breathed, setting her hands over his against her cheeks. She studied his face, his gorgeous face, and thought that he was even more beautiful than she remembered. The harsh angles of his cheekbones, the set of his jaw, and those eyes that still tortured her, even more than ever before. She kissed the inside of his palm. "I love you, Carter."

"Ahh, baby," he whispered, his eyes sparkling, his thumbs slowly caressing her cheeks. "Now, that was sexy."

When Carter embraced her in the powerful circle of his arms, she allowed herself the little luxury of snuggling against him. "Tell me again . . ." she whispered in his ear, because she needed the reassurance, needed the connection. "What you told me that night at the Club. I kept replaying your words in my head. Tell me *I'm in love with you, Emma.*"

"I'm in love with you, Emma." He bent down to kiss her, both of them clinging tight before they sensed movement beside them.

Weak-kneed with rising worry, Emma dropped down beside Ben. "I think we should call an ambulance now."

While Carter fished out his cell phone and punched the keys, she pulled Ben's dark head back on her lap and stroked his hair.

"Please be all right, Ben," she whispered in his ear. "I'm counting on your stubbornness to pull you through this time."

Chapter Fifteen

There was nothing, nothing, anywhere. Blackness. Only blackness. And pain. His every muscle screamed with pain. As Ben struggled to surface from the darkness, he realized that something was connected to his arm, to the left, beeping.

Groaning, he shifted on the squeaky bed, wanting the beeping to quiet, his head to stop pounding, his heart . . .

His eyebrows pulled low when he heard it. His heartbeat. His normal heartbeat.

He couldn't pry his eyes open; they felt leaden. But he sensed Emma sitting at his side, stroking his hair, speaking softly to someone about the accident. Ben's mind tried spinning its wheels. Accident? What accident?

The accident had been almost two years ago.

Carter's familiar laugh reached his ear. "Nothing can kill this son of a bitch. He'll pull through, pumpkin, just chill."

"But what if he doesn't?"

Her concern made Ben relax his muscles on the small hospital bed. So she still loved him?

"You know he will, sugar. This bastard's fit as a bull."

A thousand emotions assailed him when Emma's hushed reply filtered through his mind. "I can't lose him a second time, Carter."

Oh, god, baby, you'll let go. I know you will. I want you to.

"Miss Wilkins," a friendly voice said. "Would you mind giving me a bit more information? Where did this accident take place?"

Dammit, what freaking accident?

The tentacles of confusion surrounded Ben. His mind flickered with rising memories. He strained to remember, but his brain felt like exploding over the effort. The witch . . . the stupid evil witch . . . She was the worst kind of accident imaginable. Or . . . did they mean the truck that slammed into him? And everything that happened later? Every crazy thing that happened afterward, what about that? Was that the accident? His death, a new life. Confused. So confused. Had he dreamed everything?

"W-whr am I?" he grumbled, dazed and drugged as he tried cracking open his eyes.

"And he's up." Carter's rugged face shimmered before him. "How you feelin', big guy?"

"Wha' in the fuck's goin' on!"

A face replaced Carter's in his line of vision, and a pang of longing struck him when he focused on Emma. Her expressive brown eyes were turned down at the corners, her lips white and thin and being fiercely bitten by her little teeth.

Worried, she laced her fingers through his and squeezed comfortingly. "Ben, you're at the hospital. You had an accident." She spoke as if he was a baby—damn, he liked it, needed her damned foolish coddling. Her reassurance that he was . . . living.

"Y-you? Okay?" he rasped.

She nodded, and he closed his eyes when he felt the cool stroke of her fingers against the hot flesh of his neck. Ahh, Christ, her touch. Her tender touch. She'd touched her patients this way and Ben had felt jealous as a ghost, wondering when he'd feel this touch, this very touch, on his face and skin. He'd been so jealous when he came back— so fucking blind. He'd missed their comfortable breakfasts, their lazy Sundays, this. Soft. Touch.

"We're both okay, Carter and I. Worried," she said, brushing his hair back from his forehead. "How are you feeling?"

He didn't comprehend. Carter was alive—so Ben must be dead. Was this his heaven? No, damn, sinners didn't go to heaven. He was in a hospital, but why a hospital? The witch. He'd kissed the witch and had seen his old life flash before him in the space of seconds.

He opened his eyes and studied Carter inconspicuously, a strange feeling gripping his chest. The cowboy's eyes were trained protectively on Emma.

If he'd dreamed the entire thing, he'd have his life back, the old one like he wanted it. But did he want the old life? He'd thought he did, at first. But now? Fuck, he'd take anything. Hell, he'd take the new, ached with a fever to live the new. Any life. Didn't he? Why was he tired? Wanted to rest?

Maybe Carter and he and Emma could be together, could explore, could . . .

The nurse made clucking noises while she checked his vitals, and Ben wanted to rise from the bed and take the stupid board from her hands, but when he tried he was halted and shushed back in place.

"Shh, Ben, shh," Emma said.

"Sorry." His teeth ached as he spoke. He captured her hand in his, drawing her attention to his face. "Wanted to be . . . like before."

Her eyes shone with understanding, the look heavenly. The sort of look she used to give him before. Ben had walked through purgatory, had been through hell. He'd been willing to go to hell for eternity just for this. This. Her. That smile. For a chance to love her like she deserved.

His throat closed and between that and his aching jaw he could barely force the words out. "L-love you, Em."

"I love you, too, Ben."

She didn't hesitate. Didn't doubt it for a minute. Damn, why had he? Doubted?

He'd always hold a part of her heart. Always. He'd always be her first love, her champion—in her eyes he'd be the hero even if a devil had been born.

A man's strong, tanned hand settled on his right shoulder and delivered a companionable, you-go-man squeeze, and Ben met Carter's gaze. No. There was no antagonism there. No anger. No resentment. He'd never looked so much like his old friend than today.

The nurse kept fiddling around while Emma shot nervous looks in the woman's direction. When she at last stepped out into the hall, Emma let go a breath and almost jumped on Ben. "What happened? Ben, are you all right? You hit your jaw so try not to talk too much, it's still swollen."

Ben stared at Emma, then Carter, then Emma again with a sinking feeling. So he'd imagined it? They hadn't gone wild and on the dark side. He'd slammed into a carrier truck and all this time he'd probably been in a coma? Things could go back to normal. All would be all right. He'd go back home, have dinner with Emma. Spoon her. Love her. Propose marriage to her.

He didn't know how he felt about that, other than pained. Yeah, really pained. For poor fucking Carter—who'd spend his life wanting her. Struggling to move, he shifted in discomfort, feeling the twisted expression on his face. "I didn't—didn't dream?" He should be tooting a happy horn and yet—it didn't feel right anymore. It didn't. That he'd been in a coma all this time?

"Dream what?" Emma whispered as she bent over Ben. Carter's blue eyes flashed with hunger. His hand caressed her rump. "Dream what, my love?" Emma pressed.

"Us—everything."

Carter wouldn't have touched Emma like this before. Would he?

Nerves alert, Ben waited for an answer, wondering if he'd come back from the dead for real, and also wondering if this time they could work something out, the three of them, without anyone getting killed anymore. Hell, he'd make sure they worked it out. . . .

Emma's eyes swamped with tenderness, and she stroked his jaw. "No," she breathed. "You didn't dream it. . . ."

She explained to him how they'd told the doctors he'd been in a small accident, otherwise how to explain the state they'd brought him in? He'd been yelling in pain as his body adjusted. Adjusted to what? To normality?

A normal heartbeat . . .

Afraid to hope, Ben closed his eyes, and because he couldn't talk very well, he said nothing.

"The witch said it was your choice. Sure glad you chose to stay, Doc," Carter said.

When Ben raised his lashes, his friend's arm was wrapped around Emma's waist, but his gaze held steady on Ben.

"We'll work it out, whatever you want, buddy. Just want you to be okay now," Carter added, and the somberness of his friend's words gripped Ben like a chokehold.

Whatever he wanted . . .

His heart thundered. He knew, that very second *knew* the only thing he wanted. The reason he was there. "Want you . . . to be happy, Emma," he said thickly, loathing that he couldn't speak right, couldn't speak right when he had so much to say, so many things to make right, to explain, to ask forgiveness for.

How could Emma ever be happy with Ben again? He knew she loved Carter. As she'd once loved Ben. Maybe still did love him, in a way. But it hurt to be together now. It wasn't their time any longer. Hell, it would come again. It had to.

Emma gazed at him as he struggled to speak. Carter stood there. Solid. Worthy of her. In love with her.

"And I want . . . want . . . to s-say . . . be happy and I love you . . . and . . . I had to—I need to do this. . . ." He reached over to her, drew her closer, close enough to feel her breath, and her skin, her heat. She sat gently on the side of the tiny bed and bent to kiss his forehead, but he tipped his head back and he closed his lips over hers.

His insides exploded with emotion.

The kiss was the hottest thing on the planet.

Ben made it last. God, he made it last, felt it seep into his bones, their moments together, their love. Maybe one day they'd make it work, the three of them. In another time, another place. Right now this was all he deserved. *Good-bye, Emma.* Her tongue tasted his own, tangled, and danced.

He wanted so much more, to make it up to them, all the ways he'd hurt them in his desperation to belong with them once more, but this was what he'd most wanted, and suddenly he knew this was the only thing he'd get out of this second life. One last kiss.

This kiss.

Before he left them in peace forever.

And he took this kiss, prolonging it because he'd take it with him, and because letting go of this mouth, this girl, was the hardest thing he'd ever done in his life.

But Emma had Carter now, and Ben wasn't afraid anymore. She'd always love him. *No one* could ever touch what they'd had, what they'd lived together, what they'd shared, and so he kissed her.

Kissed her until his heart would shatter from the beauty of it. Until his fingers slackened in her lustrous hair, until his lips fell still against hers, and until he had to let go.

.